THE
ELEPHANT
THIEF

Elephants are amazing, but it's not just their awesome size, cool trunk-work and clever eyes: there's something profound about this wonderful animal. Jane Kerr captures it perfectly in her totally gripping adventure. *The Elephant Thief* is a story of stolen treasure, an impossible challenge and a real-life journey, but at its heart lies an unlikely and touching friendship between a boy and an elephant. You'll experience tears of rage, wonder and joy as this classic tale of hope against all the odds transports you to another time . . .

BARRY CUNNINGHAM
Publisher
Chicken House

THE
ELEPHANT
THIEF

Jane Kerr

2 PALMER STREET, FROME, SOMERSET BA11 1DS
WWW.CHICKENHOUSEBOOKS.COM

Text © Jane Kerr 2017
First published in Great Britain in 2017
Chicken House
2 Palmer Street
Frome, Somerset BA11 1DS
United Kingdom
www.chickenhousebooks.com

Jane Kerr has asserted her right under the Copyright, Designs and Patents Act 1988
to be identified as the author of this work.

Cover design and interior design by Steve Wells
Illustration © Chris Wormell
Typeset by Dorchester Typesetting Group Ltd
Printed and bound in Great Britain by CPI Group (UK) Ltd, Croydon, CR0 4YY

The paper used in this Chicken House book is made
from wood grown in sustainable forests.

1 3 5 7 9 10 8 6 4 2

British Library Cataloguing in Publication data available.

ISBN 978-1-910655-75-7
eISBN 978-1-911077-35-0

To AJ, Alexandra and Ben
With love

Based on a true story

Chapter One

SOMEWHERE IN EDINBURGH
8 April 1872

He couldn't breathe.

His lungs were pumping. His lips were open. But there still wasn't enough air.

The sack covering his head blocked everything. His nose. His eyes. His mouth. Fear burnt in his stomach, sharp and acidic.

He wondered where he was being taken. And why.

But most of all he wondered if he was going to survive the night.

Outside, the horses slowed and the carriage jerked to a stop.

'Move!'

Boy felt a rough shove in the centre of his back, and he toppled, gracelessly, from the carriage. The ground hurt. And he cursed every decision he'd made that night. If he'd been more careful, less cocky, he would have seen the two men waiting outside the abandoned boarding house where he'd been living for the last three months.

But by the time he had, it had been too late. The hood had already covered his face, and his arms had been twisted behind his back.

'Get up, you little runt.'

Heavy hands lifted him to his feet. The night breeze chilled his skin. Somewhere nearby, a door was wrenched open and instinctively, he turned towards it. Then he was pushed, almost stumbling, across the threshold.

Where was he? What did they want with him? Fear pulsed frantically in his chest.

Abruptly, the sack was torn from his head, and he gulped in air. Every mouthful tasted of damp and decay and the sea. He pivoted slowly on his heels, and tried to focus.

He was in an old warehouse. Judging by the sounds and smells, it must be close to the Leith docks. At the far end of the room, a man stood by the only window. A shaft of moonlight turned him into a dark silhouette.

'Boy. So glad you could come.'

The voice was instantly recognizable. And Boy's breath stuttered.

Frank Scatcherd. Leader of the Leith Brotherhood, a collection of Edinburgh's worst criminals and thugs. And the man who called himself the King.

'I expect you want to know why you're here.' Casually, Scatcherd pushed away from the window. As he walked, his steel-capped boots tapped on the bare floorboards. Boy waited but the King was in no hurry. It was as though he knew that every second hiked the fear a little higher. 'Well? Nothing to say?'

Now Scatcherd was so close that Boy could see the pattern of the silk scarf tied around his neck. The King liked to look good. His hair was slick with barber's oil, and a cap tilted jauntily over one ear. It was rumoured that a razor had been sewn into the peak so he could blind a man with a single head jab. But no one knew for certain if it was true.

Boy swallowed, throat as dry as dust, but he said nothing. The silence stretched for several heartbeats. Then Scatcherd slid a knife from his jacket sleeve.

'So you're still not talking.' Deliberately, he rolled the blade in his palm. Forwards and back. Forwards and back. 'What a pity.'

Boy lifted his chin and stared at the moving knife; the jagged tip was rusty with old blood. And he knew it wasn't bravery that kept him silent. Right at this moment, he wished he could make any sound at all. But he couldn't.

'Well it's lucky for you, I don't need your voice.' The knife stopped moving. 'I assume you've heard of the Wormwell auction?'

Cautiously Boy nodded. Everyone in Edinburgh knew

about the auction. Walter Wormwell owned the Royal Number One Menagerie, the most famous travelling show in the country. But two weeks ago, he'd been found lying in his study, as dead and cold as his untouched chicken supper. According to gossip, he'd left behind a large collection of zoological animals and an even larger collection of debt. Tomorrow the entire menagerie was being sold to settle those bills.

What Boy didn't understand was Scatcherd's interest. Why would the King bother with a penniless bankrupt like Wormwell? Or an auction of zoo animals? It made no sense.

'Two days before he died, Wormwell stole money from me. A great deal of money. Naturally, I want it back . . . and you are going to get it for me.'

Boy swallowed, trying to sort through the significance. A part of him was relieved. He was going to be allowed to walk out of here alive. This time, there would be no punishment. No pain.

'I've already had his house searched. Nothing. Not even a penny under the floorboards. The menagerie is the only place left. Of course, I'd prefer to go to the auction myself, but the police are sniffing around. So I've decided to send you . . .' Scatcherd's lips twisted into a smile. 'My pet thief.'

Boy flinched. How could he find a missing fortune when the Brotherhood had failed? And what would he be looking for? Coins? Bank papers? Gold? It had every sign of being a fool's errand.

'My men will get you inside the pavilion.' Scatcherd

jerked his head at the two thugs standing on either side of the doorway. 'From there, you're on your own. Keep your eyes and ears open. Wormwell hid that money and there has to be a trace somewhere. And remember . . .'

Boy waited, heart tripping. Scatcherd raised the knife and gently trailed it along Boy's arm. It stopped at his wrist, just above the ugly tangle of scars.

'The last time I asked you for a favour, you let me down. This is your chance to make it up to me.' Abruptly, Scatcherd's fist twisted, and the blade sliced through skin. Boy clenched his teeth against the pain. 'And if you fail, just imagine what I will do to you.'

Boy hung by his fingertips from the top of the high stone wall, feeling the strain through every muscle. He closed his eyes, and let go. His landing was clumsy but silent.

Finally, he was inside the auction ground.

On the other side of the wall, he heard Scatcherd's thugs muttering to themselves, then their heavy footsteps as they walked away. They'd done their job. Now it was up to him.

'. . . And if you fail, just imagine what I will do to you.'

Scatcherd's words chased through his head like night shadows. He rubbed his wrist and felt the old scars beneath his fingers. He didn't need to imagine what would happen if he failed. He already knew.

But there was no need to panic; he was good at this. Faster, smarter, better than anyone else. And the truth was that in this crush no one would even notice a pickpocket.

They were too busy staring at one of the strangest sights Edinburgh had ever seen.

Two leopards, some tigers, one battered baboon and a handful of camels trudged around Waverley Pavilion. Then came a line of antelope, two hyenas (one spotted, one striped) and a golden lioness whose tail swished as she walked.

Boy had never seen anything like them before – animals that weren't cats, dogs or rats. The only reason he knew their names was because of the auctioneer. Bartholomew Trott liked the sound of his own voice.

'. . . and finally, one Siberian brown bear sold to the London Zoological Gardens for forty guineas.' Mr Trott brought his hammer down and smiled the smile of a man making money. 'London's got a bargain there. He's young, healthy and lively as a trout.'

But the bear was already causing trouble. Jaws wide, he reared up on huge hind legs and fanned out his claws. Boy knew it wouldn't do any good. Escape was impossible. Two keepers were already pulling on his chains and, defeated, the animal fell sprawling to the ground.

Boy turned away, trying to ignore the tug of sympathy. Instead, he examined the pavilion field. Most spectators stood near the curtained stage where the animals were being brought up for auction. A little further back were rows of cages and wagons which housed the rest of the Wormwell menagerie. They were probably the best place to start.

He reached into his pocket and checked for the small blade he carried to slash open pocket linings and cut purse strings. It was still there. He was ready.

An hour later, Boy had found nothing. He'd prised open crates, crawled under wagons and plunged his hand inside several straw-stuffed cages. But just as he'd expected, it was useless. There was no gold. No jewels. No banknotes.

His only real success was hidden in the lining of his jacket – a hoard of stolen pennies, silk handkerchiefs and a lady's scarf pin. He'd even managed to sneak a tin whistle from the pocket of one of Mr Trott's clerks.

Boy reached the last of the cages and sidled around a corner. The path was blocked by a group of animal keepers talking to a man in a crumpled suit. Instinct made him pull back; he was a fraction too late.

'Oi, what d'you think you're doing, lad? Come here. I want a word.'

Spinning on his heels, Boy ran, weaving through the wagons before blending into the crowd again. Only then did he risk looking over his shoulder. The man with the crumpled suit was craning across the heads of the spectators. Boy hunched his shoulders and kept low. His heart thudded.

'Ladies and gentlemen!' Mr Trott's bellow couldn't have been better timed. Everyone turned towards the stage. Four men were lowering a cage on to a raised plinth. Behind the metal bars, a lion glowered sulkily. 'May I present Hannibal – the handsomest beast in the jungle!'

On cue, the lion rose to his feet, opened his jaws and roared. The crate lurched sideways. Boy winced at the screams.

'No need to be alarmed, ladies. He's as tame as a spring lamb and gentle as a kitten. I'd climb in there myself if I wasn't wearing my second-best coat. Now, who'll start the bidding?'

'Two hundred guineas!' shouted one large gentleman in the front row. He must be one of the guests who owned a zoological house or travelling menagerie. Boy had even heard a rumour that an American showman called Barnum had sent a buyer from across the ocean.

'Two hundred and ten!'

'Two hundred and twenty.'

'Two thirty!'

'Very well. Three hundred guineas.' It was the large man again, his face half hidden by a grey plume of sideburns. A line of gold buttons curved across his jacket. 'And I hope he can play the piano for that.'

The crowd laughed as the hammer came down.

'Sold to Mr Arthur Albright of the Yorkshire Zoological Gardens for three hundred guineas.' Mr Trott nodded to the winning bidder who smiled through his whiskers as if he had captured the lion himself. 'Congratulations, Mr Albright. He's a beautiful animal.'

Mr Trott shuffled his papers and Boy pushed a little closer, a flush of nerves prickling his skin. The final lot had been reached. His time was running out.

'And now, ladies and gentlemen, I have for you the largest and cleverest elephant ever exhibited in our great country. Maharajah the Magnificent!'

From the side of the stage, a curtain twitched and fell. Standing in the waves of purple cloth was the biggest star of the Royal Number One Menagerie. And Boy forgot every reason he was here.

With tusks as long as a man's leg, the elephant towered above the crowd. His rippled grey skin stretched over a wide back before falling into deep folds where legs met body. Each ear, large as a tablecloth, had faded at its edges as though scrubbed by an overly enthusiastic washer-woman.

If the Queen herself had emerged, she couldn't have caused more of a stir. Not only had Boy never seen anything like this creature, he'd never even imagined one existed. The elephant must be the strongest, most powerful animal to walk the earth.

But it was Maharajah's trunk which hooked his curiosity – as bizarre as a man with a third arm. It was coiled around a wooden stick that the elephant brandished like a street magician would wave a wand. Boy couldn't take his eyes away.

Then, without warning, Maharajah swung the club at Mr Trott. The crowd gasped. Boy tensed, waiting for the blow to land. This was going to be painful. But, a bare inch from trouble, the elephant slowed and gently tipped the auctioneer's hat from his head.

'As you can see, ladies and gentlemen, he loves a bit of tomfoolery.' Mr Trott didn't look amused. He scooped up the hat and pushed it back on. 'Come on, Sandev! Walk the beast about. We've not got all day.'

From the side of the stage, a slim, wiry man emerged. To Boy's eyes, he looked almost as exotic as the elephant. His red trousers were baggy at the knee and gathered at the ankle. Embroidered straps held a silver-headed cane to his chest. And a circle of white cloth covered his head, creating a peculiar type of hat. But most fascinating of all was his colour. Because this man was the first person Boy had ever seen with skin just as brown as his own.

'Well get on with it! Time's money.' Mr Trott tapped his hammer impatiently. Sandev's solemn face didn't even flicker. Instead, he held his palms together as though in prayer and bowed slowly. The entire field hushed. Impressed, Boy lifted up on to his toes. He didn't want to miss a moment.

Sandev whistled into one of Maharajah's huge ears. The elephant stomped forwards, and Boy felt the earth shake beneath his feet. The tremor seemed to reach up and wrap around his bones.

'See his noble brow. Observe his proud stature. This magnificent beast was once the personal pet of an Indian prince before he was given to the Russian Czar. I'm told he only agreed to part with the animal in exchange for six bags of gold.'

Boy could hear rumblings among the menagerists.

'I'll start the bidding at five hundred guineas.' Mr Trott peered at those on the front row. 'Gentlemen, may I remind you of the strength of this great creature. He's been known to pull the weight of twenty grown men in a wagon. For several miles. Going uphill.'

Reluctantly, Boy dropped back on to his heels. He didn't have time for daydreaming. He needed to hide until the pavilion cleared, then start the search again.

Twisting, he slid back through the crush. A sudden surge knocked him off balance, and his jacket swung open. A silver whistle tipped out. A few pennies followed. Then a hatpin. His pickpocketing blade. And one leather glove.

'You thievin' little beggar!'

A hand clamped around his neck and, for a moment, Boy was frozen. Then he fought. He kicked and punched and scratched, but nothing worked. The fist refused to loosen. Wriggling, he tried to see who held him. It was a man, solid and squat and wearing what was surely the brightest red waistcoat in the whole of Edinburgh.

'Oi, Crimple. Sling this runt up there will you? He won't be able to go nowhere.'

Another hand grabbed his collar. He was winched into the air, and brought face-to-face with a giant – one of the keepers who had tackled the Siberian bear. Hope bled away.

'Over here, Gov?' The keeper reached a tall column beside the pavilion gate. Once a marble statue would have stood there but now it was empty. Boy was thrown up. Roughly. The bricks scraped his shins.

'That's the place. He won't be shiftin' in a hurry.' Red Waistcoat was already scurrying back towards the auction stage. 'You keep an eye out. I'll deal with him later.'

Boy glanced down and his stomach lurched. The ground looked far away. For one moment he considered jumping but the cold spring had hardened the earth to rock. A fall was certain to break a bone, most likely one in his neck.

Desperately, he searched for another escape. The stage was only a stone's throw away but everyone's attention was on the sale. And even if they saw him, it was unlikely anyone would help. He was trapped, his throat so clogged with fear he needed to breathe faster to get enough air.

'. . . I must tell you that Mr Samuel MacKeith, a leading butcher in this fair city, is keen to introduce elephant steaks to Scotland. I hope that will influence your bids, gentlemen. I'm certain none of us would want to see such a fine beast on our dinner plates?'

A hand snapped up.

'Yes, five hundred and fifty guineas – now with Mr Albright. Will anyone give me five sixty?'

From his perch, Boy spotted Red Waistcoat waving furiously at the back of the bidders. A rush of anger mixed with his fear. This man was to blame. It was his fault that he was caught as firmly as a fish on a hook. Then Boy realized something; something which brought a small spark of satisfaction.

Red Waistcoat was in trouble of his own.

People had pushed forwards for the final sale, blocking

the auctioneer's view. What Boy could see, Mr Trott could not. Red Waistcoat, and his attempts to bid for the elephant, might as well be invisible.

'Five hundred and sixty from Monsieur Clemontard of the Ménagerie du Jardin in Paris. Am I offered more?'

Frantically, Red Waistcoat waved again but the auctioneer's gaze was fixed on the front row. 'Mr Albright?' A nod. 'That's five seventy from you, Mr Albright.'

The words seemed to jolt Red Waistcoat. Boy saw him whirl away from the stage like a scarlet spinning top. Puffing and panting, he broke into a waddling run, darting between the spectators. On another day, Boy would have laughed. Today he couldn't even smile. Red Waistcoat was heading back towards the column. But why?

'Raise your arm, lad. Raise your arm!' He was getting nearer. 'Do it now. Now! I'll not be outgunned by that Yorkshire cheat.'

Boy hesitated. It made no sense at all but every instinct screamed that this was a golden opportunity. So how could he twist it to his advantage?

'Just put your arm in the air and wave. He'll see you up there.' Red Waistcoat's voice was growing more desperate as he got closer. Crowds still blocked his path. 'Come on! COME ON!'

But Boy didn't wave. He did something much better. Bringing his fingers to his lips, he whistled. Loud, clear and shrill. The note soared over the heads of the spectators. They turned in one movement as though pulled by a single string. Boy made sure everyone was looking – and then he lifted his arm.

'Well, well! It seems we've a late bidder.' Peering across, Mr Trott pointed with his hammer. 'Five hundred and eighty . . . there on the column.'

'But he can't.'

'He's just a child!'

The shouts from the front row were loud enough for Boy to hear. He dropped his arm quickly. What had he done? After a lifetime trying to stay out of sight, he was caught centre stage. And there was no one to blame but himself.

'Of course he can.' Red Waistcoat had reached the column. He leant against the stone base, breathless but triumphant. 'The lad's with me. WITH ME!'

But Boy knew it was never going to be that easy. Nothing ever was. Sure enough, Mr Albright was already pushing through the crowd, his grey whiskers quivering.

'This is outrageous, Mr Trott. You can't go along with it! I was invited on the understanding that this would be a fair sale among gentlemen. Not children. And certainly not grubby street urchins.'

'I'm sorry, Mr Albright, but as long as there's money to back up the bid I have to accept it.' The auctioneer lifted his voice. 'Mr Jameson, if the boy's with you, can I be assured you have the funds?'

'I'm good for five hundred and eighty guineas. And more besides that.'

'Then let's finish this now.' Mr Albright's gold buttons rose on his chest. 'I'll give you six hundred and twenty. But that's my final offer. You won't get a better one.'

Faces turned expectantly. The sideshow wasn't over yet. Boy looked down at Red Waistcoat. Even at this distance, he could see a gleam in the man's eye.

'What say we go higher, lad? About seven hundred should do it.'

Never in his whole life had Boy imagined being in reach of so much money. It was just possible that seven hundred guineas could buy all the food in the city. He put his fingers to his lips and whistled.

'Seven hundred!' Red Waistcoat shouted. 'SEVEN HUNDRED GUINEAS!'

Boy waved again and the crowd roared. For several moments, nothing else could be heard. Not even Mr Albright's protests.

'It looks as though the boy's bought himself an elephant!' Mr Trott brought his hammer crashing down. 'Sold for seven hundred guineas to the Belle Vue Zoological Gardens in Manchester, owned by Mr James Jameson.'

For one glorious moment, Boy actually believed Maharajah was his. It was as good as dipping for a sixpence and finding a sovereign instead. Maybe it was even better than that. And then he remembered. This wasn't his victory. It wasn't even his fight. And it certainly wasn't his money.

On the ground below, Mr Jameson was bouncing up and down on short legs like an excited toad, his red waistcoat bloated with pride. 'I beat that snooty, stuck-up buffoon. I beat him fair and square.'

The crowd cheered again, so loudly that at first only Boy noticed Maharajah lumbering towards them. Then people were forced to shuffle aside. Boy envied them. If he had been on solid ground, he would have run until his legs gave out.

But he could only watch as Maharajah stopped in front of him. Gold eyes, bright as candle flames, stared back then blinked.

Suddenly, the elephant swung his trunk.

Boy jerked away, then cursed his own stupidity. There was nothing behind him but air. He was going to fall, straight on to the cold, hard earth. In that terrifying half-second, Boy wondered if it would be easier just to let it happen.

He never found out.

A tight grip stopped his dive backwards. Maharajah's trunk curled around his wrist, warm and rough. Boy's heart-beat slowed. The clever, gold eyes blinked again and when they opened, he saw himself reflected back. A scrawny boy in stolen clothes. For a moment it was just the two of them.

'My good Lord, will you look at that! The lad and the elephant. They're shaking hands.'

And later Boy realized that this was how it all began.

Chapter Two

Cold sank into his bones and fear made him even colder. The Wormwell auction might be over but Boy was still trapped on top of the stone pillar. Any excitement at winning the bidding war for Maharajah had long since disappeared.

On the ground, a collection of newspaper men fired questions at Mr Jameson.

'Gentlemen, you want to know why I bought him? Well let me tell you this. Maharajah's me crown jewel. We're already the biggest and best in Manchester. Now we're goin' to have them flocking to Belle Vue. They'll be comin' from all over the north. From the whole of the country. The whole of the empire.' He waved his arms expansively.

Boy didn't care about Belle Vue or about Mr Jameson's plans. He just wanted to get down but there wasn't a chance of escape. The pavilion was almost empty. The crowds were fading away and now the pavilion was almost empty. Within an hour, even the reporters had gone home. And still, Crimple remained on guard.

The keeper might as well be a brick wall. He had the muscles of a bare-knuckle boxer, and the face of a man who had seen everything, and then hit it. Hard. Boy wasn't going to be able to get past him, even if he had the courage to jump. His best hope was to hold out until he was back on solid ground.

But when Boy was finally lifted down, freedom seemed as far away as London. Crimple held his neck with one hand, and his arms with the other. He was able to move his legs but only in the direction he was told to go. As they followed Mr Jameson out of the pavilion, nerves made his steps clumsy.

'. . . Arthur Albright didn't know what hit him. He wanted that elephant because he knows what a big attraction he is.' Mr Jameson was managing to talk and drag on a cigar at the same time. 'But I've got him. And I'm goin' to make Maharajah more famous than the Queen herself. You'll see. I've got plans.'

Suddenly he lowered his cigar, his face as calculating as a housewife on a budget. It looked as though a decision had been made. Boy's heart thumped faster. He gave an experimental wriggle, trying to loosen Crimple's hold. Then an ankle kick. No luck.

Was he being taken to the magistrates? Terror turned his breath into quick, shallow gulps. The likelihood was probably a flogging then reform school. Or maybe hard labour in prison. Nobody survived that. Nobody *he* knew anyway.

Boy fought again, harder this time. But his arms were pulled tightly behind his back and pain spiked through his shoulders. He groaned but the grip barely loosened. Frustrated, he did the only thing he could. Twisting sharply, he spat in Crimple's face. Immediately, the keeper drew back a fist and Boy flinched at the fury in his eyes. Perhaps it hadn't been his best idea.

'Oi. Stop that!' Mr Jameson was frowning. 'Stop! There's no need for it, lad. We're all friends now. You helped me, I'll help you. Never let it be said that James Jameson didn't show a little Christian charity to his fellow man, and you've done me a good turn here.'

His words were as solemn as a vow and Boy didn't trust him for a moment. No one gave away anything for nothing. He let his face fill with contempt.

It didn't seem to bother Mr Jameson. In fact, just the opposite. He was chuckling as they stepped outside the pavilion. Boy couldn't understand it. Perhaps he was in the hands of a murderer and his mad accomplice. Or one of those do-gooders who collected orphans like trophies. He didn't know which idea was worse.

'Come on, lad. I'll give you a ride.' Mr Jameson signalled for a nearby hansom cab. 'Those reporters couldn't stop asking about you. And it's got me thinkin' ... if we play this right, it might work out well for the both of us.' He opened the door of the carriage. 'In you get.'

Boy was pushed inside with enough force to knock him off balance. Hastily, he scrambled upright but the door was already closing. Once again, he was trapped.

He leant against the cab window and tried to picture Maharajah as he'd first seen him at the auction. Strong, proud, powerful. At that moment, Boy would have given anything for the same confidence. But he was fairly certain all he had left was fear. Exactly how had he managed to jump from one catastrophe straight into another?

'... *And if you fail, just imagine what I will do to you.*'

'... *And if you fail.*'

'... *if you fail ...*'

He forced the words away.

Outside, Mr Jameson was shouting orders to Crimple. 'Take care of the elephant, and start packin' up the other animals. I want everyone ready to leave the day after tomorrow. Look lively now!'

There was little space left in the cab once Mr Jameson climbed on board. His body was almost as wide as it was squat, and in the shadows, his red waistcoat was the only splash of colour. The resemblance to a toad was even more obvious.

'So where is it that you live, lad?'

Boy crouched into the far corner, keeping himself as small as his lanky limbs allowed. It was one of the first lessons he had learnt around strangers: don't ever be a target.

'You don't say much, do you? What's your name?'

Boy lowered his chin and said nothing. Not because it was a secret but because he didn't know. He'd been called Boy for as long as he could remember. There had been other crueller, ruder names but Boy was the only one he would answer to. He'd forgotten anything else.

'Fine. We'll play this your way. It don't make any difference to me.' Mr Jameson sat back and began hunting through his waistcoat pockets. 'Now where did I put me . . .?'

Boy pulled away so violently that he hit the back wall and rocked the cab. What was the menagerist looking for? A switchblade? A cudgel? Inside, fear formed a hard ball in his gut. He tensed, already anticipating the pain.

'Easy, lad. Easy.' Mr Jameson had stopped searching. 'I'm not goin' to do you any harm. Honest.' Slowly, he reached inside his jacket and brought out another cigar.

Boy felt an embarrassed flush rise up from his neck. He might be frightened but he didn't want anyone else to know it. He eased back down on to the seat.

'Let's see now . . . where were we?' Mr Jameson lit the cigar and threw the burnt match out of the window. Boy could hardly see his face through the smoke. The taste stung the back of his throat.

'Ah, yes. A name. You've gotta have a name. I've a mind to call you Daniel after me dad, and me grandad before him. Daniel George Jameson. It's a good honest Christian name. You've got a look of a Danny about you.'

He paused, perhaps expecting some sort of response. Boy stayed silent but his heart thumped so loudly in his chest that he wondered if Mr Jameson could hear it.

'Very well then ... you point to where we've to go. I'd like to meet your people. I've got plans for you. Big plans.'

Mr Jameson blew out another stream of smoke, and rapped on the cab roof. 'Make towards Cowgate,' he shouted to the driver. 'I'm sure the lad'll let us know when we get near.'

As they moved along the streets, Boy watched the gaslights flicker through the carriage window. Gradually, the houses became more ramshackle, and the neighbourhoods far less respectable.

Mr Jameson had correctly guessed where Boy lived. It wasn't hard. Cowgate was home to Edinburgh's poorest families. Even here, on the outskirts, the poverty was obvious. Soon the lighting stopped altogether and the cab slowed over deep ruts in the road.

At last, Boy saw his chance.

Shielded by cigar smoke, he fumbled for the handle, found it, then shouldered open the carriage door. It flew wide and he jumped.

'Hey, what you doin'? Come here, lad ...'

But Boy didn't look back. Landing with knees bent, he

straightened and sprinted into the gloom. No one followed. He told himself he was relieved.

Weaving through the web of alleys, Boy headed towards the place he currently called home. It was lucky the route was so familiar. The tall tenements were wedged so close together that little light filtered through, even in daytime. Rows of broken windows were either boarded up or patched with rags. Smoke stained everything black. And tonight, the darkness was as thick as porridge.

As he ran, Boy sidestepped piles of rotting waste and foul puddles. Once, the smell would have set his stomach rolling but now he barely noticed. Even the sound of rats scurrying along the gutters didn't bother him any more.

At last, he reached the ruins of the boarding house. This time he checked carefully. No one was waiting beneath the shadowed arches. Maybe he had a little more time before Scatcherd came after him. Besides, inside this building was everything he owned.

Stooping, Boy lifted a broken door panel and wriggled through the gap. The room wasn't big, and it was already full to bursting.

In one corner, several children were practising picking the pockets of an old coat. A bell attached to the sleeve rang whenever they were clumsy, which seemed to be often as far as Boy could hear.

Watching them was a well-dressed woman, as neat and respectable as a vicar's wife. Her name was Mrs Sweets, although sometimes Boy heard her answer to Mary Cutpurse. Few would have guessed she was a thief. Her fine clothes meant she could mix with Edinburgh's wealthy housewives while stealing from their bags and purses.

Nearby, the Fergus brothers were sorting through a pile of pennies, handkerchiefs and cheap jewellery. They worked the same streets as Boy. Two would pretend to fight while the youngest grabbed whatever he could reach from those who stopped to watch.

They were good at what they did but not as good as Boy. It was why he preferred to work alone. And, until today, he'd never come close to being caught.

Head down, Boy edged around the room. He'd only just reached the furthest, darkest corner when the door crashed open. The noise fell on the room like a blanket, muffling any other sound. His stomach seized – he'd been wrong. He'd hardly had any time at all.

'Good evening.' Scatcherd's outline filled the doorway.

Heart pounding, Boy eased back into the corner. He was almost sure the King couldn't see him but that didn't stop the panic. It weighed down heavily against his chest. He had to disappear.

Slowly, Boy slid sideways along the wall. One step then another. And all the time, he stayed aware of Scatcherd. The King had already reached the middle of the room, two of his men stood on guard at either shoulder.

'The boy. Where is he?'

The only response was a nervous cough and a shuffling of feet. Boy knew it wasn't loyalty that stopped people answering, but fear. No one was ever sure what Scatcherd wanted to hear. At least, it gave him a little more time.

He shifted a fraction further and stretched out a hand. His fingers hooked around a hole in the brickwork. Finally. Quickly, he ducked inside the crumbling fireplace. Darkness closed around him. For now, he was safe.

'Well? Is he here?'

Boy heard Scatcherd pivot on his heels. Then footsteps moved closer. And closer. Suddenly a shadow blocked the light, and Boy hugged his knees more tightly against his chest. His heart raced against his ribs.

He needn't have worried. Scatcherd was facing out towards the room, his back against the chimney wall. He appeared to have no idea that Boy was behind him – barely an arm's length away.

'Anyone have an answer for me?'

'He was here just before. I don't know where he's gone now.' Mrs Sweets's voice had started strong but by the end of the sentence it was shaking.

'I see.' Scatcherd's boots lifted and shifted on the empty hearth. He was so close that Boy could have touched the polished leather. 'I hope no one minds if I make certain. Just in case.'

There were a few moments of silence, and Boy imagined Scatcherd signalling orders to his men. Then lantern lights swung around the crowded room. Boy could just see their yellow flicker, but in the hollow of the fireplace, he stayed quiet. The smell of old smoke and ashes filled his lungs.

'He's not here, boss.'

'Nothing over this side either.'

'How disappointing.' Scatcherd released a breath much like the first hiss of a boiling kettle, and a boot slammed against the bricks. Boy was sure he felt the shudder. 'Perhaps, when he returns, one of you could tell him the King expects a visit.'

Abruptly Scatcherd pushed away, and Boy counted several tracks of footsteps cross the floor before fading into the night. A burst of noise signalled that the visitors had gone. And still Boy didn't move. He didn't dare.

He wasn't sure how long he waited, but it was enough time for the room to fall quiet. People had either settled down to sleep or headed out to try their luck in Cowgate.

Cautiously, he twisted until he faced the back wall of the fireplace. He didn't need lamplight because he had done this many times before. Counting from the bottom, he slid his fingers across the bricks. Five up. Three across. One brick sat a little proud of the others. Working carefully, he eased it out, and felt into the gap behind.

The pennies were still there. All three of them. So was the silver sixpence. And the scrap of dirty silk that had once been a handkerchief. It wasn't much, but it was all he had. Quickly, he wrapped the coins in the silk and stuffed the bundle into his trouser pocket before slotting the brick back into place.

'So this is where you're hiding!'

Startled, Boy jerked. A face was peering down at him but it was too dark to see clearly. A match flared, and he almost choked on the relief. It was Robbie, the youngest of the Fergus brothers. 'I reckon you can come out now. It's as safe as it's ever goin' to be.'

Boy would have preferred to stay where he was but he couldn't hide for ever. Wriggling on to hands and knees, he crawled forward. Robbie shifted to give him space. Side by side, they sat with their backs to the chimney; it was where Scatcherd had stood just a little earlier.

'I suppose you heard.' Robbie didn't bother to lower his voice, but either everyone else in the room was asleep or they didn't want to come any closer. 'He wants to see you.'

Slowly, Boy dipped his head.

'You're going have to go. He's bound to catch up with you sooner or later. And Mrs Sweets says you can't stay here. She says none of us can afford to get on his bad side. You have to be out by morning.'

It was what Boy had been expecting but it still hurt. As usual, he was on his own. Almost without noticing, he began rubbing his wrist.

'Anyway, I've been thinking.' Robbie slid him a sideways glance. It hovered somewhere between pity and curiosity. 'The King hates that you don't talk, and he specially hates that you don't talk to him. Maybe if you'd say something then he'd stop going after you.'

He leant closer, and Boy edged back. He hated being touched, every contact pricked like nettle stings. 'Come on. Why don't you have a go? Say anything you want. Don't matter what.'

Boy wished it was that easy. Inside, there were whole speeches; an army of words just waiting for the right signal. But as hard as he tried, they refused to be heard.

Opening his mouth, he pushed out a stream of air, moving his tongue until it flapped like a stranded fish between his lips. Not a sound. It was as though everything had seized up inside him so nothing worked as it should.

'Bless me! I don't reckon you can, you sad sprunt. The King's got you all right. You're never going to escape.'

Turning away, Robbie stretched out and pulled a dirty sheet across his chest. But Boy stayed where he was, knees bent, and tried to pretend the words hadn't felt like a punch to the gut. He was trapped – trapped as surely as if he was still sitting on the stone column at Waverley Pavilion.

Boy knew sleep wouldn't come easily. Or soon. When his eyes finally drifted shut, he dreamt of silk waistcoats and pocket watches. Then Scatcherd was chasing after him, a knife in one hand and a cigar in the other. And oddly, the only obstacle that stood between them was a large elephant, with warm gold eyes.

At dawn, Boy woke with his heart racing, pumping blood into muscles that were ready to run. It had seemed so real. He rubbed a hand across his face, trying to brush away the last traces of the dream. But as much as he tried, one stubborn thought refused to leave.

By leaping from Mr Jameson's carriage, had he just made the biggest mistake of his life?

Chapter Three

PRINCES STREET, EDINBURGH
10 April 1872

Boy kept his plans simple. He had only two goals – to keep one step ahead of Frank Scatcherd, and to find out when Mr Jameson and Maharajah were leaving Edinburgh. And he knew the best place to do both.

The market on Princes Street was far enough away from Cowgate to feel safe. It was also his favourite place to go thieving. The costermongers sold everything from eels and gingerbread to cough drops and crumpets. And better still, there was a newspaper seller on each corner.

'*Herald*. Buy your *Herald* here! *Daily Record*! *The Scotsman*! Read all about Wormwell's menagerie. Get the latest on Maharajah the Magnificent! And more on the mystery of the boy who bought him!'

The stories covered the front page of every newspaper. Of course, Boy couldn't read a word, but he recognized the cartoons. One even pictured Mr Jameson and Albright in a fist fight. But his favourite was a sketch of Maharajah holding out his trunk to an angelic-looking urchin sitting on a pedestal. Boy was relieved to see that it looked nothing like him.

Impulsively, he stole the newspaper, ripped off the cartoon and tucked it inside his shirt. The paper crinkled against his skin as he strolled through the stalls, eavesdropping.

'Did you hear what happened?'

'My husband says there was a fight over the elephant, and it only stopped when a wee lad climbed on to the pavilion gate and whistled.'

'Aye, that's right. Now they're going to give him the elephant.'

'Och no, ladies. The beast's being taken to Manchester. They're heading out by train tomorrow morning. About ten o'clock. The Lord Provost's been invited to the send-off. I heard it from his cook.'

Hidden in the shadows, under the market canopy, Boy allowed himself a small smile. It was all he needed to know.

The next day, Waverley Station was louder and busier than Boy had ever seen it. He'd spent the night curled up behind a luggage cart, only to be woken by steam pulsing from the waiting train.

Minutes later, an army of animal keepers and railway workers had swarmed past. It took them a long time to sort through the waiting cargo. Not only were Mr Jameson's animals leaving for Belle Vue, but the rest of the Wormwell menagerie was heading off too.

Boy could hear squawks, grunts and hisses spill from each crate. In one pen, a tiger paced from corner to corner. Every so often, he stretched open his jaws to show red gums and sharp teeth. Two goats bleated nervously from a neighbouring cage, and a chained parrot beat its wings against the bars.

Alongside the animals were sacks of food – several hundredweight of meat, piles of fruit, and trays of bread. Boy's stomach clenched hungrily. He was an inch away from grabbing a loaf when he heard a steady stomp. The big beasts had arrived. A line of camels, baboons and bears. And at the rear was an elephant.

Boy's heart beat a little faster. He'd been wrong. Maharajah was much bigger than his memory. And much bigger than his dream. Stronger. More powerful. And certainly far more magnificent. But that feeling of kinship – of some curious connection between them – was just the same.

Quickly, Boy ducked back behind the luggage cart, wriggling so he still had a clear view of the train. Maharajah was the final animal to be boarded. He watched as the elephant was led up a ramp to the carriage. The wooden planks bowed beneath the weight.

And then the miracle happened.

Maharajah stopped on the ramp. He didn't move forward; he didn't go back. Balancing precariously, he stood on the creaking plank with the calmness of a cat choosing a spot to sleep in the sun.

Even from this distance, Boy could sense the panic among the keepers. Crimple shouted to another man and together they tried to push, but Maharajah wouldn't budge. The train gave a whistle. Time was ticking away. Maybe it wasn't too late. Perhaps this wasn't goodbye after all.

Boy stayed as still as stone. Air leaked slowly from his mouth but he didn't open his lips. He had the ridiculous thought that if he moved, Maharajah would too. And this incredible beast – who half fascinated, half terrified him – would disappear.

Then Sandev dug into his pockets and pulled out an apple. He waved it in front of the elephant's trunk. Maharajah rocked unsteadily forward. One step. And another. And another.

Boy didn't shift.

At the edges of his vision, he saw Maharajah step into the wagon. The doors shut behind him. Mr Jameson patted the backs of his keepers and smiled broadly.

'All aboard! All aboard!' The train gave another sharp toot.

And finally the spell holding Boy was broken.

He sank down on his heels and curled his face into his knees. What had he been expecting? That somehow

Maharajah would save him from Scatcherd, just like in his dream? Or that Mr Jameson would forgive his escape from the carriage and welcome him with open arms?

No. Coming here had been a stupid idea. They were leaving, and he'd missed his chance of leaving with them. It was as though he was being slowly buried underground and the last chink of light had disappeared.

The wrenching noise that filled the station a moment later took everyone by surprise. Boy lifted his head. What was it? Not the train; it was still standing by the platform, puffing out smoke. The sound came again, angry and insistent. Standing, Boy strained to see through the confusion of people. They were staring at the last wagon. What was going on?

A splintering snap followed by a ripping of wood pushed the volume even louder, and suddenly, Maharajah's head thrust out from the front of the carriage. Like a wet dog, the elephant shook himself, before jerking back to smash his legs through the rear door.

Boy's heart slowed and he grinned. Most of Maharajah was still hidden by the wreckage, but his trunk and tail poked out from either end. It was a bizarre sight, almost comical. Then the elephant kicked a leg forward, rolled back his trunk and blared out a trumpet call. Long and loud. The last of the wagon frame fell apart. And with surprising grace, Maharajah stepped on to the platform.

Boy scrambled back.

'Watch it! He's run mad!'

'Out of the way.'

'Move!'

The keepers had begun edging backwards, taking the passengers with them. One woman screamed, and a man – most likely a reporter – scribbled in his notebook. A rail worker, bristling with importance, pushed through the crowd. 'Get that beast away from my train. I want him gone now. Before he kills someone.'

Boy's pulse picked up again. Surely this couldn't get any worse? But he was wrong.

Arthur Albright of the Yorkshire Zoological Gardens stepped down from one of the first-class carriages. He stalked along the platform, gold buttons gleaming and a whip swinging in his hand. He passed so close that Boy could see the fine stitching on his waistcoat.

'Let me handle this! What that animal needs is a hard lesson to show him who's master. It's just like punishing a child.' With a flick of his wrist, Albright raised the long, leather crop.

Boy didn't even hesitate. He had only one thought: to get the whip.

Quickly, he scrambled up to the top of the luggage cart. From the top, he looked straight down on to Albright and his plume of grey hair. He took one quick breath. And jumped.

Albright had no warning, so despite his size, it was easy. He crumpled like paper when Boy's weight landed heavily on his back. The whip slipped from his grasp. Boy rolled upright and grabbed the handle. Victorious, he clutched it to his chest.

Only now did he stop to wonder why he'd even bothered. What had made him be so stupid? To risk everything – and for an elephant?

Albright was already staggering to his feet, his face red and furious. 'Give me that, you little runt.'

'No!' Mr Jameson was pushing through the crowd. 'Leave him.' Boy's heart skipped with relief but he didn't let go of the crop. It was the only weapon he had. Should he stay and fight, or leave and run? Indecision kept him frozen.

'Jameson! I might have known the brat would be with you. It appears you've taken on another troublemaker for Belle Vue.'

'He's no troublemaker. In fact, you'd be amazed at how helpful he's goin' to be.' Mr Jameson folded his arms. Boy shuffled nearer. Of the two men, instinct told him who was more likely to be on his side. He just prayed he wasn't wrong.

'Is this another one of your ridiculous schemes? Don't you ever learn?'

'There's nothin' ridiculous about what I've got planned. You'll see.'

'Well, no one cares about the boy. He's not important.' Albright stabbed a finger in Maharajah's direction. Spittle flew from his mouth. Boy could almost feel his fury. 'It's that elephant who's a dangerous menace. Someone could have been killed. You ought to have him destroyed.'

'Don't be ridiculous. He was just scared of that tiny carriage space, that's all. No one would want to be stuck in there for seven minutes, never mind seven hours. He's harmless.'

'It didn't look that way to me. He's caused complete chaos. People are terrified. You've wasted your money on a beast you can't control. I'm only grateful you're stuck with him, and not me.'

'Give over! He destroyed a wagon, not a person. He's as gentle as a lamb. He'd never hurt anybody. Why even a child could control him. And I can prove it.'

Boy flinched when Mr Jameson grabbed his shoulders. He tried to pull free but the grip was too hard. What was going on? A strong shove pushed him along the platform towards Maharajah.

'Go on, lad. Show them there's nothin' to be scared of.'

Bewildered, Boy stood within a few feet of the elephant. He wasn't sure what he was supposed to do. Nothing about this was making sense – even his own decision to come here seemed muddled. Then to his horror, Maharajah began to rock and wail. It sounded worse than it had in the carriage. Nerves rattled in his chest like marbles in a tin box.

'The birch. Get rid of it.' Mr Jameson's sharp whisper carried easily through the station. And Boy realized he still had tight hold of the whip. Hand trembling, he placed it on the floor and kicked it backwards. Maharajah stopped wailing. His ears fanned out. They stared at one another. For once in his life, Boy had no ideas. He waited for more instructions but Mr Jameson said nothing.

Over the elephant's broad back, Boy spotted a man standing in the remains of the wrecked carriage. It was Sandev, hiding so far into the shadows that it was unlikely anyone else could see him. Silently, the keeper lifted one arm in the air, spread his hand wide and brought it down in a smooth, sweeping motion.

Boy stared, confused. Sandev did it again. And finally Boy understood; but would it work? He lifted his chin, looked into the elephant's eyes and copied the movement. A faint whistle blew through the station, gentler than a breeze in spring. And Maharajah dropped to one knee.

Somewhere behind there was a cheer, but Boy didn't turn to look. He was too stunned. Sandev pushed his other hand firmly downwards, so Boy did the same. Immediately, the elephant's right knee bent and he lowered his head to the floor. And then there was only relief as Maharajah bowed before him, as obedient as a scolded child.

'Here, lad.'

Instinctively, Boy caught what Mr Jameson had thrown. An apple. This time he didn't need Sandev to show him what to do. Opening his palm flat, he inched a little nearer. And then a little nearer still. Quicker than a wink, Maharajah lunged and grabbed the fruit with his trunk.

Boy reached out, heart slamming. With the tips of his fingers, he stroked the wrinkled skin around one tusk. It felt warm. Rough. Comforting. Curiosity overcame the last of his nerves. He leant forward to rest his cheek in the same spot. He could feel the elephant breathing.

In and out.

Out and in.

This close, Maharajah's eyes were as deep and gold as fire. Behind them, Albright snorted. 'Circus tricks. That's all. It doesn't mean anything. He's still dangerous.'

But Boy could feel the tension ease. There was some laughter and a ripple of applause.

'Take a bow, lad,' Mr Jameson said quietly. Boy did as he was told, even though he felt ridiculous. The clapping grew.

'Delightful!'

'How charming.'

Albright frowned. 'So the beast's calm now. But he's not much use to you in Edinburgh. How d'you think you're going to get him to Manchester? There's no rail company that would be willing to take him after today.'

Mr Jameson was silent. Boy watched his face. He appeared deep in thought but in his eyes Boy thought he saw a glint of triumph. His mouth curved into a sly grin.

'He'll walk. He'll walk to Belle Vue!'

'You're going to walk that elephant more than two hundred miles through Scotland and England?' Albright was scathing. Boy wasn't surprised. It sounded like a ludicrous idea. 'You're a madman, Jameson.'

'He'll do it and he'll be quick about it. I bet you anything. Anything you like.'

'So you'd stake your reputation on that?' Albright's gaze flickered over the crowd. He looked to be making a quick calculation. Something about it woke Boy's sixth sense for trouble. 'Perhaps you'd be willing to make a small bet in front of these good witnesses?'

'Go on. I'm listenin'.'

'I say you'll never make it there in less than seven days. But if you're so confident perhaps you'd care to wager all you've bought in Edinburgh? Better yet, what about all of the animals at Belle Vue?'

'That would close us down.'

But Boy noticed Mr Jameson didn't refuse. Perhaps he was weighing the odds. There was silence; the kind of silence that comes before big decisions are made. With every breath in his body, Boy willed the menagerist to say no. Why would anyone risk losing all they owned? If he only had half as much, he'd be rich. Sometimes people didn't know when they were lucky.

'Put your money where your mouth is, Jameson. I'll stake my menagerie against yours. But if that beast is not at Belle Vue by the nineteenth of April at ten o'clock in the morning, then your livestock is mine.' Mr Albright extended his hand. 'You start tomorrow. Agreed?'

Mr Jameson hesitated then reached out. They shook. And so when Boy watched the 10.05 express roll out of the station fifteen minutes late, Maharajah was not on board. Because he would be walking to Manchester.

Chapter Four

WAVERLEY TRAIN STATION
11 April 1872

'James Fredrick Henry Jameson, you're a fool. And an idiot. And I don't know why I married you.'

The woman who spoke had her hands on her hips and towered above her husband. She was also furious. Boy could understand why. As far as he could tell, Mr Jameson had spent seven hundred guineas on an elephant that he might end up giving away.

'What do you think you're playing at? You'll cost us everything.' She prodded Mr Jameson's chest with a sharp finger. 'All that we've worked for.'

To Boy's embarrassment, the couple had begun this argument on the platform at Waverley Station. Or at least,

Mrs Jameson was arguing. Mr Jameson just stood like a child waiting for a hoop to stop spinning. Boy wished he felt as calm. He still had no idea what was going on.

Mrs Jameson was tall and thin, with faded brown hair pulled so tightly to the top of her head that the skin across her narrow face stretched tight. At the moment, she reminded Boy of a spitting alley cat trying to protect her territory. All claws and hiss.

She'd emerged from one of the carriages just before the train set off, and announced that if Mr Jameson was staying in Edinburgh then so was she. A conductor had to be sent scurrying to retrieve her luggage from first class.

It was soon obvious to Boy that she didn't entirely trust her husband – and that was even before she'd learnt about the bet.

'Sheer stupidity. That's what it is. Whatever possessed you? You'll have to back down.' She took a deep breath and finally gave Mr Jameson a chance to speak.

'Me dearest dove, I know what I'm doin'. This will be the makin' of Belle Vue. I promise you.'

'But, Jamie, you can't win. That elephant is no racehorse. He's slow and heavy, he can't cover that distance in seven days. What if he gets ill? What if there's an accident? It's impossible, even for you, and Albright knows it. Why do you think he made the bet?'

'Poppycock, me sweet love.' Boy was amazed Mr Jameson's confidence didn't waver. 'This'll be the biggest, most talked about event since the coronation. And this is the lad who's goin' to make it happen. Him and Maharajah.'

He gestured Boy forward. Boy shuffled nearer. He'd been waiting here since the train steamed out of the station. Part of him – the small, optimistic part that seemed to have survived against all the odds – still hoped this was the chance he'd been waiting for. But his other self, who knew nothing ever came for free, sneered at the idea.

'This here is Danny. Danny, this is Mrs Jameson herself. The kindest, most lovin' wife a man could want.'

'Don't try that flannel with me.' Mrs Jameson folded her arms over her chest and glared down at her husband. 'I want to know what's going on.'

She wasn't the only one. Boy was desperate to find out as well. What could he possibly do for Belle Vue that was so important? His only skills were as a pickpocket. He knew nothing about animals and certainly nothing about elephants. It didn't make any sense.

'Come on, Jamie,' Mrs Jameson demanded. 'Sandev's already agreed to look after Maharajah until we get to Manchester. If you need more help, we could ask him to stay on. At least he knows what he's doing.'

'No, me love, you don't understand. I've got it all worked out. Once we get to Belle Vue, we won't need Sandev. Because we'll have Danny.'

'What are you talking about?'

'The boy, me darlin'. He's me secret weapon. After he's been cleaned up and had a bit of trainin', he and Maharajah will be the biggest draw in the park. You'll see.'

Mrs Jameson snorted down her long nose. 'Don't be ridiculous! He's nothing but a dirty, scrawny urchin.'

Boy didn't even blink at the insult. He'd heard lots worse. All his attention fixed on Mr Jameson. Exactly what was his plan? However much he turned over the possibilities, he just couldn't work it out.

'There might not a great deal to him now, me dove, but he's worth his weight in gold. Thanks to the auction, there's stories of him everywhere. Him and the elephant. Look at the front of *The Herald*. And *The Scotsman*. People would pay thousands for publicity like that. And I can bet anything you like, there'll be more tomorrow.'

Mr Jameson swiped his hand in the air as though reading a newspaper headline. 'Can't you see it? – "Elephant Boy Tames Wild Beast". "Orphan Saves Maharajah from a Vicious Whippin".'

'Don't you bet me anything, James Jameson. That's what got us into this trouble.'

'Me pet, you know as well as me, that what the public really love is a story. A drama. A tale of triumph over adversity. Well, we can give it to 'em thanks to Danny here. He's the boy that bought an elephant. The urchin who's a friend to wild creatures. The only one that could calm a raging beast. And he's the boy that's going to ride Maharajah all the way to Manchester.'

Ride an elephant! Nerves quivered in Boy's stomach. And yet underneath it all he felt a spark of something that might actually be hope. He moved a little closer. But not close enough that he couldn't still escape.

'Think about it,' Mr Jameson paused. 'That journey's more than two hundred miles, through Scotland and England. Think of all those towns and villages. All those people. All those newspapers. All those customers.'

He rolled out the last word so it lingered between the three of them. Mrs Jameson's anger seemed to fade a little. Her arms loosened from their tight hold against her chest.

'That's all very well. But if you think Arthur Albright is going to sit back and let us win, then you really are a fool.'

It was too late. Even Boy could sense she was weakening. Mr Jameson put a hand around her waist to pull her close.

'I've already thought of that. Whatever he tries, I can handle. Trust me, me dove. Just trust me.'

Gently, he kissed her cheek. The skin turned pink. For a moment, Boy could picture Mrs Jameson as a young girl, soft and full of laughter. There was a sigh.

'Very well, Jamie. You've got your wish. And I hope you don't drag us all down with you. I'll never forgive you if you lose Belle Vue.'

'I won't, Ethel May, I promise you that.'

Boy's insides cramped as Mr Jameson stepped nearer. At long last, this was the opportunity he'd been waiting for. He couldn't have been more certain if a herald of angels had flown down to Waverley Station to sing it out loud.

'First of all, I'm glad you came back to us, lad. I had a feeling in me gut that you would. And I'm hardly ever wrong.'

Mr Jameson put a hand on Boy's shoulder. Boy worked hard not to flinch. The contact prickled. He couldn't imagine ever wanting to be touched.

'Now I've got somethin' I need to ask you – and it's important. Is there anyone here in this city who you'd miss? And who'd miss you?'

The question was so blunt it was almost cruel. A succession of faces filed quickly through his mind. Robbie, Mrs Sweets and the other Fergus brothers were all there. And the mystery woman who he only ever saw in his dreams.

But the truth was, no one would really care if he disappeared – and it was entirely possible that only Frank Scatcherd would actually notice. Blinking, Boy lifted his chin and shook his head. The pat on his shoulder was brief so he allowed it.

'Then this is a golden opportunity I'm offering you, lad. A chance for fame and fortune. A chance of a lifetime, some might say.' Mr Jameson's voice turned silky. He slipped a gold sovereign from his wallet, and dropped it into Boy's hand. It was hard and cold and comforting.

'That's for you. There's only one now, but I can promise you if you stick with us, there'll be more. I want you to come to Belle Vue. You'll have enough food to fill your belly twice over. A fine suit of new clothes. There'll be a real bed with cotton sheets. And in the winter, we always have fires burning in every hearth.'

A sly look crossed his face. 'And there's the elephant. You'll have Maharajah. He'd be yours to look after. And you can ride him in style all the way to your new home. So what d'you say?'

Boy knew Mr Jameson must have worked out exactly what to offer. Comfort. Safety. And Maharajah. Nothing had ever sounded more tempting but could he believe it? It seemed too incredible to be real.

Of course, in the end, the decision was easy – because he didn't have much of a choice. This was what he wanted. A chance to escape. He curled his fingers around the sovereign then nodded.

'That's wonderful, lad.' Mr Jameson grinned. 'And remember you're Danny from now on. I want you to have a name in those newspapers. I want people to know who you are. And where you come from – Danny from Belle Vue. They're both names to be proud of. Remember that.'

Boy didn't return to Cowgate. If this worked out, he'd never have to go back there again. And he'd never have to see Scatcherd. Or feel his fists. Or the cut of his knife. Every time he realized the possibilities, his heart seemed to lift right out of his chest.

Instead, Boy left Waverley Station in a hired carriage alongside the Jamesons. There was a lot to be done, according to Mrs Jameson, and very little time to do it. She ticked off the jobs on her gloved fingers.

'A bath. A decent meal. And most definitely a lesson in basic manners . . . but first we'll have to arrange some new clothes.' She swept a look from Boy's head to his feet.

'Perhaps a suit in green silk? You'll need something elegant but that'll also attract attention.'

'He'll be sittin' on an elephant, me dove,' said her husband. 'If that's not goin' to attract attention, I don't know what will.'

A little later, the carriage stopped at a parade of wealthy shops. Boy recognized George Street. He'd been here once before but a grubby pickpocket stood out among the rich shoppers like a cat in a dog race so he hadn't returned.

Out of habit, he looked around for thieving opportunities. Grocers and chemists clustered next to clockmakers and drapers. On one side, an emporium stretched three storeys high, and every window was full of bedding, glassware and china. Next door, a cobbler worked on a pair of lady's shoes, while the smell of peppermint drifted from a nearby sweet shop. Boy's mouth watered. But he wasn't allowed to linger.

Like a battleship in full sail, Mrs Jameson stormed through one doorway. A bell jangled as they went inside.

Boy swallowed a gasp.

The room was filled, floor to ceiling, with shelves of folded cloth. Each fabric had been sorted according to colour and type, from muslin and cotton to velvet and tweed. He'd never seen such choice.

The clothes he stood up in were all that he owned – a tattered shirt earned by bartering with a fellow thief; trousers and a jacket stolen from a busy washerwoman; and, his proudest possession, some ill-fitting boots. They weren't a matching pair, but still worth every hour he'd spent scouring Edinburgh's rubbish dumps.

Yet here, amid this rich finery, Boy felt every inch of what he was – a dirty, ragged pickpocket. In the slang of the streets, he was nothing more than a tea leaf. A dipper. A fine wirer. A tooler. A thief.

A small man, sharp-featured and pale, came out from behind one of the shop counters.

'Welcome to Fairgreave and Sons, tailors to the gentry. Can I help you, madam?' He bowed to Mrs Jameson and turned a calculating eye on her husband. 'Sir?'

He ignored Boy. Boy tugged at the sleeve of his shirt and tried not to care.

'I need a suit of clothes made up, the best you have, for Danny 'ere. We're thinkin' of somethin' bright, in silk maybe.'

The tailor didn't even pretend to think it over. 'Sir, I'm afraid it's just not possible. We're a high-class establishment, serving refined and fashionable tastes. We don't cater for beggar children.' He gave a loud sniff. 'And to put it frankly, the boy smells. I suggest you go elsewhere.'

A familiar feeling flooded over Boy. He wasn't good enough. Not good enough for this place or anywhere else that would ever matter. He hated that the tailor's reaction even bothered him. Why hadn't he learnt by now?

'He smells, but he can have a wash. You're a fussy snob, but there's nothin' you or I can do about that.'

Shocked, Boy stared at Mr Jameson. It was the first time

he could remember anyone ever defending him. In Cowgate, asking for help was a certain way to disappointment; he'd got used to standing on his own. Warmth unfurled in his chest.

Mr Jameson took out his wallet, and tipped a handful of coins on to the counter. 'Perhaps these could change your mind. I'm a cash man, meself. Don't believe in credit.'

The tailor's fingers closed over the money before it could roll to the floor. He gave a smile so thin it looked like a line had been drawn across his face.

'On reflection, sir, we might be able make an exception. I'll see what I can do. Just this once.' He gestured to one of his assistants. 'Fetch the silks, Turpin. The jewel colours.'

'Yes, Mr Fairgreave.' The man scurried off towards a ladder at the back of the shop.

Turning to Boy, the tailor pulled a measuring tape from around his neck. His nose twitched. 'Legs apart and raise your arms.'

Boy glanced at Mr Jameson who nodded. So, bracing himself, he did as he was asked. The urge to run had rarely been stronger. Mr Fairgreave made a series of rapid measurements, scribbling notes as he worked.

'He's very . . . brown, isn't he?'

Boy was used to people talking around him – and about him. He always listened. But this time, he waited for Mr Jameson's answer with more than normal interest. Of course, he knew he wasn't the same colour as everyone else. His skin didn't freckle in the sun, or turn pasty white, even in winter. He looked different. What he didn't know was the reason why.

'Well what's not dirt is all him. So I expect he's got some foreign blood in him somewhere.' Mr Jameson had settled himself into an armchair. Now he raised an eyebrow. There was a challenge in his expression that Boy was glad wasn't directed at him. 'Have you a problem with that?'

'No! No, sir. Of course not.' Mr Fairgreave blinked rapidly. 'And what style of clothing were you considering, sir? For what sort of occasion?'

'A suit of Sunday clothes for a start. Then somethin' more in the Indian style. Those big trousers. Like ladies' bloomers. They might be the most comfortable. He's goin' to be riding an elephant.'

'An elephant?' The tailor's pencil jabbed into Boy's arm. It hurt, but Boy didn't mind. The expression on Mr Fairgreave's face was worth it. He looked appalled.

'Yes, the story will be in all the papers. If I were you, I'd watch out for it tomorrow in *The Herald*. And *The Scotsman*. You could make your name sewin' clothes for this lad. He's goin' to be famous.'

'Famous, you say?' Boy could almost hear the deliberations going on in Mr Fairgreave's head.

'Yes, no doubt about it. You'll see.'

Mrs Jameson had been examining swatches of silk at the counter, now she came to stand by her husband. He patted her hand. 'What d'you think, me dearest?'

'An Indian wardrobe would certainly attract a great deal

of attention, Jamie. And maybe a waistcoat – one in each of the coloured silks. With a white shirt beneath.'

'Perfect, me dove. And slippers to match every outfit, I reckon.'

For the rest of the morning, Boy was pulled and prodded. Lengths of cloth were flung across his shoulders, while patterns were cut and tacked. He endured it only because he knew he had to, but each touch felt like a hot iron.

Finally, to his relief, Mrs Jameson seemed satisfied. She nodded to her husband, who rose from his seat and opened his wallet again.

'I need at least one complete costume for tomorrow. I don't care how you do it but it must be delivered to my hotel by seven o'clock in the mornin'. The Cavendish on Albany Street.' Mr Jameson placed another stack of coins on the counter. 'There'll be a bonus on top of that if you do.'

'Certainly, sir.' Mr Fairgreave was all politeness now. He cleared his throat. 'It's been an experience to serve you, sir. I don't think we've ever outfitted a person for an elephant ride before.'

Mr Jameson blew out a cloud of cigar smoke as he opened the shop door for them to leave. Boy heard the bell set tinkling again before Mr Jameson replied.

'Oh, this is not just a ride, me good man. *This is an adventure!*'

Chapter Five

THE CAVENDISH HOTEL, EDINBURGH
11 April 1872

'I f he causes trouble, he's out.' The man behind the hotel desk glared at Boy as though he was only one move away from committing a particularly monstrous crime.

'He won't.' Mr Jameson took a puff of his cigar and leant a little further over the desk. 'And can I say how grateful we are that you were able to put us up for an extra night. Me and Mrs Jameson always stay at the Cavendish when we're in Edinburgh. We'd have hated to take our business elsewhere.'

He let the threat hang in the air for a moment but it took the landlord a little time to appreciate the message. Then he smiled nervously.

'You know we're always glad to have you, Mr Jameson.' He jerked his head. 'The maid will show him up to the room. The Indian fella's already arrived. The boy's sharing with him.'

It took three flights of steep stairs to reach the attic chamber. The room was small and plain but compared to what Boy was used to, it was a palace. Tonight would be the first time he'd ever slept in a hotel. Or in a room with a fire in the hearth. Or without mice and rats. The list could go on and on.

There was only one bed – which Sandev had already claimed judging by the abandoned suitcase – but a mattress had been laid out on the floor, near the fire. Boy sat and felt the softness of the cotton sheets with something close to wonder.

He had nothing to unpack. His only belongings were the bundle of pennies, the newspaper cutting and Mr Jameson's sovereign. He pushed them all under the pillow, making sure everything was well hidden.

But Boy had no more time alone. Footsteps stomped along the corridor then Mrs Jameson marched in, towels tucked under one arm. Behind her, two maids carried a tin bath, and others followed with buckets of hot water.

'Over there, please. Quickly now.'

Boy watched as the tub filled and the steam rose. This would be a new experience. He did wash but not often, and only when the stench became so strong that even he noticed. Usually, he stripped to the waist in a trough of rainwater, except for one summer's afternoon spent scavenging in the River Leith with Robbie. He still remembered how the cold had stolen his breath, and chased goosebumps across his skin.

Mrs Jameson was brisk. 'Take off your clothes. Put them in a pile over there. The sooner you're clean the better.'

Boy hesitated. He wasn't shy. No one living in the slums could stay prudish, but trusting other people was hard.

'Don't worry, there's nothing you've got that I haven't seen before. I brought up two younger brothers.'

She rolled up her sleeves and knelt to test the bathwater. All but one of the maids left the room. Boy peeled off his trousers, shirt and jacket, and grabbed a towel. Naked, he huddled inside the folds. On the floor, his clothes were a heap of dirty rags. He struggled not to feel ashamed.

Mrs Jameson rose to her feet and glanced at the pile.

'Burn these,' she said to the maid. 'All of them. And throw away the boots. Then bring a plate of bread and cheese, maybe a little ham.'

'Yes, ma'am.' The girl left hurriedly, holding a hand to her nose and the clothing at arm's length.

'Well, get in, lad. You're not going to get clean just by looking at it.'

Gingerly, Boy stepped into the tub, and lowered his body into the water. He knew some of the other slum children would have run screaming from the idea of a bath, but he had a fierce desire to be clean. He was sick of stinking like the Cowgate alleys.

'Mr Jameson said you weren't a great talker but do you know what this is?' Mrs Jameson held out a cake of soap. Boy nodded, a little insulted to be asked. 'Then use it. I want you smelling like a spring garden by the time you're finished.'

Warily, Boy took the soap. He still couldn't quite believe his good fortune. At any moment, someone was bound to burst in and say it had all been a terrible mistake. That all this was not for him but for another, more deserving child.

He kept his eyes on Mrs Jameson as she moved around the room, warming the towels by the fire and lighting the oil lamp. She began to sing softly: '... the lilies so pale. And the roses so fair ...' Her voice was surprisingly sweet. A whisper of a memory drifted into Boy's head and then disappeared.

He sat back in the tub. The soap bubbled up between his wet fingers. He spread it over his skin and the dirt ran in streaks down his arms. The bathwater clouded.

Closing his eyes, Boy held his breath and sank beneath the surface. He lay there, feeling cocooned and safe. When he sat up again, his muscles were as soft as butter. He rubbed soap into his scalp, and scrubbed so hard he couldn't believe any grime could possibly remain.

'Come on, up you get.'

Mrs Jameson held out a towel. Boy stood and wrapped it around his middle. He watched the water stream off his body. Now that he was clean, his skin seemed even darker. The colour of strong tea, Mrs Sweet had once said, not altogether unkindly.

But that wasn't the only reason he looked different.

Underneath the layers of dirt, there was clear evidence of the life he was leaving behind. And it wasn't pretty.

Scars dotted his skin, some old, some new. Most of them had been earned in fights with other thieves. He'd been lucky to survive one knife wound which ran the length of his shoulder. But by far the worst were the marks on one wrist, so deep they would probably never fade. Boy blocked out that memory. He didn't want to think about Scatcherd now.

For several moments, Mrs Jameson's gaze moved over his injuries. Boy waited for the revulsion. He was surprised – and beyond grateful – when her expression didn't change. He'd hate to be pitied.

'Your food's over there by the hearth,' she said at last. Her voice sounded rougher than before and she had to clear her throat before continuing. 'I want to see a good bit eaten by the time I come back. I'll go and get you something to wear.'

By the time Mrs Jameson returned, Boy had already stuffed down most of his supper. He pulled the plate close to his chest, worried that she might take the rest away. But instead, another twist of bread dropped into his lap.

'For you,' she said. 'It looks like you need it. And I've brought one of Mr Jameson's shirts. It'll do for now. I expect your new clothes will arrive in the morning.'

Awkwardly, Boy tugged on the nightshirt. The hem hung below his knees. He sat on the bed and pushed the rest of the food into his mouth. Mrs Jameson watched until the last scrap disappeared.

'Now into bed with you, lad.'

The sheets on the mattress had been drawn back and Boy slid between them.

To his surprise, Mrs Jameson smoothed the covers carefully around him before reaching to brush his forehead. Instinctively, Boy pulled back. A soft sigh touched his cheek.

'Get some rest. Tomorrow will be a busy day.'

She left with a bustling sweep of skirts. The room grew dark, and Boy's eyes drifted shut. Much later, he heard Sandev slipping into the room and then there was nothing but the comfort of sleep.

Boy stood in front of the mirror and stared. The stranger was like him, but not like him. He had the same dark eyes and brown skin. The same hair with the cowlick curl that refused to lie flat. But still, he couldn't quite believe it.

Like Sandev, he was wearing trousers that were loose at the knee and gathered at the ankle. A green waistcoat covered a white silk shirt, and on his feet were matching leather slippers that curled up at the ends.

The clothes had arrived promptly at seven o'clock this morning. He'd tugged them on in the small dressing chamber next to the Jamesons' hotel room and then turned to face the mirror. Five minutes later, he was still trying to get over the shock.

He reached out again and touched the glass. His reflection did the same.

'Danny.' He mouthed the name experimentally, watching his lips move. It was strange but not awkward. From now on, this is who he was. He had a real name. A real identity. He wasn't Boy any longer.

He was Danny from Belle Vue.

Behind him the door cracked open. 'Come on, Danny,' Mr Jameson shouted. 'Let's have a look at you.'

Four faces turned as Danny stepped into the next room. He heard Mrs Jameson gasp, and saw Sandev's eyes widen. But Crimple was the first one to speak. 'Bleedin' Nora! I'd never have recognized him.'

Mr Jameson just grinned. 'Splendid. Absolutely splendid. We'll have everyone eatin' out of the palms of our hands.' He stuck his thumbs into the pockets of his waistcoat. 'So now that we're all here, let's start plannin' a hullaballoo.'

Danny had no idea what a hullaballoo was but he knew it was likely to be big. The Elephant Race was due to begin in two hours, and nerves were already taking hold of his stomach. He lined up beside the others and waited.

'Now listen carefully because I'm countin' on each one of you.' Mr Jameson had begun marching up and down the room like an army general. 'You've all got jobs to do. Sandev's joinin' us from here until Belle Vue. And on the way, he's goin' to teach Danny everythin' he needs to know about Maharajah.'

Lightly, he tapped Danny's arm. 'So lad, I want you to listen and learn well. In seven days I'm expectin' you to have that beast purring like a pet cat. He's your responsibility. Your job's to look after that elephant like he's more precious than the Crown Jewels.'

Swallowing, Danny nodded. The collar of his new shirt rubbed against his neck and he reached to tug it back. This wasn't just about escaping from the slums or from Scatcherd and the Leith Brotherhood. He actually had a job to do. And if he didn't get it right, he'd be back where he started.

Mr Jameson continued pacing. 'I've managed to get us one of Wormwell's supply wagons. It was goin' cheap at the auction. Crimple will be the driver – he's the muscle. He'll sort the stuff that needs fixin'. Food, security, broken equipment, that type of thing.'

He rubbed his hands. 'I'm goin' to work the publicity. I want this story on every front page. "Maharajah the Magnificent and the Boy who tamed him." Nobody's ever going to forget seein' us strollin' down their high street.'

The flaw in this plan was obvious. Danny hadn't tamed anyone or anything – and especially not Maharajah. He swallowed again, throat suddenly dry.

'We'll have posters sayin' we're comin' through every town and village. Me and Mrs Jameson will be travellin' with you as far as the Borders. After that I've a man in mind who'll help the rest of the way. He's an animal doctor by the name of Saddleworth. Got lots of zoological experience and he's lookin' for permanent work. He'll join us in a couple of days.' Mr Jameson looked around. 'So any questions?'

It was Crimple who asked what Danny had been dreading to hear.

'It's like this, Gov.' The keeper shifted his weight from foot to foot, and curled his hands into fists. 'I can see you've got the boy kitted out with fancy clothes, and I'll admit he looks better. But what do we know about him? He can't even speak, he's just a dumb mute. And he's foreign-lookin'. I don't trust him. He could slit our throats and rob us in our beds.'

For one angry moment, Danny wanted to take a swing at Crimple's face. Then the nerves dancing inside his stomach took a swooping dive. This was when everything would be taken away from him. He'd been stupid to believe he could start a new life.

A hand clasped the back of his neck and Danny tried not to recoil. Mentally, he measured the distance to the door. He could still escape. It was not too late.

'I'll say this to you loud and clear, Nelson Crimple. I don't care where this lad came from or about the colour of his skin. He's one of us now. Part of Belle Vue. Besides, he can't be that dumb.' Mr Jameson's voice sharpened. 'He's here with us, isn't he? And it's going to be the cleverest choice he's ever made. You mark me words.'

A dull flush crept across Crimple's face. 'Once a thief, always a thief, that's what I say. The boy's a dipper. We might as well call him Dan the Dip, cos that's what he is.'

'Dandip. Is it not a good name for an elephant's thief?'

The voice was light and musical, each word pronounced

so exactly that the overall effect was almost too perfect. And with a start, Danny realized it was first time he'd heard Sandev speak.

'Dandip. Dandip . . . yes, I like it!' Mr Jameson's eyes glittered. 'It's got something. We could use it. Let's see . . .'

He gazed into the distance. Danny wasn't sure what was happening. But everyone else stayed quiet, even Mrs Jameson. Although she didn't look happy. Two lines creased her high forehead, and her fingers knotted tightly together.

'You're Dandip,' Mr Jameson said at last, pointing at Danny. 'An Indian prince, orphaned as a baby, whose only friend was an elephant cub. But you're torn apart when he's brought to England. You follow him and . . . and you're reunited at the Wormwell auction. Just as Maharajah's being sold! It's a bloomin' miracle. Now you're both goin' to Belle Vue to make your home together.'

He pulled a cigar from his jacket. 'What a story! The newspapers will love it. And so will the payin' public. It'll explain everythin'. You're a foreigner. You've got no English. It's a touch of genius, even if I do say it meself.'

Danny struggled to think. Surely no one could possibly believe such nonsense? There were so many holes in the story it was difficult to know where to begin.

Crimple tried. 'But nobody'll believe he's royal, Gov.'

'Poppycock! He can be the son of an Indian princess and an English army officer. He was killed in battle, and she died of grief shortly after givin' birth. All you have to do is tell the story with enough confidence and everyone will believe it. And I'll tell you why – because everyone will *want* to believe it.'

In the whole of his life, Danny didn't think he'd ever heard such rubbish. He'd never be able to fool anyone into believing he was a prince. But Mr Jameson stopped any more objections with a sweep of his hand.

'We can sort the detail later. And I don't want any of this talk goin' further than these four walls. Remember that. We keep this private, just between us here. Our job is to entertain the public. And you gotta think big, not small. Because this is not everyday life. It's an adventure of a lifetime.'

Once again he gripped Danny's shoulder. Danny could feel the pressure bite through his skin. He wanted to pull away.

'So are you in, lad?'

Chapter Six

WAVERLEY PAVILION, EDINBURGH
12 April 1872

'Ladies and gentlemen, today is the start of a fantastical journey. And one day, you can tell your children and grandchildren that you were here. Right at the beginnin' of the Elephant Race.'

Throwing open his arms, Mr Jameson shouted to the crowds from the top of the steps at Waverley Pavilion. Word must have spread because there were hundreds of people staring up at Danny, Maharajah and the rest of the Belle Vue party.

Danny suspected most of them had seen the newspaper stories about yesterday's drama at the station and were hoping for more excitement. Mr Jameson had practically bounced with delight when he'd read the headlines aloud over breakfast. 'What did I tell you?' he'd said, kissing his wife. 'It's workin' already.'

Fidgeting in his new clothes, Danny stood next to the Jamesons. This was his first official outing as Prince Dandip, and no one from his old life would have recognized him today. It was the main reason he'd not made any fuss, even when Mrs Jameson had used henna paste to dye his hair. Now there was no hint of brown, only a flat, toneless black.

To complete the disguise, a strip of white cloth had been wrapped around his head so that it matched Sandev's turban. Three peacock feathers waved from the crown, and a black curl kept falling in his eyes. Danny tried to push it back, but it wouldn't stay. He felt ridiculous.

At least Maharajah was also dressed up for the occasion. A jewelled harness covered his head and neck, and a glittering red bead hung from the centre. The collar had been designed especially for him, Mr Jameson explained. On very grand occasions, a plume of ostrich feathers could be fitted to the top.

It certainly looked impressive and Danny had stared at the jewels enviously. His fingers itched to touch but Crimple had curled his lip.

'He's had that harness for years, boy. Wormwell had it made up for parades and such like. But there's nothin' for you there. Everythin's paste and glass so you can keep your thievin' hands off.'

Even if the jewels had been real, Danny wouldn't have taken the risk. Besides, he already had Mr Jameson's sovereign safely tucked into the cuff of one of his new shirts, alongside the bundle of pennies. At the moment, he had no intention of running but he liked knowing they were there.

'. . . a grand and marvellous occasion, ladies and gentlemen. And I can promise you, it'll be one you'll never forget.' Mr Jameson had just finished his speech when Arthur Albright strode up the pavilion steps.

'I'll do something you won't forget if you don't hurry up.' Albright held up a pocket watch and flag. 'You've only ten minutes before ten o'clock, and don't expect any extra time if you're not ready.'

'Now, now. Don't get yourself upset, Arthur.' Danny could tell Mr Jameson was enjoying himself. Albright's rudeness seemed to bounce off him as harmlessly as soap bubbles. 'Everything's under control. We were just waitin' for you. Now that you're here, we can start.'

He nodded to Sandev who manoeuvred Maharajah forward. The elephant knelt on the top step. Danny had been warned what to expect but that had been talk and hot air. This was the reality. And Maharajah was bigger than a mountain.

Anxiously, Danny brushed his wrist, feeling the scarred tissue beneath his fingers. He stopped as soon as he realized what he was doing. He didn't have time to be nervous.

Hooking a slipper on to Maharajah's bent knee, Danny grasped the wrinkled skin behind one ear. He slid a leg over the elephant's neck and shuffled to sit just behind his head. Stretching, he gripped the harness. Almost immediately, Maharajah rose.

It was like riding a wave – there was the sheer terror of going under and the relief of bobbing up again. The strength tossed Danny forward and back, until finally he came to rest, stiff but upright. He hoped he didn't look as panicked as he felt.

At least, the audience seemed to like it; there was a ripple of applause and some gasps. But, to Danny's relief, Maharajah remained perfectly still. He released a breath. They'd passed the first test. And if anyone deserved thanks it was Maharajah. He suspected it was only the elephant who had stopped them from looking like fools.

Gathering his courage, Danny looked down. On the ground, Mr Jameson and Albright were answering questions from the newspaper men.

'Do you think you can make it in seven days, Mr Jameson?' one shouted.

'Of course, young man. And with time to spare.'

'Mr Albright, are you confident you can win the bet?' asked another.

'I have absolutely no doubt that in a week's time, Maharajah, and the other Belle Vue animals will be joining us at the Yorkshire Zoological Gardens in Leeds.' Albright's chest of gold buttons expanded. 'In fact I invite you all to see them there.'

The boast might have rattled another man but Danny

was sure Mr Jameson would have a trick up his sleeve. He was right. Puffing on his cigar, the menagerist blew out a long stream of smoke, and clapped a hand around the shoulders of the nearest reporter.

'I believe you're from *The Herald*, young fella? Well you can let your readers be the first to know.'

He pointed a finger at Danny. 'That there boy – he's an Indian prince. Name's Dandip. Make sure you spell it right. That's D-A-N-D-I-P. He followed Maharajah all the way from Delhi and now they're goin' to Manchester to make their home at Belle Vue. Tell your readers, they can see them there in a week's time. We're open all year round.'

Danny held his breath. He waited for someone to point out the lie – to say they'd never heard anything so ludicrous. So stupid. But no one did. Instead, Mr Jameson was immediately surrounded by reporters.

'How did the Prince travel from India?'

'Is he planning to stay?'

'Will he be meeting Her Majesty during his visit?'

Amazed, Danny watched them scrabble for information. Mr Jameson had been right; they believed it. And if they believed, surely he was safe? No one could harm Prince Dandip of Delhi. Not even Frank Scatcherd.

Eventually, Mr Jameson broke away from the press men. Sandev appeared with a last apple for Maharajah. The tower clock ticked down the final minute. And Danny straightened his shoulders. The adventure was about to begin.

If he'd ever felt like this before – a churning mix of giddy, excited and terrified – he couldn't remember it.

'So are you ready, lad? Albright's not happy. He didn't like being upstaged. But he's goin' to wave the flag, then you're away.'

If it had happened like that, Danny thought later, perhaps everything would have been fine. But there was no dignified send-off; no gentle signal as the clock struck the hour. Because Maharajah didn't wait.

As though his life depended on it, the elephant ploughed down the steps and into the shrieking spectators. They scattered like ants. All Danny could do was bounce on Maharajah's back and panic. He tightened his grip on the harness. What had gone wrong? This was supposed to have been easy.

He scrambled to remember his instructions. Nothing surfaced. Behind him, there were shouts, mingled with screams. Albright was roaring something but the words grew faint as Maharajah moved further and further away.

Desperately, Danny searched for help. On the far side of the pavilion Crimple sat at the reins of the wagon, but he was hemmed in by the crowd, and Mr Jameson and Sandev were nowhere in sight.

Maharajah was now veering in the opposite direction, out on to Edinburgh's steep streets. This was not the route that had been carefully plotted on the map. Danny felt a flush of sweat glue the new silk shirt to his skin. He'd assumed elephants were slow animals but Maharajah had sprung into a trot that was getting faster and faster as they went up and down hill.

Ahead were roads bustling with market stalls, shoppers and carriages. Bounding towards all that, was a fully grown elephant, ridden by someone whose training had lasted less than two minutes. And right now, the only advice Danny could remember was from Sandev: '*Do not worry. I will be with you.*'

It didn't help.

The path cleared and, for one glorious, hope-filled moment, Danny thought all would be fine. He relaxed slightly, loosening his death grip on the harness. At the roadside, two small children laughed and pointed as he and Maharajah bumped past.

Then the elephant turned down the cobbled curve of Victoria Street, and into the Grassmarket, home to one of the city's busiest street markets. Now there was no laughter, only screams. And Danny had the briefest impression of faces wide-eyed with disbelief as they charged by.

'What . . .?'

'Watch it!'

'Get away . . .'

The first casualty was a tray of pies, carried by a baker's boy with such fierce concentration that he didn't notice anything else. Not even the elephant stampeding towards him. By the time Maharajah had passed, the food lay in the mud. A crate of kippers was next, smashed and ground under the elephant's feet. And that was just the start.

Danny watched helplessly as sacks overturned, spilling cabbages and potatoes across the street. Further on, a stall of cooking pots toppled when shoppers scrambled to safety. And the noise grew louder as a flock of chickens escaped their damaged cage.

In the middle of the chaos, a wagon driver tried to calm his horses. Danny could tell it wasn't doing any good. They reared up, sending a cartload of barrels bumping down the hill. One bounced, cracked and split. The spicy scent of beer soaked the air, mixing with the smell of fish.

Danny closed his eyes and wished himself a hundred miles away. Ten hundred. He opened them again. But he was still here. Riding an elephant through Edinburgh, dressed like a fool.

He tried again to remember what Sandev had said. Something about using his head. Danny struggled to think through his panic. No, it was Maharajah's ears. He tugged roughly on the wrinkled skin then pulled at the harness as hard as he could. It made no difference. Maharajah didn't stop.

He tried again, this time digging his knees into the tough hide, and kicking with all his strength. Perhaps pain would register. But it was useless. Nothing worked. Danny had as much control as a string puppet in a seaside show. It was only by some miracle that no one had been injured. At least not yet.

Some instinct made him glance up. A few feet away, jutting out into the street, an apothecary sign swung from a shop canopy. The large wooden board was hanging almost exactly at Danny's height. And they were heading straight towards it.

Danny ducked, pressing against Maharajah's back as if it was possible to merge into the hard skin. A heartbeat later, there was a whoosh of air as the shop sign flapped harmlessly above them. But it was long seconds before Danny could bring himself to sit up. Chicken feathers settled on his turban. His throat felt dry.

Then, just as quickly as it had begun, the mad dash stopped. Maharajah drew to a halt and strolled towards a barrow of apples. His trunk hovered over the fruit before plucking one from the tray and tossing it into his mouth. Danny felt the gentle motion as he chewed.

Relief surged through him, but horror followed just as quickly. He gazed back up the street. The market was destroyed. Almost all the stalls were overturned, and some lay in pieces.

Worse still, an angry crowd had begun to gather. Danny could see threats written on every face. One large costermonger brandished a splintered plank; another swung a fist. Danny's heart raced as they moved closer.

'Hey, lad. Over here!'

Startled, he glanced around. A little distance away, Mr and Mrs Jameson were clambering from a hansom cab. Danny didn't know whether to be relieved or terrified. The grand send-off had been a disaster. The rampage through the market was an even bigger catastrophe. He was bound to be punished and sent back to Cowgate.

And to make matters worse, it was obvious Mr Jameson was grief-stricken. He was running ahead of his wife, flapping his arms like a plump, anxious bird. As he got nearer, Danny saw a tear slide down one ruddy cheek. He braced himself.

But once again, nothing was as it seemed.

'What a send-off, boy. You should have seen Albright's face.' Dumbfounded, Danny realized Mr Jameson wasn't crying, he was roaring with laughter. 'Funniest thing I've ever seen.'

It was the wrong thing to say, Danny knew that straight away. The stallholders were closing in and they were looking for someone to blame. Mr Jameson was the obvious target; Danny only hoped the fight would be quick.

It was.

There was a brief scuffle; some grunts, a punch which came from nowhere and Mr Jameson fell to the ground. Danny waited for him to get up but the menagerist didn't move. The big costermonger was holding the broken plank to his throat.

'There's nothin' funny about what happened here. That beast wrecked our barrows. And if he's yours, you'd better put your hands in your pocket to pay for the damage.' He must have pressed harder because Mr Jameson let out a groan. 'Or perhaps you need a wee bit of encouragement.'

'How dare you! Get away from my husband.' Mrs Jameson had arrived at last. 'Move aside. Now!'

Using her umbrella, she batted her way towards her husband. Danny could just see the top of her bonnet and then the crowd closed in. It was enough to kick-start a fresh wave of panic. He needed the Jamesons as much as they needed him. And if he didn't do something quickly, his future would slip away as quickly as sand through fingers.

Desperately, he tried to think. Another whisper of Sandev's advice surfaced: '*Be soft, but be sure*'. It was all he could remember. He'd already tried force, perhaps gentleness was the answer.

He leant forward and stroked the top of Maharajah's head. Nothing happened. He tried again; still no response, but the movement nudged another memory. Sandev had whistled – once at the auction and again later, at Waverley Station.

It was worth trying. Danny rounded his lips and blew. A shrill whine emerged, more like a squawk than a whistle. He tried again. This time more softly, and it was as if he'd turned a key in a lock. With a jerk, Maharajah lumbered forwards.

People scattered, leaving Mr Jameson lying in the dirt. Only the costermonger remained, apparently unaware of the animal headed towards him. Danny smirked. That wasn't going to last.

Maharajah's trunk wrapped around the man's shoulders and he was pulled like a weed from a flower bed. Danny saw shock transform his face. The crowd laughed, a little nervously, but no one came any closer.

Thank goodness Mr Jameson was not a man to waste an opportunity. He scrambled upright, dusty but intact. His wife began brushing down his waistcoat.

'I'm fine, Ethel May. Stop your fussin'.'

'You're only fine thanks to Danny and Maharajah. Perhaps you should try thinking before opening that big mouth of yours. You great fool!'

'You're right, me dove. Lord knows, you usually are. But I don't think I can change now.'

Pulling away, Mr Jameson scanned the circle of stall-holders. 'Don't worry, none of you will be out of pocket. I always pay me debts. But just you make sure you tell the newspapers. The elephant's name is Maharajah, the boy's Prince Dandip. And the menagerie's Belle Vue. Don't forget!'

He tugged open his purse and began handing out coins. One by one, the market traders left with their money. Danny was glad to see them go. There was only one problem left – and he was wrapped in Maharajah's trunk. Danny whistled again just to see what would happen. Immediately, Maharajah relaxed his hold. The costermonger dropped free and slunk off.

'That was priceless.' Mr Jameson tucked the wallet back into his jacket. 'Worth every penny. And more.'

Danny stared at him in disbelief. Surely this morning had been a complete disaster? Maharajah had destroyed the market, the stallholders were furious, and the damage had cost a small fortune to set right.

Mrs Jameson finished inspecting her husband for dust. She smiled. 'You have to understand, Danny, Mr Jameson believes in drama and show. He's convinced that every time you make the newspapers, for good or bad, the publicity helps Belle Vue. And there's nothing he loves more.'

'Apart from you, me dearest love. Apart from you.' The menagerist held out an arm to escort his wife. 'Come on, we have to find the others. We've time to make up. Let's start the Elephant Race. And if we're lucky this won't be the last of the excitement.'

Chapter Seven

ON THE ROAD TO STOW
12 April 1872

When Mr Jameson had planned the route to Belle Vue, Danny hadn't been able to help. For a start, he wasn't exactly sure where Manchester was, or even in which direction they would have to go.

So Mr Jameson had shown him on the map, tracing the path from Edinburgh with a stubby finger. They would follow the Waverley rail line as far as was possible, he'd said. Moving through Scotland from Edinburgh to Langholm, then across Cumberland towards Kendal, dropping down into Lancashire, and then south to Manchester.

Of course, once he'd seen the distances, doubt had hit Danny with the force of a steam train. It looked impossible.

They would have to walk two hundred and twenty miles in only seven days, with an elephant who had already destroyed a rail carriage and a street market. The uncertainty must have shown on his face.

'We'll do it, lad,' Mr Jameson had smiled. 'Don't you fret. I made you a promise and I'm not losin' Maharajah to Arthur Albright. Now let's get out of this city.'

After the chaotic start, it took more than an hour to cross Edinburgh – mainly because Maharajah couldn't take a step without attracting a large crowd. And every moment, Danny half expected one of Scatcherd's men to stop the parade and drag him away.

But at last, they reached the city outskirts and he looked to where Edinburgh touched the sky – the old castle squatting high on the hill, above an assortment of tall towers and spires that pierced the smoke. Somewhere beyond that horizon was his new life. This mad adventure, built from half-lies and half-truths, was really going to happen.

A part of him wanted to laugh. Never in his wildest, most fantastical dreams had he imagined leaving Cowgate like this: riding an elephant, dressed as an Indian prince. But the rest of him was terrified. Was he making a huge mistake? Abandoning all he'd ever known to trust in strangers? Could life really be better anywhere else?

A shaft of sunshine cut through the clouds, and Danny lifted his face to catch the warmth. Then and there, he made a vow. Trust his instincts, depend solely on himself and disappear at the first sign of trouble. It had brought him this far. Now it had to get him to Manchester.

At first, the road south was awash with houses but then they trickled away, and the countryside took over. It was the first time Danny had ever been outside Edinburgh, and from his seat on Maharajah's back, he had a sweeping view of all that he'd been missing.

Wide, green moors rose up to crags that looked like pieces of jagged glass against the sky. Streams had carved gullies through the dark rocks. Best of all, the air smelt different. No smoky fog or stinking alleys. Every breath tasted fresh and cold and clean.

But what Danny couldn't quite believe was the space.

It seemed incredible that in Cowgate he'd had to share a room with more than twenty people. While here, everyone he knew could have a home of their own and there'd still be plenty of land left over. Mr Jameson had even said that somewhere in Scotland, the Queen owned another grand castle with towers and turrets. But despite straining his hardest, Danny couldn't see any sign of it.

He gave up trying, and watched Mr Jameson flag down one more traveller. Now that they were on the road, the menagerist was as excited as a week-old puppy. Every time he spotted someone, he'd clamber from the wagon and start up a conversation.

'Take a look at this great beast. Have you ever seen anything like him? Well just you come along to Belle Vue, there's even more to marvel at. You mark me words.'

The miracle of meeting an elephant was more than enough to make people stop. But nothing prepared Danny for the first village. He'd only seen crowds this big when the Royal Scots Regiment held a homecoming parade through Edinburgh.

There must be hundreds lining the road. Old ladies. Mothers with babies. Shopkeepers. Farm workers. And everywhere he looked, children were pointing and giggling.

'Are you really a prince, mister?' one lad shouted. He was running alongside Maharajah, trying to copy the elephant's long steps and swinging his arm like a trunk.

'Nah. He can't be. Where's his crown?' another boy smirked. 'But I reckon he must be rich. Just look at them jewels.'

To Danny's horror, the boy took a running jump and lunged for Maharajah's harness. There was no chance of success but, after what had happened in Edinburgh, tension tightened his nerves. Maharajah was certain to lose his temper. He braced, waiting for the explosion. It never happened.

The boy fell back, laughing, into the arms of his friends, and Maharajah walked on without missing a step. He didn't roar. Or bellow. There wasn't even a flicker of irritation.

Amazed, Danny leant forward and stroked across the hard dome of Maharajah's skull. A throaty rumble vibrated through the bone, deep and warm. It was the sort of sound no one could possibly hear, only feel. And in that moment,

Danny would have bet his life that Maharajah was happy.

'Prince Dandip!'

Hastily, Danny straightened. Mr Jameson was glaring at him from the wagon. It obviously wasn't the first time he'd shouted. 'Come on, Your Highness! Everyone's waitin' for you. Give them a wave.'

He looked around, suddenly aware of all eyes on him, but for once in his life, the stares were friendly, not suspicious. Hesitantly, he lifted an arm and waggled his fingers. A roar erupted. He waved again. Another cheer. His mouth curved up. This was simple. He could be a prince quite easily, if all it took was nodding, waving and saying nothing.

It was a long time before Danny, Maharajah and the rest of the Belle Vue party were allowed to leave Danderhall and even then, children continued to trail along behind them. It was the same in the towns and villages that followed. The newspapers had spread the story, and word of mouth had done the rest. People wanted to believe.

Danny just hoped they never found out who he really was.

When they finally reached Stow for the overnight stop, Danny slumped over Maharajah's neck with relief. Every part of his body ached, and his hands were frozen into claws from gripping the harness. For the last few miles all he'd thought about was sleeping in a real bed. He might have guessed there'd be other plans.

'I want you and Maharajah to do something for me,' Mr Jameson announced. The wagon had stopped outside the village inn where Danny imagined there were plenty of comfortable mattresses and soft sheets. Mrs Jameson had already gone inside to book them all rooms.

'It's past time that you started your trainin'. We need to add in a few tricks. Get the crowds goin' a bit more. I want you to work on it tonight with Sandev. A couple of hours should do it.'

Danny's spirits sank but he had no choice. This was part of the deal. Besides, it was important. He needed to make absolutely sure he was irreplaceable. No one was going to have any reason to send him back to Cowgate.

The light was fading as Danny followed Sandev and Maharajah along a path leading away from the village. As well as his silver-headed cane, Sandev carried a food sack and another stick, slightly smaller than his own. He stopped in a small clearing, edged by trees.

'Here is good. Away from houses and people.' Sandev's precise, clipped speech made every sentence sound like an order. It was only around Maharajah that his voice seemed to soften. 'You have much to learn. And in only seven days. Observe and concentrate.'

Danny pulled back his shoulders and stifled a yawn. He'd try his best, even though his eyes stung with tiredness, and feeling was only just returning to his fingers. Sitting on the grass, he propped himself upright to watch.

Sandev held a slice of apple in an outstretched palm. Immediately, Maharajah lunged for it but before he could touch, the keeper raised his cane and whistled. The elephant stopped. Sandev whistled again and, with one quick swipe, Maharajah snagged the fruit and tossed it into his mouth.

'Well done, my friend. That was good.'

Gently, Sandev rubbed Maharajah's trunk, and Danny's exhaustion lifted. This was much better than Munro Dougall's begging dog who performed for pennies in Edinburgh. He couldn't wait to try, and it looked simple enough. He reached for the bag of fruit.

'No!'

Quickly, Danny pulled back his hand. Sandev looked even more serious than usual. Wrinkles creased the skin around his dark eyes and his mouth was a solemn line. Not for the first time, Danny found himself wondering about Sandev. Where was his home? His family? Or, like Danny, did he have no one?

'You may think you know how to command elephants. But do not imagine it is so easy that even a street thief can do it. It takes many years to become a mahout.'

A mahout? Danny's confusion must have been obvious.

'Mahout is the Indian name for an elephant trainer. Like me.' Sandev held a hand to his chest. 'Some are good. Some are bad. The foolish ones use knives to train elephants. They keep their animals in chains. Never free to move. There is no skill in what they do. No cleverness.'

He pointed to Maharajah's front legs. Near the bottom, circling each foot, was a ridge of puckered skin. 'Look. Calluses. These happen when elephants are chained for too long. They become sore and bleed. Sometimes there is infection.'

'And here.' This time Sandev ran his hand down the elephant's side. Danny peered closer. A long strip of raised skin, darker than the surrounding area, slashed across Maharajah's stomach.

'This happened many years ago when Maharajah first arrived at Mr Wormwell's menagerie. He was cared for by another mahout. He used pain to make his elephants work. But Maharajah was stubborn. One day, the mahout became angry and stuck a knife into Maharajah's belly. He left Maharajah to die.'

Sandev rubbed the scarred skin again. 'But Mr Wormwell found him. He ordered the man to leave. And he gave Maharajah to me. By God's grace, he lived.'

Danny's stomach hollowed out. Maharajah was the most powerful creature he'd ever seen. He couldn't imagine anyone being strong enough to harm him, but it was obvious that even his size hadn't stopped the cruelty.

Danny smoothed the scars on his own wrist. He remembered the pain as though it had happened only hours ago. Shame lingered. He'd always thought it had been his own fault. That Scatcherd had hurt him because he'd been too weak. Too stupid. Too frightened. Now he wondered. If it could happen to Maharajah, then it could happen to anyone.

Reaching up, Danny stretched his arms wide and laid them against the elephant's side. He turned his face into the rough warmth. Maharajah shifted a little as if finding the most comfortable spot, and then he settled. They stood together. After years of trying not to touch anyone, it felt strange to be so close to another living creature. Danny didn't want to let go.

'You begin to understand,' Sandev said at last. His clipped voice had mellowed slightly. 'Maharajah responds best to kindness not to pain. Remember that, and perhaps you will learn.'

Guiltily, Danny recalled how he had kicked Maharajah to stop his mad dash through Edinburgh. Force had not worked but gentleness might have done.

'So we begin training. Approach the elephant always from the side. Never from the front. Remember what I said – be soft but be sure. Copy me.'

Danny relaxed his hold but he didn't want to lose contact. He trailed a hand across Maharajah's skin and felt the rough, wrinkled warmth. His last remaining fear of this great creature fell away. And all that was left was wonder.

'Here he is most sensitive. The ears, the trunk, the shoulders and around the eyes and mouth. He feels like you and I feel. If a fly sits on his back, he knows it. He can sense it. But it is his mind that is most clever. And he remembers everything. I will show you.'

Sandev picked up the smaller cane from the ground and tossed it to Danny. 'For you. Every mahout must have one. It is called an ankus.

The stick was smooth and polished, with one slightly

curved end. It might not be as ornate as Sandev's silver-headed cane, Danny thought, but it was still beautiful. He ran his hands down the grained wood. It glided easily beneath his fingers.

'Most ankus have hooks. I took off the hook after Maharajah was injured. I do not need it. And neither will you.' Danny knew he wasn't being given a choice. It was clear Sandev would not tolerate failure. 'I will teach you the most important commands first. "Stop" and "forward". When you know these, we will move on.'

Danny was surprised to discover the training plan was actually very simple; give an instruction and reward the result. Years ago, Sandev had taught Maharajah that if the elephant touched the ankus, a whistle would blow. And if the whistle blew he would be given a treat.

After that the commands became more complicated. Different movements of the ankus could be used to indicate different instructions, Sandev explained. Pick up. Drop. Catch. Leave. While the whistle told Maharajah that he would earn a treat for obeying.

It didn't take long for Danny to realize that the theory might be easy but the practice was hard. The gestures were sometimes so subtle they were impossible to copy. Danny's attempts often confused Maharajah. He didn't think he'd ever get it right.

'Again,' Sandev said after a series of failed efforts. 'I told you. Concentrate!'

With a sigh, Danny picked up the ankus but immediately it was plucked from his grasp. When he glanced up Maharajah was holding the cane in his trunk and pointing at the bag of food, his eyes sharp and unblinking. This time the elephant was giving the orders.

Danny hesitated, but instinct told him not to surrender. He held out an apple and reached for the ankus. For a while it was a contest of wills. Danny refused to let go, and so did Maharajah. Then suddenly the elephant released his hold, and Danny stumbled backwards, ankus in hand. He looked up. Maharajah was munching the fruit, his gold gaze glittering. It felt like a breakthrough of sorts.

'Perhaps you have a little talent.' It was as near to a compliment as Sandev was likely to give, and Danny felt the warmth blossom in his chest. 'Come. Let us try again.'

The lesson was hard work. Sandev made Danny repeat the whistles and gestures again and again, until he wanted to weep with exhaustion. Midnight was fast approaching and tomorrow was likely to be another long day. But at last, Sandev seemed satisfied. 'Enough. We will finish now.'

Danny was hooking the ankus into his belt when he glimpsed a slight, shadowy outline among the trees. They were being watched, but this wasn't like the friendly curiosity of today's crowds. This felt different. Concentrated and fierce.

'What is it?' Sandev turned to see what had caught his attention. Immediately the figure spun away, melting back into the woodland. For a heartbeat, Danny hesitated but Sandev had already broken into a run. All he could do was to follow.

Together, they plunged between the tall pines. Grasses and thorns scraped Danny's legs, and a low branch ripped a hole in his silk shirt. He ran on anyway. But it was useless.

The intruder was too far ahead to catch and, without a lantern, it was impossible to see which direction he'd taken. Reluctantly, Danny pulled to a stop. His chest heaved and his lungs burnt with the effort of breathing. At his side, Sandev hardly seemed winded.

'We must tell Mr Jameson in the morning. You and I will stay with Maharajah tonight in the barn. To be certain there is no trouble.' A frown deepened the wrinkles again. 'Perhaps it was a curious villager. No more than that.'

Perhaps. But Danny remembered the stranger's intense scrutiny, uneasily. He looked again into the darkness where the man had disappeared. Now nothing disturbed the shadows. And the only reason Danny knew he'd been there at all was the odd, anxious feeling inside his stomach. It felt like a warning.

Chapter Eight

STOW

13 April 1872

Danny was certain he didn't get much sleep overnight but at some point he must have drifted off because he was bumped awake by an insistent nudge against his side.

Blinking, he pushed it away and struggled to sit – then almost immediately jerked back. Maharajah was standing over him, his trunk swinging loosely. Sandev was nowhere in sight and, for a moment, Danny wasn't sure what to do. Then he remembered the mahout's advice. *Be soft but be sure.*

He whistled gently, trying to remember everything he'd learnt last night. Maharajah's head tilted to one side. It looked for all the world like he was making a decision. Then slowly he stretched out his trunk. Danny smiled, hooked a palm around the warm, wrinkled skin, and let himself be pulled to his feet.

By the time the sun rose, he and Maharajah were ready to leave, and the rest of the Belle Vue party were not far behind. Outside, the hotel landlady waited to wave them goodbye. She bobbed a nervous curtsy. 'Your Royal Highness, it's been a pleasure to have you as a guest in our humble home.'

Danny thought of the night he'd spent in the cold barn among the straw, and nodded his head regally. It was almost painful to think that a short distance away there had been a soft, comfortable bed waiting just for him. But at least there had been no trouble.

'I hope everything was satisfactory, sir. Your room was a wee bit disturbed this morning. It's our very best bed-chamber. Was there a problem?'

Puzzled, Danny frowned. What did she mean? He hadn't even been inside the inn, let alone into any of the bedrooms. His scowl deepened, and the landlady shrank back. 'I . . . I wasn't complaining, Your Highness. I just thought . . . it looked a bit muddled. Messy, you know. I just didn't want to think . . . that we hadn't . . . that it wasn't good enough.'

'Everythin' was perfect, madam,' Mr Jameson interrupted. He flashed a warning glare at Danny. 'Prince Dandip thanks you for your hospitality, and invites you and your family to

Belle Vue as his honoured guests. See that you spread the word.'

Crimple flicked the reins and the wagon set off. Flushed pink, the landlady curtsied again. Perhaps she carried on bobbing up and down much longer after that, but Danny wasn't paying attention. Questions were too busy whirling through his head.

If he hadn't been in the room, who had? Could it have been the prowler they'd chased last night? The stranger who had run off into the night? Or, most worrying of all, had Frank Scatcherd finally found out he'd left Edinburgh?

The temperature dropped as the road zigzagged towards the next stop at Hawick. Sitting on Maharajah's back, Danny felt the sharp whip of the wind from every side.

The rest of his new clothes were due to arrive by train this evening, and he was looking forward to the warmth of the woollen jacket. Although he had to admit that his strange costume – and the ankus tucked into his belt – had been a blessing. So far, to his amazement, no one had questioned the story of Prince Dandip and his elephant.

But still something felt wrong. It was the same feeling he'd got before a police raid on Cowgate, a sense that danger was hiding in the shadows. The trouble was he had no real evidence. There had been no damage. Nothing had been stolen. And no one had been hurt. There hadn't even been any delays to the Elephant Race. And Mr Jameson hadn't seemed at all concerned about their night-time visitor.

'I doubt it was anyone who meant any harm,' he'd said. 'Probably just a young lad wantin' to have a nose at Maharajah. And even if it were one of Albright's men, you two chased him off. He'll know he can't mess with us. We'll carry on the night watch just to be safe. Don't worry. Everything's goin' splendidly. Just look at the crowds we're gettin'.'

Danny let himself be convinced, because it was easier than worrying. And for the next few miles, the Elephant Race continued without trouble. Everywhere, Maharajah and Prince Dandip were welcomed with warmth and curiosity.

Of course, it didn't last.

Two miles from Hawick, Danny was the first to see the toll house, tucked into a bend on the road. A wooden fence stretched across the front, stopping travellers from moving on until they paid a fee. He'd become used to this. They'd already passed through several tolls without charge. Most collection officers were too fascinated by Maharajah to ask for payment. This was unlikely to be any different.

A large man stomped from the house. Like Crimple, he had the build of a boxer, and a face that appeared to have been ironed flat. Danny had met this type before – the Leith Brotherhood was full of thugs who swung a punch to solve a problem. Usually, they'd been with Frank Scatcherd, happily carrying out his orders to break a few bones.

'You can stop right there.' The man leant his big fists on the gate and looked up at Danny. His eyes were too small for his head, and his ears were too large. 'What's your business?'

Behind Danny, the rest of the party had caught up. Mr Jameson clambered down from the wagon and scurried forward.

'Me good fellow, don't you know who this is? May I introduce Prince Dandip of Delhi and his elephant, Maharajah the Magnificent. I'm surprised you haven't heard of them. There's been a lot in the papers.'

'I don't care if you're the Prince of Wales. You aren't getting through this gate without paying.' The toll man swept an assessing glance from Maharajah's trunk right to his tail. 'That'll be five shillings.'

'Five shillings? But that's ridiculous. I could drive a cow through here for eight pence.'

'That beast's a wee bit bigger than a cow now, isn't he? I reckon five shillings is a fair price.'

'I think not, sir.' Mrs Jameson had joined her husband. She had her hands on her hips and her voice quivered with anger. 'We will certainly not be paying such an outrageous fee. It's nothing short of robbery. I demand to see a list of your tolls.'

The man stabbed his finger at the gate where the charges were pinned. Even Danny could see – horses, cows, donkeys and sheep were pictured, but not elephants.

Mrs Jameson smiled triumphantly. 'If the animal's not on the list, you can't charge a fee. What's your name, sir? I would like to know who to report to the local magistrate.'

'I'll not be tellin' you that. Besides, I can charge what I like. It's my toll.' He curled a lip. 'Anyhow, the price has just gone up to ten shillings. You should have paid when you had the chance.'

A clatter of wheels signalled the arrival of another carriage. Several travellers climbed out and Danny watched their mouths drop open when they saw Maharajah. One of them – a smartly dressed gentleman, with sandy whiskers and a woollen suit – took out a notebook from his bag. His pen moved busily over the paper as the argument continued.

'. . . how dare you raise the price? I want your name now, sir,' Mrs Jameson demanded.

'I'll not give it to you.'

'Och, don't be so shy, Samuel Peppershank. Tell the lady who you are.' The shout came from the carriage driver. Danny could see he was enjoying himself, and none of his passengers seemed to care about the hold-up. Everyone was too caught up in the quarrel.

The toll officer reddened. 'I will not. And you'll not be coming through here now. I can promise you that.' He pumped a fist at Maharajah. 'That creature's not gettin' past my toll. Not ever. I'll have his head, if he does.'

'And I'll have your head, if he doesn't!' Mr Jameson banged on the fence; and it didn't even rattle. 'Sandev!' he shouted.

'Sir?' The mahout bowed.

Mr Jameson gestured to the toll gate. 'I want it gone. You

know what to do.'

An emotion flashed across Sandev's face that might easily have been annoyance. Or perhaps alarm. Danny found it difficult to tell. Then his expression resumed its normal calm. 'I do not think it wise, sir. Perhaps we should turn back. Find another way.'

'No. I won't be bullied into givin' up. And another road would take too much time. Go on. Quickly now!'

Sandev paused and for a moment Danny thought he would do nothing, but then he raised his ankus and blew out a signal. In one fluid movement, Maharajah swung his trunk and knocked the gate straight off its hinges. Astounded, Danny watched it crash to the ground. He wanted to clap, but, beneath him, Maharajah was already moving, splintering the gate under heavy feet.

'What are you doing?' Peppershank spluttered. 'That's my property. You can't . . . !'

'I've changed my mind,' Mrs Jameson took out her purse. 'Here's your ten shillings, Mr Peppershank. As my husband often says – it was worth every penny!'

With a sweep of her cloak, she climbed back on to the wagon with her husband. And they followed Danny and Maharajah through the broken toll.

They didn't get far. Footsteps pounded on the ground. Danny looked back. The sandy-haired gentleman was sprinting after them, the notebook still clutched in one hand.

'You there!' he shouted. 'Stop!'

Danny wasn't stupid. They'd argued with the toll officer, wrecked the gate and delayed other travellers. He didn't expect they were going to be thanked. He whistled for Maharajah to go faster, hoping the wagon would follow. But the man wasn't giving up. Instead, he seemed to lengthen his stride.

'Stop, please! I mean no trouble.' His face had turned pink. 'Please. This is a marvellous opportunity. It'll be to your advantage to listen . . . Almost certainly make you famous . . .'

Danny's heart skipped. Those were exactly the right words to get Mr Jameson's attention. Sure enough, the menagerist was already ordering Crimple to halt the wagon. Reluctantly, Danny signalled for Maharajah to stop too. He hoped it wasn't a huge mistake.

Leaning against the wagon, the man tried to get his breath back. 'May I introduce myself?' he said at last. 'My name is Hardy. Heywood Hardy. I'm an artist, currently on a sketching trip in Scotland.' Another gulp of air. 'Your little skirmish certainly livened up my day. And I was wondering if you'd allow your animal to be the subject of one of my paintings? Perhaps with his keeper . . . and the Prince?'

A painting? Danny couldn't believe it. Portraits were for rich, powerful people. Lords and ladies with more money than sense. Or royalty with palaces to fill. Not for someone like him.

Mr Jameson looked thoughtful. 'I'm listenin'. Tell me more.'

'The painting would be of the utmost taste. And I can assure you of my qualifications, sir. My work has been exhibited by the Royal Academy. The Queen herself has admired it.'

'The Royal Academy, you say?' Mr Jameson's excitement was growing. 'The Queen?'

'Yes, indeed. I believe this scene would be the perfect addition to my other work on this trip. I'm considering calling it "The Disputed Toll". I'm sure it will prove most popular. If I could be a little immodest, I do have quite a following.'

Danny might have guessed Mrs Jameson would be more practical. 'How long would it take?' she asked. The worry lines had appeared on her forehead again.

'Not long at all, madam. I've already completed a sketch. I would like to do a small watercolour now. But I can do the bigger canvas at my studio in London.'

There was never any doubt that Mr Jameson would say yes. Danny knew it and so did Mrs Jameson.

'Very well,' she sighed. 'I'll give you an hour, Mr Hardy. But not a minute longer. We can't afford any more delays.'

'Thank you, ma'am. That's very generous.'

Mr Hardy set up his easel a few hundred yards from the toll house. No one seemed to think it was a good idea to get much closer. Danny could see Peppershank prowling outside, inspecting the damage to his gate and gesturing angrily to every passer-by.

Within minutes, a small crowd of travellers had

surrounded the painter. Danny heard one man introduce himself as Alfred Kibble of the *Hawick Express*, sent to cover the Elephant Race for the local newspaper. Once again it looked like Mr Jameson's publicity machine was working.

And so, Danny sat while Maharajah posed and Mr Hardy painted. It should have been a welcome rest from the journey but something was gnawing away at the back of Danny's mind. A puzzle waiting to be solved. Below him, Sandev whistled to Maharajah to raise his trunk, and in that instant he knew what it was.

This afternoon it had been Sandev who'd told the elephant to break down the toll gate; all he needed was the right instruction from the right person. So if Maharajah could do that, then it would be very easy to order him to destroy a rail carriage – a carriage exactly like the one at Waverley Station.

On that morning, Sandev had disappeared just before Maharajah smashed up his carriage. And when the mahout reappeared, he'd been standing inside the wreckage. Which meant he'd been there with the elephant all along, whistling instructions.

If Danny was right, the entire journey was nothing but a con trick. There had never been any need to walk to Belle Vue because Maharajah would have stood calmly in the train all the way to Manchester.

This was a hullabaloo entirely created by one person. And Danny strongly suspected that person wasn't Sandev, but James Fredrick Henry Jameson. The man who wanted the world to know about Belle Vue.

Heavy footsteps stopped the track of his thoughts, and Danny flinched as a large figure loomed behind Mr Hardy.

'I've just been wonderin,' Peppershank said, pointing to the artist's easel. 'Could I be in that painting too?'

Chapter Nine

HAWICK TRAIN STATION
13 April 1872

The girl standing at Hawick Station had hair the colour of marzipan – the pale gold sort that Danny had seen through bakers' windows but never tasted. He thought they were probably around the same age, but it was difficult to tell. Everything about her was spotless. She looked more like a china doll than a real person.

Briefly, he wondered who she was. The train was about to steam out of the station and, aside from the mountain of cases and hatboxes at her feet, she seemed quite alone.

'Danny!' He turned, and promptly forgot all about the girl. Mr Jameson was striding along the platform. 'Stop day-dreamin', lad. I found your new clothes in the parcel office.

The tailor must have sent them down on an earlier train. But there's still no sign of Saddleworth.'

Impatiently, the train pulsed out another cloud of smoke, and a passenger emerged from the final carriage, tugging a large travelling case. He was probably of average height but compared to Mr Jameson he looked much taller, and he had the ruddy skin of someone who spent most of his time outdoors.

'There you are! Good heavens, man. You're cuttin' it fine. You nearly went off with the train.' Mr Jameson nodded towards Danny. 'Prince Dandip of Delhi. This is Mr William Saddleworth, Belle Vue's new animal doctor.'

'I'm delighted to meet you, Your Highness. You've caused quite a sensation in Edinburgh.' Mr Saddleworth smiled briefly and offered a polite handshake, but Danny noticed he didn't bow. Instead, his clever blue eyes slid from Danny's turban to the tips of the new leather slippers. For the first time since Edinburgh, Danny wondered if his disguise was quite good enough.

'Well now that you're here, we can start makin' plans. I've booked rooms in the local inn. Grab your trunk and let's get going.'

'But what about Henrietta?'

'Henrietta?'

'My daughter.' Mr Saddleworth gestured along the platform. The girl with the golden curls was gliding towards them, a red velvet cape swirling gracefully from her shoulders and a jaunty hat tilted over one ear.

'I didn't realize you were bringin' anyone.' Danny was sure Mr Jameson's eyebrows had risen a full half-inch.

'I sent a message ahead. I assumed you already knew.'

'No. I got no message. But I thought I'd made it clear. This isn't a pleasure trip. It's probably best if Miss Henrietta goes back to Edinburgh. At least until we reach Belle Vue. You can send for her then.'

'I'm sorry. It's too late. She has to come with me.'

'You do realize that time is tight? We can't hang about – even if somethin' goes wrong. It'll be dirty and tirin'. It's really no trip for someone so young and—'

'But Mr Jameson. *He's* here.' The interruption came from Henrietta. She'd hooked a hand into her father's arm and was staring at Danny as though he was a specimen in an apothecary jar – foreign, mysterious and slightly disturbing. It made him want to bare his teeth and growl.

'Yes. Well . . .' Mr Jameson spluttered. 'Of course, what I meant to say is . . . this isn't a journey for a gently raised young woman, Miss Henrietta. Like yourself. It's different for Danny. He's a–a . . .'

'A prince of royal blood? The son of an Indian princess?' She wrinkled her small, freckled nose. 'A BOY?'

'Er . . . that's right. Yes.'

Henrietta's eyes flared. For a brief moment, she reminded Danny of Mrs Jameson when he'd first seen her in Edinburgh – as though she was spitting mad, and ready to draw blood. A part of him was impressed.

'Just because I'm a girl, Mr Jameson, doesn't mean I'll hold you back. And I won't get in the way. I promise. I simply don't see why I shouldn't be allowed to come.'

'Maybe. But it still won't work. There's no room in the wagon for all your cases and hats and whatnot. We've already got Maharajah's kit in there. There's no space for more.'

'Well that's easily solved.' Henrietta glanced at the pile of luggage behind her, then lifted her chin. The angle was defiant. 'I'll leave them behind.'

'Oh . . . very well.' Mr Jameson must have realized the fight wasn't worth it. 'I suppose we can manage. You can be company for Danny here. Maybe teach him some proper English manners.'

'Thank you. You won't regret it.'

A sly smile flickered over Henrietta's face so quickly that it was almost never there. No one except Danny seemed to notice. He clenched his teeth against a grimace. She was going to be trouble.

The first two days of the Elephant Race had not gone exactly to plan. So in the dining room of the Bridge Hotel in Hawick, the next five days were arranged with meticulous care. Danny listened attentively. He wanted to make certain he knew every detail.

The Jamesons were to travel as far as Langholm, and then take the train to Manchester, leaving Mr Saddleworth in charge. His job was to make sure Maharajah covered at least thirty miles a day; anything less could risk them losing the bet.

Back at Belle Vue, Mr Jameson would begin organizing the welcome reception for their arrival. It was set to be the biggest event Manchester had ever seen, and just the thought made Danny's heart flutter.

'But while we're gone, I want the papers to carry on followin' the race,' Mr Jameson said, waving his cigar around so wildly that Danny had to duck. 'Everyone's already talkin' about us. So let's give 'em some stories.'

'True enough. The whole world seems to know about Maharajah.' Mr Saddleworth sipped his ale. He'd spread out a map, marked with their route, on the dinner table. 'But you've got to be careful, you can't always control publicity.'

'Nonsense. There's nothing that could damage Belle Vue now. It doesn't matter what the story is – good or bad – as long as they're talkin' about us. And when they talk about us, they'll want to see for themselves. And when they come to see, we've got 'em. Hook. Line. And sinker.' Mr Jameson banged the table between each word so hard that the glasses bounced.

'I still don't think . . .'

The conversation stopped when the food arrived. As honoured guests, they were being served by the landlord himself: Mr Hamish McDonagh. Danny suspected he had good reason to be grateful. His business must be booming thanks to Prince Dandip and his elephant.

All night, people had been lining up to shake Danny's hand. One woman even grabbed a peacock's feather from his turban as a souvenir. It had seemed ridiculous to Danny but she'd clutched it as though it were made of gold.

And still, not one person had questioned his identity. Everyone believed he was Prince Dandip of Delhi. He wondered how they would feel if they knew the truth – that he was nothing more than a slum urchin with as much royal blood as the hotel cat.

'Your Highness.' Bowing clumsily, Mr McDonagh presented Danny with a plate of lamb, gravy and roasted potatoes, then shuffled backwards. He was bent double by the time he reached the door but managed to prise it open by hopping on one foot.

If Danny hadn't been so distracted, he would have laughed. But he was too busy with his dinner. For as long as he could remember, food had been the main focus of his life. It had taken four days of regular meals to stop the constant hunger but he still ate quickly so nothing could be taken away.

Cupping an arm around the plate, Danny pushed as much as possible into his mouth before swallowing. Across the table, Henrietta had cut her meal into small bites and was chewing delicately. She said, 'Thank you,' when she was given a glass of water; and, 'Yes, please,' when she was offered bread.

It was obvious to Danny that she'd never gone hungry. He curled his lip. She probably imagined missing breakfast was halfway to starvation. He couldn't think of anything they would ever have in common. Worst of all, she wouldn't stop staring.

Abruptly, Danny pushed away his empty plate and jumped up. Perhaps he should check on Maharajah. Crimple seemed unlikely to bother – he was sitting at the bar, nursing a beer and spinning stories for some of the other drinkers. Danny half listened as he brushed past.

'. . . so I pulled his jaws wide open and put me fist right in.'

'You never did! So what happened next?'

'Wait up and I'll tell you. Just let me get another drink.'

But a moment later, a roar erupted, outraged and angry. Danny swivelled to look. Crimple was patting his jacket as noisily as a soldier's drum.

'That lad. He's taken me money. The thieving beggar. I knew he was trouble.'

Crimple's chair crashed to the floor as he stood. 'Where are you, boy? You'd better come here, before I find you first.'

Danny didn't hesitate. He'd been in this situation many times before and he knew what to do. Run.

Instinct and reflexes gave him a head start but, judging from the shouts, he was already being followed. 'I'm going to get you, you good-for-nothin' little runt.'

Danny bolted through the hotel lounge, jumping over feet and around tables. In the far corner, a door led to the yard. He headed towards it. Behind him, there were crashes and curses. Crimple hadn't stopped. So neither did Danny.

He plunged through the door, feeling the cold air on his face. His legs had begun to burn and cramp was slicing into his chest. He glanced back. Crimple was still pounding across the cobbles, ugly and determined. How long before he gave up? They could be running around in circles all night. To make matters worse, hotel guests had drifted outside to watch. Half of them looked appalled to see a large drunk chasing after the royal guest of honour. The other half were obviously delighted.

Danny had just finished a second lap of the yard when he spotted Henrietta Saddleworth at the front of the crowd. Not that he expected any help from her direction. She might be pretty to look at but he didn't imagine she could ever be useful.

Then to his shock, Henrietta did something that changed everything.

She stuck out a dainty foot just as the keeper ran by. It was an old trick, often used in Cowgate's dark alleys to topple a chasing constable. Simple but effective. And if Danny hadn't seen it with his own eyes, he wouldn't have believed it.

Crimple was oblivious to the danger. He tripped, fell and landed in a sprawl at Maharajah's feet. Drunkenly, he struggled to rise but his boots slid on the cobbles. Danny didn't wait for him to try again.

He pulled the ankus from his belt and whistled. Maharajah obeyed instantly. Curling his trunk around Crimple's leg, he lifted the keeper into the air so he swung upside down like a clock pendulum. His face turned a vivid purple.

Laughter erupted from the audience. In the centre, Danny spotted Mr Kibble of the *Hawick Express* scribbling notes with his pen – this would be another drama for the papers.

Then a clatter sounded as something fell from Crimple's jacket and coins rolled in every direction.

'You had your money with you all the time, you daft clod,' said one of the bar drinkers, scooping up a loose shilling. 'The boy didn't steal it from you. It's right here.'

'Och, the man's too drunk to find the nose on his face.'

'Aye, but someone else's nose has found him.'

The laughter didn't stop until Mr Jameson stalked down the hotel steps. He was smiling but Danny could see the annoyance in his eyes. He clapped his hands for silence.

'Ladies and gentlemen, I hope you enjoyed our little performance. The show's over for tonight but remember you can see much more at Belle Vue.' He nodded to Danny. 'That's enough, Your Highness. You can let him down now.'

Warily, Danny lowered the ankus and Maharajah dropped the keeper to the floor. But Crimple didn't get up. Instead, he sat with his head buried in his hands, while the crowd cleared around him.

'I think you owe Prince Dandip an apology for that little misunderstanding,' Mr Jameson said just loud enough for any remaining guests to hear. Then more quietly, he hissed, 'And keep off the drink! You're watchin' Maharajah tonight. And I want no more trouble.'

Staggering, Crimple pushed to his feet. Resentment rippled from him in waves. But he did as he was told, barging Danny's shoulder as he passed. 'Get out of me way, boy!'

Danny's anger simmered. He knew he'd made an enemy, but he didn't care. Even when he was being honest, people didn't believe him. So why should he bother trying?

To make matters worse, Henrietta Saddleworth was still staring. Danny glared back, hoping she'd go away. He knew he should be grateful but he just wanted to be left alone. Instead, she stepped so close that Danny could see the smattering of freckles dotting her small nose. For some reason, it made his temper fade.

'You should be thanking me, not scowling. My Aunt Augusta says good manners show good breeding and there's no excuse for being without either.' She lifted her chin. 'Anyway I've decided I'm going to be your friend. I think you need one. But don't ever call me Henrietta. My name's Hetty.'

Chapter Ten

ON THE ROAD TO LANGHOLM
14 April 1872

'I've read about you in the newspapers. What's it like in India? I imagine it's similar to Scotland, only hotter and with more elephants.'

Hetty had not stopped talking since breakfast. In fact, Danny couldn't remember when she'd last paused for breath. She talked as though the sun was drying up words, and there would soon be a long and silent drought. Danny had never met anyone quite like her.

The best part was that she didn't expect him to say anything. She seemed perfectly happy for him to stay quiet while she did the talking. Which meant that in the last few hours he'd learnt more about Henrietta Saddleworth than anyone else he'd ever met.

Her mother had died three years ago so Hetty had been sent to live with an elderly aunt in Edinburgh.

'The problem is I don't think Aunt Augusta really likes children. And she doesn't approve of "*frivolous events, frivolous people or frivolous talk*".' Hetty made her voice loud and shrill so she sounded like a haughty old lady. 'We didn't go out much, or meet anyone interesting. Although we did go to church all the time. Every day. And twice on Sundays. So I suppose she must approve of God a great deal.'

From the moment Hetty had been sent away, she'd begged her father to return. Danny wondered how Mr Saddleworth had managed to hold out for three years. He'd already seen how easily she could win an argument.

'You see Papa wasn't able to look after me when Mama died because of all the travelling. He's extremely clever and goes all over the world to treat sick animals. Paris, Frankfurt, Vienna. Everywhere. But now Papa has promised that I can live with him, and he says we must settle down in one place. That's why we're going to Belle Vue.'

Hetty dropped her voice to a whisper. 'And I know you and I shall be great friends. I felt it almost straight away. Although you mustn't think I like everybody. I study people carefully first, then I make up my mind. And I can tell Crimple has a mean streak. He has watery eyes just like Reverend Hepple. Aunt Augusta once found him lying on the floor in the vicarage with an empty bottle of sherry.'

Danny didn't much care about Crimple's eyes or Aunt

Augusta's vicar, but he wasn't expected to respond. They were both sitting on Maharajah's back, riding towards the next stop at Langholm. Danny had already given himself a headache trying to be certain they didn't make contact. Touching people still made him feel prickly.

'Anyway, I shall call you Danny. Everyone else does, and Prince Dandip of Delhi is far too grand. I'm not sure Aunt Augusta would approve, but even the Queen must be called Victoria sometimes.' Hetty giggled. 'Although I don't know who would dare.'

Danny shifted uncomfortably, feeling his legs cramp as he moved. For the first time since agreeing to become Prince Dandip, he wished he could tell the truth. It didn't seem right to fool Henrietta Saddleworth – not after she'd helped him escape Crimple. If he thought it was possible, he would have said he felt guilty. But he'd never had much of a conscience, so it couldn't be that.

'. . . and I'm glad I asked to ride Maharajah. Everything looks so different from up here, don't you think? People don't seem very important when you can see the mountains.'

Hetty was right, although Danny could never have described the feeling out loud. The countryside was so vast that it was difficult to imagine there was anything else. For miles, all he could see were the bumps and dips of hills. Better still, there was no sign that they were being followed. In fact, Danny had begun to think he'd been worrying for no reason.

Just to make sure, he checked again, lifting up on to his

heels until he was practically standing on Maharajah's broad back. No, there was nothing but clouds of dust. The last few days had been dry, turning the road into a sandy track. A layer of grime covered everything. The bright colours of his silk costume had dulled to grey, and Maharajah's skin was muddy brown. Even Hetty had begun to look grubby.

So when the road dropped to a river, it was impossible to resist temptation. Now that he'd got used to being clean, Danny wanted to stay that way. He whistled for Maharajah to kneel, and he and Hetty clambered down.

'Good idea, lad. We'll stop here for some rest and a bite of food.' Mr Jameson waved everyone to a halt.

Danny pulled the ankus from his belt and started to unbutton his jacket, but the sound of a heavy splash stopped his fingers. Maharajah had beaten him into the water, and already he was shoulder-deep. Fascinated, Danny stared, nearly certain he could feel the elephant's happy rumble.

Sinking low, Maharajah rolled from side to side until every inch of skin was wet. When he finally stood, the water fell away in fat streams. Then using his trunk, he sprayed a shower so high that it arced across the river, nearly reaching the far side. Delighted, he did it again.

And again.

Danny grinned – so Maharajah wanted to play. Hurriedly, he wriggled out of his jacket, and toed off the slippers. Beside him, Hetty dipped one foot into the shallows and squealed as she waded deeper. Danny started after her, his feet slipping on the wet stones.

'Wait!' Mr Saddleworth stepped into his path. 'I'd like a word . . . please.' Despite the politeness, it wasn't a request. Reluctantly, Danny stopped. Over Mr Saddleworth's shoulder, he could see Hetty moving further and further away.

'I want to be clear. My daughter is very important to me. She's had a sheltered life and she's in need of a friend. It looks like she's chosen you. And I'm hoping that whoever you are, you won't let her down. Do you understand what I'm saying?'

Danny nodded. Of course he understood. It was a warning. Mr Saddleworth wasn't convinced by the story of Prince Dandip, and he was quite prepared to protect his daughter.

He kept his face blank, but inside Danny could feel anger windmilling with hurt. However hard he tried, he was never quite good enough. Not for Crimple. Not for Hetty's father. Even Mr Jameson wanted him to be someone else. Someone better. Someone higher-born.

'Good. I'm glad that we agree.'

Turning his back, Danny waded through the shallows. Strong currents swirled in the centre but here it was calm and clear. Sunlight winked off the surface and he traced the flickering patterns until they disappeared. He closed his eyes.

Almost immediately, a shower of water stung his skin. He spluttered at the shock. Maharajah was flicking his trunk. If he'd been human, Danny would have thought he was laughing. Perhaps he was.

'Oh, look at you!'

Giggling, Hetty scooped up a handful of water. But Danny was ready this time. He splashed back, scattering drops over her hair like wind-blown petals. She gasped then smiled with such joy that Danny couldn't look away.

'This is fun. I never knew water could be this fun. I always thought it was just for getting clean.'

Danny remembered the afternoons he'd spent paddling in the Leith with Robbie, scavenging for any scraps worth selling. Robbie was probably the closest he'd ever had to a friend. Then he looked at Hetty. Their lives had been so different. He had more in common with Maharajah. Even their scars matched.

'Watch, Danny.' Hetty had tucked up the hem of her dress so it floated around her knees. 'Watch this!'

She curled Maharajah's trunk around the backs of her legs and sat down as though on a swing. Gently, the elephant moved, back and forth, so her toes trailed in the water.

'That's a great trick for Belle Vue, Miss Henrietta,' Mr Jameson called. He'd walked down to the river's edge to watch. 'People will pay good money to have a go on an elephant swing.'

'Jamie! What ridiculous nonsense.' But even Mrs Jameson was smiling.

Danny suspected they stayed at the river for longer than

they should. Apart from Mr Saddleworth's warning, it had been as near to perfect as he could imagine. He wished he could fold away the memory, just as he had done with the newspaper cartoon of himself and Maharajah. Eventually Mrs Jameson stood and held out towels.

'Come on! We must be going. Hetty, Danny – dry yourselves and put on your shoes. We need to get to Langholm. Mr Jameson and I have a train to catch.'

Everything had gone smoothly today, and Danny knew that sort of good fortune never lasted for long. He was right. A few miles on, their luck ran out.

The road leading across the river stopped. The bridge no longer existed. Two columns remained but the supporting arches had crumbled, spilling stones into the water. Danny examined the gap between one side and the other. He didn't need anyone to explain that it would be impossible to cross.

'I don't understand why we knew nothin' about this.' Mr Jameson's face had turned ruddy. 'I told McDonagh we were heading for Langholm. He should have warned us last night when we were at the hotel. Did he say anythin' to you, Crimple?'

'No, Gov. Not a thing.'

'Sandev?'

'No, sir.'

Danny could almost see the frustration seeping out of Mr Jameson. 'If I thought he was capable I'd have said Albright was behind this. But even he couldn't have knocked over half a ton of stone.'

'Oh, Jamie. You'll find a way.' Mrs Jameson linked her arm though her husband's and bent her head towards his. 'You always do.'

'Of course, I will, me pet. I'm not goin' to be beaten by a bit of water.' Mr Jameson patted her hand, absent-mindedly. He was staring at the bridge as though it could magically repair itself but Danny was certain only a small army and a miracle would be able to do that.

Mr Saddleworth had unfolded his map to trace the route. 'The River Esk stretches a long way across country, I'm afraid. The nearest bridge is about fifteen miles back up north. It'll probably cost us half a day, there and back. Maybe a little more. But it might be our only option.'

'No, we can't afford the time, and I'm not a man who believes in goin' backwards.' Mr Jameson narrowed his eyes and looked over at the far bank. 'I reckon if we can't go over the water, we're going to have to go through it.'

A short time later, Danny stood with the others on a small beach of stones. The men had cut back a tangle of under-growth to reach it, and the wagon had very nearly over-turned coming down the bank. But eventually, thanks to luck and the carthorses, they'd made it.

Mr Saddleworth strode into the river until the water hit his knees. Danny watched his forehead furrow.

'It's worth trying,' he said at last. 'This stretch is much shallower, and the current doesn't look as strong. If we can get across, we shouldn't lose any more time.'

Crimple was shaking his head. 'I don't like it. I'd hate to get stuck out there. We'd be sittin' ducks if anythin' went wrong.'

'I agree.' Sandev said. He slid his ankus back into his belt and folded his arms. 'Sometimes it is wiser to be cautious.'

Mr Saddleworth's frown deepened. 'I admit it might be difficult, but anything else would delay us.'

Danny took another glance across the river, suddenly impatient. If they wanted to beat Albright, there wasn't time to argue. They had to keep moving, and they had to be quick.

Before there was a chance for second thoughts, he pulled himself on to Maharajah's back. The elephant lifted his trunk.

'Hey, what are you doin', lad?' Mr Jameson shouted. Behind him, Sandev had started shaking his head.

Danny drew his ankus and held it like a soldier brandishing a sword. He pointed to the opposite bank. Nerves fluttered in his stomach but he ignored them. Someone had to guide the way and it might as well be him. And besides, much to his surprise, he wanted to prove something to all those who had doubted him – that he could be reliable and trustworthy. A person others could depend on. He just needed a chance to show it.

Mr Jameson shaded his eyes. Danny felt the scrutiny as though he were back in the tailor's shop being measured for size. He pulled back his shoulders and straightened his spine.

'Fine, if that's what you want,' Mr Jameson said at last. 'We'll follow after you. But if you've any doubts, come back – straight away. I've told you before, I need Prince Dandip. I've big plans for you.' He patted Maharajah's flank and stepped away.

Danny focused on the far side of the water. This was his chance; he couldn't back out now. He whistled and Maharajah stepped into the river.

'Good luck!' Hetty shouted. A golden curl shook loose, whipping against her cheek. 'See you at the other side.'

The shallows were easy to navigate, barely tickling Maharajah's feet. This was no different from paddling in puddles, Danny thought. It was going to be fine. Then suddenly they dived deeper, and he could feel Maharajah straining to push through the current. The roar of the water rushing downstream deadened any other sound.

Danny clenched the harness tightly. He'd never realized how powerful a river could be. The Esk was a monstrous beast with jaws and teeth that could swallow them whole. But Maharajah was stronger, Danny told himself. He just had to be.

The water turned from grey to black as they reached halfway. Abruptly, Maharajah stumbled and Danny was jolted from his seat. Heart pounding, he slid towards the swirling current, and for one horrifying moment, he thought they would both plunge below. Then, by some miracle, Maharajah regained his balance, struggled upright and trudged on.

The worst was over.

Danny's relief when Maharajah reached the opposite bank was paralysing. Lying flat along the elephant's back, he tried to recover his breath and his nerves. Only when he was sure his heart rate had returned to normal, did he try to sit up. They'd done it.

They'd actually done it.

He waved to the group on the other side. Now it was their turn.

The Wormwell wagon had not been built for river crossings but the base was lined with canvas, and the large wheels were reinforced with metal rims. It would have to be enough. Shielding his eyes, Danny watched them. Crimple took the reins, with Mr and Mrs Jameson sitting alongside. Hetty was wedged between them, while Sandev and Mr Saddleworth waded into the water on foot, roped to either side of the wagon.

Their progress was painfully slow, or so it seemed to Danny. The wind had picked up and was whipping along the river. And now, after days without rain, the clouds burst open. The Esk rose to swell and crest in the downpour. The water was almost up to the men's chests and climbing higher, but the wagon was more than halfway across.

Danny felt his mouth lift into a half-smile. They were going to make it. He could feel the bubble of relief rise in his chest.

Then suddenly, the cart lurched to one side and stopped. The horses pulled frantically at the reins, as eager to get out of the river as anyone, but the wagon wouldn't shift. The wooden frame slumped awkwardly. Taking a deep breath, Mr Saddleworth plunged beneath the water. Danny waited. And waited. He could see Hetty pressing a hand to her mouth. Then abruptly Mr Saddleworth's head surfaced.

'It's no good. One of the back wheels is broken.' He was shouting but Danny still struggled to hear. 'The horses won't be able to pull it free. We'll have to set them loose. They're panicking and they're no good to us in this state.'

As soon as the reins were cut, the animals grabbed their chance for freedom. They swam across the final stretch and raced past Danny, water streaming off their flanks. They were safe but what about everyone else?

Danny looked at the stranded wagon. Mrs Jameson had lifted her skirts out of reach of the circling water. Hetty's face was pinched with cold, and the men were soaked and shivering.

And out of nowhere, he remembered Mr Trott's boast at the auction: '. . . he's been known to pull the weight of twenty grown men in a wagon. For several miles. Uphill . . .'

And Danny knew there was no choice. He whistled to Maharajah and they plunged back into the Esk. It felt colder than before, and the current seemed even stronger. The rain was falling so hard that the drops bounced off the river.

Mr Saddleworth was quick to catch on. 'Good thinking, Danny.' He hauled himself against the wagon, and reached inside. 'I'll toss you the training rope. Put the loop over his head, and tie it to the harness. That'll give the best grip. Just wave when it's secure. Then get Maharajah to pull like the devil.'

Mr Saddleworth threw the rope but Danny could hardly feel his hands. He missed it on the first attempt. And the second. But he managed on the third try.

Grasping Maharajah's ears, Danny shuffled forward so that he was leaning as far as he could reach. He widened the loop to its furthest point and tried to flick it over the elephant's head. No luck. The noose was not big enough. He did it again. It was not going to work. Panic was starting to grip.

'Let Maharajah help,' Mr Saddleworth shouted. 'Maybe you can do it together.'

Danny tried again but this time he held out the ankus. Obediently Maharajah lifted to touch it and his trunk coiled like a hook. Danny threw. The rope caught and settled low around the elephant's neck. It tightened and held. This might actually work, Danny thought, fumbling to knot the ties. He made the signal. And Maharajah began to pull.

The wagon gave a loud groan that could be heard even over the noise of the river, then it shifted unsteadily before shuddering to another stop. Mr Jameson and Crimple scrambled down to lighten the load a little more. The water reached their necks.

Danny whistled and Maharajah tried again. This time with more success. Gradually, inch by inch, the wagon moved. Progress was slow, the wheels often catching on the rocks and stones, but finally they reached the other side.

'Good work, lad.' Mr Jameson panted, his face pink from the effort. 'Well done.'

Relief and pride bubbled inside Danny, and he was certain his chest was puffed up like a peacock's. He wanted to enjoy the feeling a little longer but the job wasn't over yet. The wagon needed to be dragged up the bank from where it slumped in the shallows.

The men wrapped the rope around their waists and heaved from the front, while Danny guided Maharajah back into the Esk to push from behind.

And then suddenly the world collapsed.

One moment Danny was sitting safely upright. And the next, he was slipping backwards as Maharajah buckled beneath him. Desperately, Danny grabbed for the harness but it slid through his frozen fingers. And now there was nothing to stop his fall.

He tumbled into the icy water.

The shock of it stopped him still. He drifted, unable to move his arms and legs. The river flipped him over and over. Around and around. But Danny couldn't fight against it. Then the numbness dissolved, and terror took hold. He began thrashing, not knowing which way was up and which was down. Once he saw a glimpse of sky but however much he tried, it was always just out of reach.

The pressure to breathe was burning his lungs, and finally Danny gave in. He opened his lips and his mouth filled with water. At the edges, his vision blurred to black, and there was an irresistible urge to sink down.

The thought came to him with complete certainty – this was how his adventure would end, just as it was beginning.

Chapter Eleven

THE RIVER ESK
14 April 1872

The realization that he was likely to die struck Danny only a heartbeat before he was offered the chance to survive. So for a brief moment, he was balanced between two quite different worlds – like a spinning coin flipping from heads to tails, and back again.

Suddenly, a tight band hooked around his chest and he was yanked upwards. Breaking through the surface of the river, his lips opened on a gasp. Water heaved from his stomach and he tasted air. Wonderful, great mouthfuls of fresh air.

Then he was lifted. Cradled in a powerful grip. And Maharajah was wading across the water with all the force and strength of a sea storm.

'Danny!'

'Thank the Lord!'

'Is he . . .?'

But the question was never finished. Hands reached for him, pulling him back on to solid ground, and he was enveloped in warmth. It wasn't nearly enough. Every part of his body shook, despite the cocoon of towels and blankets.

'Thank the good Lord!' Mrs Jameson was pale. 'We thought we'd lost you. We thought you might be . . .'

This time when she brushed her fingers over his forehead, Danny didn't flinch. He was just too tired. And when he tried to turn his head, dizziness came in waves.

'There, lad. Don't move. You're all right now.' Mr Jameson patted his arm awkwardly. 'You really are all right.'

It was a few moments before Danny realized he was lying on a grass embankment. He could hear the rumble of the River Esk nearby. How long had he been in the river? Two minutes? Two days? It might have been anything.

Mr and Mrs Jameson knelt on one side, and Hetty sat on the other. He was desperate to shrink away from the attention but he didn't have the energy.

'I've never been so scared.' To his amazement, he realized Hetty was holding back tears. She hadn't quite succeeded. One leaked down her cheek, and he watched, curiously. It was odd to see someone crying over him; odd but not unpleasant. 'I–I thought you were dead. If it hadn't been for Maharajah—'

'Yes. All's fine now, Danny,' Mr Jameson interrupted.

'You're safe. I've just sent Sandev and Mr Saddleworth for help. Shouldn't be too long. Langholm's only about a mile away. Crimple can stay here. See to the wagon. And then we can...'

But Danny stopped listening. His concentration was fading like daylight at dusk. He wanted to sleep but the trembling wouldn't stop and every time he closed his eyes, his chest tightened and he couldn't breathe.

A farm cart clattered down the lane a short time later. Mr Saddleworth was sitting upfront, directing the driver. Danny knew he should get up but his legs wouldn't do what he told them, and neither would the rest of his body. In the end, he let the men carry him.

The farmer drove straight to Langholm Station. Danny wasn't sure why until Hetty explained that the Manchester train was due within the hour. He'd forgotten Mr and Mrs Jameson had planned to return to Belle Vue. Not that anything was making much sense. His last memory was of Maharajah collapsing underneath him. After that everything was hazy and confused. The water seemed to have washed away his mind as well as his strength.

From the back of the cart, he stared up at the sky. Grey clouds scuttled across the weak sun, and suddenly it came back to him in terrifying colour. He remembered the shock, the terror and the urge to give up – to let the water pull him down.

When the cart finally drew up next to the train platform, Danny was trying hard not to be sick. Hetty hovered next to him, tucking in the towels whenever they came loose. If she'd been talkative before, it was nothing compared to now.

'. . . you should have seen us, Danny. We didn't know where you were and everyone was looking. Then Sandev whistled but Maharajah had already gone into the water. And he saw you and scooped you up with his trunk. I've never seen anything like it.'

Hetty loosened the towel that covered his head, pulling it away from his face so he had room to breathe. 'You might have died if he hadn't . . .'

Abruptly, she stopped, staring as though seeing him for the first time. Danny couldn't quite read her expression. Shock? Anger? Or was it hurt? He was too muddle-headed to be sure.

'Danny, me boy! You're lookin' better already.' Mr Jameson's face popped over the side of the cart, startling them both. He was grinning around another large cigar. 'Glad to see you're on the mend. You'll be as right as rain in no time. You'll see.'

Danny didn't need a mirror to know it was a lie. He felt terrible, but at least he'd got control over his stomach. He didn't think he was going to be sick. Not yet, anyway.

'Before we head off, I need a word about Belle Vue. The welcome reception's goin' to be big. Flags. Banners. Balloons. Everythin'. That sort of hullabaloo. I'm invitin' the press men and the Mayor. Maybe the Lord Lieutenant as well. So I reckon you'd be best to arrive with about five minutes to spare. Create a bit of excitement. "Will they or won't they make it?" You know the sort of thing.'

He turned to his wife. 'What do you think, me dove?'

'As long as Maharajah arrives before ten o'clock, I don't care if he flies,' Mrs Jameson said tartly. Elbowing her husband out of the way, she smoothed a hand over Danny's forehead. He tried to sit upright but she pushed him back down gently.

'No. Lie still. Rest is what you need, young man. We need you fit and well, and home at Belle Vue by Friday. We're relying on you.'

Her last-minute instructions came so thick and fast that Danny could barely take them in. He didn't really mind. Her fussing felt like being wrapped in another warm blanket. They were to make no more unscheduled stops; Crimple was not to touch a drop of ale; and Danny was to be taken straight to the nearest hotel and put to bed.

She was only just winding down when Mr Jameson pulled Mr Saddleworth to one side. Danny strained to listen.

'. . . The lad seems well enough so I want you to start off early tomorrow. We can't afford any more delays. And it'll do no harm to let the newspapers know about the Prince's river adventure. They love a bit of drama. So let's give 'em some . . .'

They walked away, out of earshot, but Danny didn't need to hear any more. Even a near-drowning couldn't stop the Elephant Race. In fact, it had probably only attracted more publicity. He only hoped there wouldn't be any more disasters.

Finally, the Manchester train arrived and the Jamesons climbed on board. Danny managed to prop himself upright to wave goodbye. Mr Jameson poked his head from the carriage window. He was still puffing on the cigar.

'Remember what I said. Drama. That's the key. Everyone loves a bit of excitement . . .'

The rest was lost as the train steamed out of the station. Beside her husband, Mrs Jameson waved until she was a dot in the distance. Danny felt a tug in his chest as he watched them disappear. For the last four days, the couple had guided his life like a compass. It felt strange to be without them.

Despite her absence, Mrs Jameson's orders were obeyed as if they had come from the Queen herself. Wrapped in blankets, Danny was carried into a room at the town's hotel. He lay back on the bed and sank into the warmth. It felt like floating on clouds.

Almost immediately, Mr Saddleworth herded Sandev and Crimple outside but Hetty didn't seem to want to leave. She'd folded and refolded one towel twice already.

'Very well. Stay if you must, Henrietta. But don't tire him. He needs rest. He did well today.'

'Yes, Papa.'

'And Danny.' Mr Saddleworth hesitated at the door. 'About what I said before . . . Maybe Henrietta did know what she was doing. Choosing you, I mean. Well done, lad.'

At any other time, Danny would have grabbed at the compliment; he'd wanted to prove himself, and he'd succeeded. But the silence when Mr Saddleworth left was awkward, and he wasn't sure why. Hetty had barely said a word to him in the last half-hour – not since Mr Jameson had interrupted them at the station. Warily, he watched her stalk to the washstand and pick up a hand mirror.

'I think you should see this.'

She pushed the towel away from his face and lifted the glass so Danny could see. He stared at his reflection.

It was much, much worse than he had expected.

The river had destroyed his disguise. The turban had unravelled and, now that his hair was dry, it stood in stiff, spiky clumps. Worse still, the black dye had leached away in patches, blotting one cheek. Even the scars on his shoulder were visible through a rip in his shirt. He looked more like a battered clown than Indian royalty.

Danny slanted a glance at Hetty. She was staring at him.

'You're not really a prince, are you?'

Slowly Danny shook his head.

'Have you even been to India?'

He shook his head again.

Hetty blinked rapidly. When her eyes met his, they swam with a mixture of anger and hurt. 'I just wanted to believe it was true. I've never been anywhere or done anything exciting. And it all sounded so incredible.' She snatched the mirror away. 'You must have thought I was stupid. Everyone must.'

This time, Danny rocked his head more forcefully. Whatever else he thought of Hetty, she wasn't a fool. She was quick and clever. And he suspected she'd have made a better thief than half the pickpockets in Cowgate.

Hetty slid the mirror back, then propped herself against the washstand. It was as far away from him as she could get in the small room. Danny held his breath. Now that she knew he wasn't a prince, would she even want to speak to him? He was surprised to find that it mattered.

'I don't know who you really are,' she said at last. 'Or where you come from. And I know you can't tell me. But I keep my promises. You're not...' She seemed to struggle for the right words. 'You're not by yourself any more.'

Even if he had been able to talk, Danny wouldn't have known how to reply. She'd stolen away his breath with just a few words. He wanted to speak, so badly. Inside, a war was going on. One side of him was battling to be heard while the other had given up trying.

Hetty watched his face for a few moments then sighed and pushed away from the dresser. 'Well, I suppose we'd better get you cleaned up.'

With Hetty's help, it didn't take long for Danny to repair the river damage. He tugged on a fresh silk shirt, and she fetched a damp flannel so he could wash his face. Then together they managed to wrap a length of cloth around his head so the worst of the ruined dye-job was hidden.

'That's better.' Hetty smiled slyly. 'Some people might even say you were handsome. Not me, of course.'

Danny's cheeks flamed and he was glad when a knock on the door cut short his embarrassment. Hetty went to answer.

'May I come in?' Danny couldn't see the visitor but the voice was vaguely familiar.

'I'm sorry I'm afraid it's not a good—'

'Please. I really must see the Prince. It's important.'

Danny heard Hetty sniff. 'Very well. But you can't stay long.' She opened the door wider and a man slid inside. His eyes flicked quickly around the room before reaching Danny. He bowed so low his slight body was almost folded in half.

'I hope you remember me, Your Highness. Alfred Kibble, of the *Hawick Express*. I've been following the Elephant Race for the newspapers.'

This close, Mr Kibble barely looked old enough to shave. He had smooth skin, blond curls and blue eyes wide with innocence. Danny imagined old ladies loved him. He probably had no trouble getting people's stories.

'May I sit, Your Highness?'

Danny nodded cautiously. He was curious to find out what the reporter wanted.

'Thank you,' Mr Kibble grabbed Hetty's empty chair and perched beside the bed.

'Please forgive my intrusion, but Langholm is ablaze with stories about your river adventure. You're certainly attracting a great deal of interest. In fact, that's why I'm here.'

His cheeks flushed pink. '*The Times* of London has asked me to write a series of articles about you. The editor loved my account of the disputed toll, and he wants more stories for his own paper. They're thinking of calling it "The Life and Times of an Indian Prince". So I was wondering…' He leant nearer. '… if I could interview you?'

Danny's throat dried. This was a disaster. The Prince Dandip story would never hold up to close inspection. The more detailed it became, the more likely the lies would be found out.

Hetty answered for him. She walked in front of Mr Kibble, blocking his view of the bed. 'As I'm sure you know His Highness doesn't speak English. I'm afraid it's just not possible.'

Relieved, Danny slumped back into the pillows. Hetty wouldn't let him down. She understood. They had to get rid of the reporter as quickly as possible so he couldn't discover the truth.

'That's a great pity, Miss Saddleworth.' Like a hound on the scent of a fox, Mr Kibble switched his attention to Hetty. Panicked, Danny realized he wasn't giving up. 'The whole of the country is interested in His Highness's adventures. And no one else has managed to secure the Prince's personal story. Surely there must be some way it can be done?'

'I don't think—'

'Of course, I'd make certain to mention Belle Vue. The extra publicity would be sure to attract more visitors.' Mr Kibble's breath hitched slightly. 'And to be frank, this would be a big opportunity for me. My wages support my entire family, and a reporter's job is not always secure.'

Danny could actually see Hetty soften. Her shoulders no longer looked quite so rigid, and a hand fluttered to her throat. He tried unsuccessfully to catch her eye.

'Well . . . I suppose I could translate. My Papa is a famous animal doctor. He and I lived in India for a year, while he was looking after the King's elephants. And I know enough of the language to get by.'

Hetty told the lie without even blinking. Danny stared at her, horrified. What was she doing? She only spoke English, and he couldn't even speak! Just how were they going to get away with this? He pulled hard on her sleeve. But Hetty sat down on the bed and ignored him.

'I could act as a translator. Although, as you can see, His Highness is very tired and shaken after his ordeal. His voice is terribly weak. He'd have to whisper his answers to me.' She smiled prettily at the reporter. 'Would that be acceptable?'

Mr Kibble frowned. 'It's a little unusual but I see no reason why we shouldn't try.' From his bag, he pulled out a notebook, and an elegantly carved ink pen.

Hetty inclined her head. 'So what would you like to ask Prince Dandip?'

Danny cursed inwardly. He'd been expertly trapped.

There was no way of wriggling out of this, as much as he would like to. Without speech, he had about as much power as he'd had against the river.

At first, the interview was conducted in a strange triangle. Mr Kibble would ask a question and Hetty would lean forward for Danny to 'whisper' in her ear.

'His Highness says he does indeed have a great love of Scotland and its people. They have been very welcoming. He would love to return one day,' she replied to one query.

'. . . Yes, the Prince says he would be most pleased to invite the British royal family to visit. He's sure they would have a lot in common.'

'. . . His Highness is certainly enjoying his journey through the countryside and says he's convinced they will arrive in time to win the bet.'

Eventually Hetty didn't even pretend to consult Danny. To his alarm, she took the half-story that Mr Jameson had fed to the Edinburgh papers and let her imagination run wild.

'How did the Prince's parents meet?' She considered the question. 'Well it's a very romantic story. The Prince's father was a captain in the British army. He met the daughter of an Indian maharajah and it was love at first sight. But their love was frowned upon, so they ran away and were married. Eventually her father forgave them. He sent messengers begging them to return. But it was too late.'

It was very possible Hetty had actually forgotten anyone else was in the room, Danny thought. She seemed to be lost in a dream world.

'The captain died fighting the Maharajah's men, believing they'd been sent to take his wife. The princess shut herself away and refused to forgive her father. Months later, she died giving birth to their son. The Maharajah was grief-stricken. He couldn't even bear to see his grandson. So when the Prince was old enough, he ran away. His only friend was an elephant calf. That elephant was Maharajah. Named, of course, after the Prince's grandfather.'

She broke off and patted Danny's hand. 'His Highness told me himself that without the elephant he would not have survived.'

What a pile of poppycock! Danny wanted to roll his eyes but Mr Kibble was watching them too closely. He didn't dare do anything but smile and nod.

Hetty peered over at the reporter's notebook. His pen lay on the paper. 'Are you writing this down, Mr Kibble? You don't seem to be making many notes.'

'Yes, yes, of course. I'm just finding it so . . . so incredible. *The Times*'s readers will be amazed. It's almost impossible to believe.'

The alarm ringing in Danny's head became louder and more insistent. Hetty's ridiculous fantasy could destroy everything. Mr Jameson might think any publicity was good publicity but Danny knew people didn't like being treated like fools.

'It may be hard for you to believe, Mr Kibble. But my Aunt Augusta always told me how it important it is to tell the truth. And she's been a great influence on me.' Even

Danny had to admit Hetty wasn't lying about that. She cleared her throat. 'Besides, this will make a fascinating tale for your readers.'

'Well, yes. I suppose so.' The reporter glanced down at his notes. He picked up his pen again. 'I'd like to ask you about more recent events. Edinburgh and the Wormwell auction. Did you, or the Prince, ever meet Mr Wormwell himself?'

Hetty looked surprised. She glanced at Danny. He shook his head. The questions were making him more and more uneasy.

'Why no, we never met him. Although my father did. He said . . . now how exactly did he put it? He said Mr Wormwell was a good man but dreadful with money and a terrible judge of character. His death was horribly tragic.'

'I suppose it was.' Mr Kibble didn't sound particularly sympathetic. He scribbled something on his pad. 'If I could return to the auction. I understand that as well as the elephant, Mr Jameson bought several other animals?'

'Yes, my Papa shall be in charge of them, along with rest of the menagerie at Belle Vue. But they all went by train to Manchester. It was only Maharajah who refused to go.'

'So the express was delayed while the elephant was taken off the train, along with all the other items bought in the same lot? The ropes, the harnesses, all the other essential equipment for Maharajah? Paperwork perhaps?'

'Yes. I suppose so.'

'That must have taken some time?'

'I imagine it did, but I wasn't there. Sandev and Crimple made sure everything that was needed came with us in the wagon. All I know is that we have to arrive in Belle Vue by the nineteenth of April – seven days from leaving Edinburgh. Otherwise Mr Albright wins the zoological collection.'

Mr Kibble made another note. 'And it was in Edinburgh that the Prince was reconciled with his long-lost friend? How fortunate that he reached the auction just in time to see Maharajah being sold. And how lucky that the train was delayed so they could be reunited. Some might call it an incredible coincidence, don't you think?'

'Yes. You could say so.' Hetty shifted uncomfortably. It was obvious to Danny that she was far happier spinning stories about his past than lying about more recent events. 'But this has been reported in great detail already, Mr Kibble. It was in all the Scottish papers.'

'You're quite right.' To Danny's surprise, the reporter snapped his notepad shut. It seemed an abrupt end to the interview, although he'd certainly be glad to see the back of Mr Kibble. 'I've taken up a lot of your time. I'm very grateful to you.'

'Can you tell us when *The Times* will publish the story?' Hetty asked politely.

'I'm afraid I can't give you an exact date. I've a little more research to do. To make certain all the details are correct. Now if you'll excuse me? Your Highness, Miss Saddleworth. It's been a pleasure.'

He gave a brief nod and left the room in swift strides. Hetty waited until the door closed before jumping up excitedly.

'Well I think that went very well. Everyone will be even more fascinated by Prince Dandip. And Mr Jameson will be delighted with the publicity, don't you think? I hope Papa will be pleased too. I mentioned several times that he's an animal doctor, and how people always want his advice. Imagine us appearing in *The Times* of London ...'

Hetty was giddy but Danny didn't share any of her excitement. He was even more certain than ever that it could only be a matter of time before the truth came out. And then he would be back, exactly where he'd started. At Frank Scatcherd's mercy.

Chapter Twelve

LANGHOLM
15 April 1872

They got ready to leave Langholm at sunrise. Danny still felt weak and he had to force himself out of bed, but he knew they couldn't stay any longer. Time was becoming more and more precious.

At least there were no more signs of trouble. Crimple had met them for breakfast after a night repairing the broken wheel with the blacksmith, while Sandev had kept watch over Maharajah in the stables. No one had seen anything unusual.

Light was already streaking across the dark sky as they arrived to collect the wagon. The blacksmith yawned as he unbolted the gates to his yard. Danny's jaw itched in sympathy. He was so tired he could have slept standing up.

No one else appeared any brighter; Crimple was grumpy from lack of sleep; and both Sandev and Mr Saddleworth seemed caught up in their own thoughts. Even Hetty was quiet. The two carthorses stamped impatiently in the cold, their breath creating clouds in the spring air.

Only Maharajah was unconcerned. Danny gave him an apple, and felt a gentle nudge in return. A wave of affection swept through him. This animal had saved his life. In that moment, Danny knew there was nothing he wouldn't do in return.

'We left the wagon through here,' Crimple led them to the back of the blacksmith's yard. 'And I checked everythin' before I left last night so I know . . .'

He stopped suddenly, blocking Danny's view. Then he stepped aside.

Horrified, Danny stared. The wagon stood in the centre of chaos. Its cargo had been ransacked; every box and bag pulled out and overturned. The contents spilt across the floor in a sprawling tangle.

Ropes and harnesses were now mixed with buckets, chains and cleaning brushes. Sacks of food had been tipped up and shaken, leaving fruit, vegetables and some sugar cane rolling across the yard. One large hay bale looked as though it had been pulled apart, straw by straw.

'Who . . . who would do this?' Hetty's shock echoed Danny's. There was something about the destruction that was almost spiteful. 'And why?'

'It weren't like this when I left. I promise you.' Crimple looked dazed. 'I know it weren't.'

Mr Saddleworth picked up an apple sack that had been slashed open. His face was furious. 'Well whoever it was, if they were hoping to find valuables, they won't have had any luck. There's nothing here worth stealing.'

Danny knew Mr Saddleworth was right because he'd already checked. The scattered cargo was mostly equipment needed to clean, feed and train Maharajah, plus some day-to-day essentials for the trip – battered pans, old camping blankets and towels. Nothing that would have raised more than a few shillings at an Edinburgh pawnbrokers.

But last night, the intruder had torn everything apart. They'd missed nothing. One large crate hadn't even been opened since the auction. Now papers streamed across the floor. A corner of a book peeked out from the mess. Leaning down, Hetty cleaned off the cover.

'It's a scrapbook of newspaper cuttings.' She turned the pages. The dust made her sneeze. 'They're all stories about Maharajah. Here's one from the *Blackpool Gazette* – "Mayor Welcomes Elephant Sensation to North Pier". And another from the *Liverpool Daily Post* – "Miracle Maharajah Lifts the Weight of Ten Men". It's even got a cartoon!'

As Hetty flipped through the rest of the scrapbook, Danny noticed several rolls of paper curled under the wagon. Curious, he tugged one free.

The poster was bold and bright and instantly recognizable. Maharajah stood in a circus ring alongside his keeper. Two large hoops were hooked over his trunk, and a blue feather sprouted from his headdress.

"'Maharajah the Magnificent Appears Tonight, Courtesy of Wormwell's Royal Number One Menagerie. Come and Marvel at the Strongest Beast in the British Empire'", Hetty read aloud over his shoulder. She reached out a hand. 'Look Danny. That harness is the one he's wearing now. And Sandev, that's you! You both look wonderful.'

'Thank you, Miss Henrietta.' Sandev made his elegant bow. 'Those were happy times. But I am sad to say Mr Wormwell was a gambling man. When he died, the menagerie had to be sold. There was no money left to carry on. And no job for me.'

'I'm so sorry. I didn't realize.'

'Do not worry. I have other offers. Everything will be well.' As usual Sandev's solemn face gave nothing away. If he was upset about leaving Maharajah behind in Manchester, Danny couldn't tell. An uncomfortable twinge twisted his stomach. He was pretty sure it must be guilt. If it wasn't for him, Sandev would probably have a job at Belle Vue.

'But I'm sure if I asked Mr Jameson, he'd give you—'

'Henrietta, leave Sandev alone. It's his business, not yours.' Mr Saddleworth was still sifting through the clutter. 'We need to concentrate on clearing this. Danny, you collect the papers with Henrietta. Sandev, sort out Maharajah's equipment. Check it carefully. Crimple, you do the rest.' He rubbed the back of his neck. 'I want to speak to the black-smith, ask him to check the wagon.'

Danny was surprised how quickly they managed to turn the chaos into some sort of order. Many of the food sacks were torn, a brush had been snapped in half and some of the fruit was badly crushed. But much of the rest was salvageable.

The blacksmith gave them a new crate for the papers, and Danny rolled up one of the posters to keep for himself. Within an hour, they'd reloaded the supplies and were ready to get back on the road.

Crimple finished harnessing the horses. 'Find any problems with the wagon, Gov?' he grunted, giving a final tug on one of the leather buckles.

'No, it's all clear. No sign of anything unusual.' Mr Saddleworth climbed up and took the reins. 'What do you think, Crimple? Could Albright have been responsible for this?'

The keeper shook his head. 'Don't see why Mr Albright would bother. It held us up a bit, but we soon got it sorted. If he were wantin' to stop us properly, he'd do something a bit more permanent. I reckon it was just kids.'

Danny wasn't so certain. Perhaps the intruders had been disturbed. Maybe they would have damaged the wagon if they'd had more time. The edgy feeling had returned. He'd even started to wonder if Frank Scatcherd had something to do with it. But the idea was ridiculous. He was miles away and, so far, no one else had realized that the boy pickpocket from Cowgate was Prince Dandip of Delhi.

Or had they? Fleetingly, he thought of Alfred Kibble, and his precise, exact questions.

'Will you report this to the constable, Mr Saddleworth?' asked Sandev.

'No, it would only delay us. I can't find anything missing, and we don't know who's responsible. Maybe it was children, or a local villain who's seen the publicity and was looking for money. But I want you all to be especially vigilant from now. We don't need any more setbacks.'

Crimple flicked the reins, Danny whistled to Maharajah and they left Langholm behind.

The country road rose up into the hills before dropping down to follow the River Esk once again. It was cold, wet and exhausting. And when they finally crossed the border into England, Danny didn't feel excited. He was just too tired.

At least people were still turning out to greet them. In Longtown, crowds lined the streets, spilling into the market square and beyond. If Mr Jameson had been here, he would be dancing a jig: this was exactly what he wanted.

But as they crossed the town's arched bridge, the faces blurred away and all Danny could see was the water. Coiling around the rocks, churning along the shore and slamming against the bank. And he remembered the strength of the current, dragging him under.

He wiped a damp palm across his shirt. His heart raced. Air was pumping in and out of his lungs as fast as butterfly wings. It was no good, he couldn't do this any more.

On shaky legs, Danny slid down from Maharajah, not

even bothering to call him to a stop. The dismount wasn't graceful. He almost fell beneath Maharajah's feet and it was only by luck that he wasn't hurt.

'What's the matter?' Hetty scrambled from the wagon. 'Danny? What is it?'

Reaching his side, she tried to shield him from the curious spectators, but Danny hardly cared. Feelings were shaking loose inside him and he couldn't calm enough to pin them down. Confusion. Fear. Shame. Crouching, he let his chin slump on to his chest. How stupid to be terrified of water when he'd faced so much worse.

Something rough rubbed the back of his neck, and a strong grip wrapped around his chest, pushing him off balance. It was Maharajah. Danny tried to pull away but the elephant wasn't letting go. If anything, his grasp only tightened.

Then, dumbfounded, Danny realized what was happening. Maharajah was rocking him, just like a mother would cradle her baby. In Cowgate, he'd seen women nurse their children in the same way while they gossiped across the alleys. He'd always wondered what it felt like. And now he knew.

He curled into the warmth and let himself be held. His fear dissolved like dust in rain.

Danny didn't climb back on to Maharajah after they left Longtown. Instead, he walked at the elephant's side, trying to stretch his stiffened muscles. The shakiness was gradually disappearing, and it was good to have solid ground beneath his feet.

He tried to match his strides to Sandev's. The mahout seemed to have the energy of ten men. So far, he'd walked every step of the way, without a rest in the wagon, or a single word of complaint. It made Danny want to do the same.

Hetty strode between them. Her clothes were no longer spotless. Dirt and dust circled the hem of her dress; another smear streaked down one sleeve; and her hair hung in an untidy plait. The jaunty little hat was long gone. Danny couldn't believe she was the same girl who had arrived at Hawick Station. He liked this one much better.

'This is the best adventure! Aunt Augusta would never let me go anywhere. She says curiosity is vulgar, and young ladies should only show interest in sewing and the weather.' Hetty flung out her arms and spun in a circle. 'But one day I want to travel the world. Maybe I'll go to India with my papa and see elephants just like Maharajah.'

Danny felt a tug of longing at the idea. More and more, he was realizing that this journey wasn't only about reaching Manchester, but about a hundred other places he could visit once he got there.

'That is not possible, I am afraid.' Just for a moment, it looked as though Sandev's mouth might curl into a smile.

'Why not?' Hetty stopped mid-stride. Her hands settled on her hips, in a way that Danny recognized meant business. 'Don't you think I can do it?'

'No, Miss Henrietta. Forgive me. I think you could do

anything you want. But I am afraid you will not see elephants like Maharajah in India. Because he is an African elephant. They are much larger. More powerful, with bigger ears and tusks.'

Hetty's brow furrowed. 'I don't understand. I thought Maharajah was from India.'

'You are not the only one to think so. Maharajah was young when he joined Mr Wormwell's menagerie. Smaller and not so strong. But people loved him. For years, we travelled the country together. He and I even performed for Her Majesty.'

'Maharajah has met Queen Victoria?'

'Yes, most certainly. Of all the animals, he was her particular favourite.'

Danny's jaw loosened, and pride uncurled in his chest. Of course Maharajah was special, but to be recognized by the Queen surely proved it. Lightly he brushed a palm along the elephant's trunk, feeling the thick ridges of skin bump against his fingers. Maharajah curled towards the touch.

'Come on!' Mr Saddleworth shouted. 'I've already told you. We haven't got time for dawdling. It's the fourth day and we're not even halfway to Belle Vue yet. Let's go!'

It seemed to Danny that their pace quickened after that. Crowds greeted them in every town but Danny practised his royal wave – polite but distant – and he kept Maharajah moving.

Finally, just before midnight, they arrived at the George Hotel in Penrith. It was Crimple's turn for the night watch so he disappeared to the stables with Maharajah, while everyone else waited for Mr Saddleworth to book rooms. Bone-weary, Danny slumped into a corner of the reception hall. He hadn't planned on falling asleep but his eyelids fluttered closed without waiting for permission.

He was jerked awake by the heavy tread of boots, and deep voices that didn't sound local. Two men were talking to Mr Saddleworth at the front desk. The older one had a crumpled face that matched his crumpled suit, and Danny was almost sure he'd seen him somewhere before. And then he remembered.

It was the same man who had been talking to the animal keepers at the Wormwell auction. The man who'd chased him away from the wagons. But what was he doing here, miles away from Edinburgh? Suddenly Danny didn't feel quite so tired any more.

Edging closer, he slipped behind an armchair near the reception desk. His sixth sense for trouble was screaming like a siren. He peered around the chair. The older man was shaking hands with Mr Saddleworth.

'I'm Inspector Clarence Quick from the Edinburgh City Police. I believe you're with the Belle Vue party. I'm looking for Mr James Jameson. Is he here?'

'No, I'm afraid he and his wife travelled ahead of us to Manchester. They left by train yesterday.'

'That's a pity.' The inspector frowned. 'I'm anxious to speak to him. I have some questions about his purchase of an elephant from Wormwell's Royal Number One

Menagerie. I believe the animal's name is Maharajah. And he's being ridden by an Indian prince called . . .' He glanced at his colleague for help.

'Dandip, sir.'

'That's right. Prince Dandip. A rather urgent situation has arisen.'

'Can I be of any help?' Hetty's father sounded curious but not particularly concerned. He'd probably never had reason to be wary of the police. Unlike Danny. 'My name's William Saddleworth. I'm in charge while Mr Jameson's away.'

'Thank you. Unfortunately, I expect he's the only one with the answers we need. We'll have to reach him at Belle Vue. I wish you a safe journey.'

Inspector Quick tugged the brim of his hat, and Danny thought he would leave without another word, but then he stopped. 'A friendly warning, Mr Saddleworth. If I were you, I'd watch how you go on from here. There are a lot of unscrupulous characters about. And not everyone is exactly who they seem. Do be careful.'

Danny leant his head against the back of the chair, and tried to bring his panic under control. But already his imagination was running in wild loops.

Had the police been sent after him? Did someone suspect that Prince Dandip of Delhi was really a street pickpocket from Cowgate?

Or was it just possible that Inspector Quick was on the trail of something much, much bigger?

Chapter Thirteen

PENRITH
15 April 1872

'What do you think you're doing, lad?'

Danny jerked back against the chair. Mr Saddleworth was peering down at him, his face lined with suspicion. Straightening, Danny yawned and stretched out his arms, hoping he looked like he'd been napping, not eavesdropping.

'Well, if you're that tired, perhaps you should go to bed. I've booked us all rooms and Sandev's already gone up.' Mr Saddleworth gestured towards the stairs. 'I almost forgot. Have you seen my map? The one marked with the route to Belle Vue? It's not in the wagon.'

Frowning, Danny shook his head. Mr Saddleworth was

rarely without his collection of maps and charts. His detailed planning was the main reason they'd managed not to stray off course.

'I suppose it must have been thrown away with all the mess from the break-in. I've a spare copy. It just means I'll have to spend the next hour marking out the route again. And I've enough to do.' Mr Saddleworth sighed. 'Go on. You get to bed.'

It was more of an order than a suggestion but Danny wasn't tired any more. The restless uneasy feeling was growing. On its own, a lost map was insignificant but added to the list of mishaps over the last few days it suddenly seemed far more important.

As well as last night's break-in at the blacksmith's yard, he'd come as close to drowning as he ever wanted to. He and Sandev had chased off a prowler, and it was very likely that someone had ransacked his room at the pub in Stow.

Could Arthur Albright be behind it all? And what would be the point? There'd been no major delays, apart from the setback caused by the damaged bridge. The Elephant Race was still on schedule. More or less.

Then there was a nagging worry that Danny still hadn't shaken off. He was almost certain they were being watched. Had someone seen through his disguise and set Scatcherd on his trail? Or were Inspector Quick and the Edinburgh police keeping track of their journey? And if so, why? And the last, most disloyal thought – the one he'd been trying hard to avoid – was this: could Mr Jameson have arranged the accidents to get more publicity for Belle Vue? He'd already done it before, at Waverley Station, Danny was sure of it. But had he tried again?

Danny climbed the hotel stairs, dragging his toes against each step. Then a sudden panicked thought sent him whirling back – through the reception hall and out into the yard. If someone was serious about stopping the Elephant Race, there was only one certain way to do it. Through Maharajah.

Heart hammering, Danny sprinted towards the barn where Maharajah had been bedded down for the night. He burst through the doors and spun around, not entirely sure what he was expecting to find. But it certainly wasn't this: silence. Peaceful, unbroken silence.

Carefully, he edged towards the back of the building. Stopped. Looked both ways. And pivoted on his heels just to make sure.

Nothing.

No trouble. No upset. No sign of disorder.

Maharajah lay sleeping in the straw, breathing heavily. Even the Wormwell wagon stood undisturbed in the darkness. Solid and sturdy after the blacksmith's repairs.

Danny's chest eased. Everything was fine. There had been no need to panic. He was becoming ridiculous, jumping at shadows and imagining trouble that wasn't there. But, just as he'd let down his guard, footsteps rustled through straw and something collided heavily with his back. He wasn't alone.

Automatically, Danny turned, grappling blindly in the

dark. His arms hooked around a small, slight body and held on tight. Sliding a hand upward, he slapped a palm across an open mouth. Sharp teeth sank into his skin. Jerking, he loosened his grip, and hissed out a silent curse.

'Serves you right! It's me, you idiot. Who did you think it was?'

Danny's pulse slowed. An embarrassed flush spread over his skin and he blessed the cover of darkness. He should have known Hetty would come after him. Deliberately, he stepped back, hoping she hadn't noticed the slight shake of his fingers. He could still feel the blood rushing through his body.

'I just wanted to talk to you.' Hetty paused, and her eyes searched the shadowed corners of the outbuilding. Danny recognized her edginess because it matched his own. Then she brought her attention back to him.

'Do you know the police have been?'

Danny nodded.

'Well, I've been thinking about the last few days . . . about the break-in and everything else that's happened. What if the police have discovered something. What if . . .'

Despite himself, Danny's heart picked up. He leant closer.

'What if Albright has been paying someone to slow us down. And what if that person is someone close to us. Someone who's near enough to know all our movements.' Hetty paused. 'And what if it's—'

But she didn't get a chance to say any more. Behind

them, the door creaked open. Lamplight spilt across the floor. Crimple stood on the threshold.

'Oi, what are you two doing here?'

Hetty's shocked gaze caught Danny's, and in that moment, he knew exactly what she was thinking. Then she turned and put her hands to her hips.

'What do you mean? We've been watching over Maharajah, because you weren't here. The question should be – where have you been?'

Crimple glowered and Danny was near enough to smell the beer on his breath. 'A man's got to eat, hasn't he? Anyway, what I do is none of your business. Get back to the hotel.'

The following morning was grey and gloomy, much like Danny's mood. He'd had no further time alone with Hetty. Last night Crimple had marched them both back to the hotel, and straight into Mr Saddleworth's temper.

'Henrietta! Danny! There you are! You should have been asleep hours ago. Up to your rooms now.'

Danny had obeyed reluctantly. But he'd spent most of the night tossing and turning.

Could Hetty be right? Was Nelson Crimple behind all those odd events and near catastrophes? He turned over the possibility carefully.

Instinct had already convinced him someone was trying to cause trouble. Ever since the first night in Stow, when he and Sandev had chased the prowler, he'd felt uneasy. But not all the pieces fitted.

Crimple had seemed as shocked as everyone else to find the ransacked wagon this morning. And he definitely couldn't have been the prowler. That man had been slight and wiry, not big and thickset.

Yet, whenever anything had gone wrong, Crimple had always been nearby. He was at the reins of the wagon when the wheel broke; he was in the hotel when Danny's room was disturbed; and he was only a short distance away when Danny had fallen into the river.

By sunrise, Danny's head swam, and he was happy to get back on the road. He needed wide, open spaces. They were climbing up and over Shap, the highest point on their route. Walking alongside Maharajah, Danny could feel his muscles stretching and tightening with the march uphill. But, at the top, the view was worth every ache.

Sunlight split the clouds, brightening the moors to a vivid green. In the distance, snow showered the mountains and the wind whipped across Danny's face, stealing his breath. It was like standing on the roof of the world. He stepped right up to the edge and looked down. Cowgate's dirty, choked streets were a lifetime away. And despite everything, he felt his spirits lift.

On the other side of the peak, the wind dropped from a gale to a gust, and it was easier to breathe. They stopped to eat in the shelter of some rocks, close to a stream. Crimple stayed in the wagon. But before Danny could catch Hetty's attention, he was called away to help Mr Saddleworth check and clean Maharajah.

Strangely, this had become the favourite part of Danny's day. While he worked, Mr Saddleworth would tell stories of his adventures. Most were about animals that Danny had never heard of, and countries he didn't even know existed.

Today he welcomed the distraction.

'Paris is beautiful.' Mr Saddleworth said, running a hand over Maharajah's front feet. 'Not now, perhaps. The city's still getting over the Prussian war. I was there last year but, to be truthful, I wasn't much help. No one was interested in saving the zoological animals. Most were killed to feed the starving. I even saw a butcher selling camel steaks and slices of elephant's trunk.'

A week ago, Danny wouldn't have turned a hair at the idea – when he'd been hungry, he'd eaten anything he could beg or steal – but now the thought made his stomach churn. He wiped a cloth down Maharajah's back leg, taking extra care to be gentle.

'And in some countries, elephants are not killed for food but for money. Hunters chop off the trunks, skin the heads and cut away the tusks for ivory. It's barbaric. I've seen them used to make ladies' fans and chess sets. And some tusks are kept as trophies. It's cruel and ugly and—'

Mr Saddleworth stopped abruptly, and Danny realized Hetty was standing just behind them. From the horrified look on her face it was obvious she'd been listening.

'I'm sorry, Henrietta.'

'No, Papa.' Hetty was shaking her head vigorously. 'Don't. I'm not a little child, and I'm not going to faint away whenever I hear anything unpleasant.'

'I'm your father. It's my place to protect you.'

'Then how will I learn anything important? I need to know what goes on in the world even if it's bad. Anyway, I need to talk to you.' She took a deep breath, and flicked a glance at Danny. He knew immediately what she was going to say, and part of him wanted to hold her back. It was too soon.

'I think Albright has been paying someone to sabotage the Elephant Race. Ever since we started, odd things have been happening. I don't mean big delays, but small things. Like the wagon getting stuck in the river. Or Danny falling into the water. Then there was the break-in, and now your map's disappeared.'

She'd begun to talk more quickly. 'And I think it's Nelson Crimple. He's always watching us and acting suspiciously. He doesn't like Danny. And I don't think he likes Maharajah much either. And—'

'Enough, Henrietta! Stop.' Mr Saddleworth was frowning. 'This is ridiculous. You might not like Crimple but that doesn't mean he's done anything wrong. He's one of Belle Vue's most loyal staff. Losing the Elephant Race would mean losing his job. And besides, how would he have been able to ransack the wagon? The blacksmith was with him all night. I know because I checked.'

'But Papa!'

'As for the rest of it – the map, the river, the bridge. Let's be logical. We're walking more than two hundred miles across country, there are bound to be a few accidents. But that's all they are. Accidents. Nothing more. You've created a drama out of nothing.'

Hetty's chin had come up. 'What about the police? Why were they here?'

'They came to see Mr Jameson, not to speak to Crimple. And if there was any evidence against him, I'd know about it.'

Mr Saddleworth lifted his hands to Hetty's shoulders, and Danny knew the moment she realized the argument was lost. Frustration stiffened her spine.

'I agree we have to be more careful – all of us – but these accusations are completely unfounded.' As Hetty arched away, he sighed and dropped his hands. 'I'm trying to be a good father to you, Henrietta, and I've allowed you a lot of freedom on this trip because I doubt your Aunt Augusta gave you very much. But I'm warning you, if this behaviour continues you will lose it.'

Hetty's eyes flared. Danny could almost hear the battle going on inside her head.

But in the end she turned away. And he knew he'd failed her. When a few words of support might have made a difference, he couldn't say anything. What good was he as a friend if he couldn't even do that?

Chapter Fourteen

ABBEYSTEAD HALL

16 April 1872

The fifth night of the Elephant Race would be different from the others. Instead of stopping at a village inn, they'd been invited to stay at Abbeystead Hall. Danny wondered if it was as grand as it sounded. He couldn't believe a few days ago he'd been living in slums and tonight he would be the guest of an English lord.

'Lord Cawthorne loves animals,' Mr Saddleworth explained. 'He has his own collection, and he's been writing to Mr Jameson for advice on which animals to add to his menagerie. When he heard about the Elephant Race, he insisted we stop at Abbeystead. It's quite an honour.'

They'd pushed hard to arrive by late evening. Eventually

Danny had given up walking and climbed back on to Maharajah. Now his arms ached, and his shoulders were stiff from keeping upright. But at last, Abbeystead's tall chimneys could be seen, poking out from between the trees.

Danny and Maharajah led the way, trooping up the long, gravel driveway while darkness fell. As they drew nearer, the house unfolded like a paper fan, becoming larger and even more impressive. Danny couldn't quite believe it was real. Every window blazed with light, illuminating the courtyard in the dusk. Water gushed from a fountain of stone lions, and the wide, smooth lawn looked as though it had been ironed flat.

A man stood on the front steps, dressed in black tie and tails. He might have been smiling but it was difficult to see beyond the large moustache that curled above his lips. At his heels, several dogs yapped noisily.

'Welcome, Your Highness. Welcome, everyone.' His voice was a boom. 'I'm delighted you were able to visit. I've been reading about your progress. I'm Cawthorne.'

He strode towards Maharajah then circled him before coming back to the point where he'd started. 'So this is the animal that the whole of the country is talking about. I can see why. He's an incredible creature. A quite remarkable specimen.'

Lord Cawthorne reached out to touch Maharajah's trunk but the elephant jerked away. He seemed oddly skittish. Danny gently smoothed a palm across one ear.

'So how big would you say he is? About twelve feet to

the shoulder? And fully grown?'

'Roughly that, Your Lordship,' Mr Saddleworth replied. 'But Mr Jameson could tell you more.'

'Yes. It's unfortunate that he couldn't be here. We've never actually met but I've enjoyed our correspondence.' Lord Cawthorne glanced towards the steps where another man had appeared. Gold buttons glittered on his waistcoat. 'However I believe you already know one of my other guests. Mr Arthur Albright of the Yorkshire Zoological Gardens?'

'No. I'm afraid I haven't had that pleasure.'

Mr Saddleworth didn't look pleased. He wasn't the only one. Danny tensed as Albright walked down the steps towards them. Instinctively, he slid an arm on either side of Maharajah's neck and curled his body over the warm skin. The urge to protect was surprisingly fierce.

'Mr Saddleworth, I presume? What a fortunate meeting!' Albright smiled – the kind of smile that showed all his teeth but no warmth. 'And Your Highness. I'd certainly not expected to see you all here. Surely by now, you should be miles further on?'

Dinner was served in the grandest room Danny had ever seen. A huge gaslight dripping with glass beads hung over the long table. Hetty said it was a chandelier. Whatever it was called, he'd never seen anything so magnificent. He only managed to stop staring when Hetty elbowed him in the ribs.

Sandev and Crimple had not been invited to eat with them. Instead, they were sent to the Abbeystead kitchens. Danny might have been more worried if he hadn't heard Mr Saddleworth's whispered order to Sandev. 'Stay with Maharajah in the stables tonight. Do not leave his side.' As it was, Albright's presence at Abbeystead was already making Danny uneasy – and he still had to get through dinner.

As guest of honour, Prince Dandip was seated next to Lord Cawthorne; Hetty was on his other side.

Sitting opposite – almost hidden by gold-edged china and a huge vase of flowers – were Mr Saddleworth and Albright. And at the far end were the two other dinner guests. They were introduced as the local vicar, Reverend Edgar Applerow, and his wife Beatrice.

Mrs Applerow was a smaller, softer version of Mrs Jameson. She had a gentle manner and a kind smile. Danny was more suspicious of her husband. His face was all straight lines, and he bowed his head to pray with a passion that Danny had only ever given to his food. It was the first time he had ever been asked to say grace before a meal, and he fidgeted uncomfortably.

'. . . and may the Lord make us truly thankful. Amen.'

As several footmen carried in bowls of soup, Danny felt his unease grow. He looked down at the cutlery lined up on the stark white tablecloth. There were so many pieces he didn't know which to choose.

'Copy me,' Hetty whispered. She lifted one of the silver spoons, so Danny did the same. In his other life, he would have slipped it into his sleeve and then sneaked out of the house but he couldn't do that any more. However tempting.

There were seven courses in all, each one announced by Ogden, the Abbeystead butler, in a heavy, solemn voice. After the pheasant soup came a fish course of turbot and tartare sauce, then a choice of creamed lobster or wild duck, both wrapped in pastry.

As each plate was brought in, Danny watched Hetty carefully to check he didn't make any mistakes. At last, the main dish arrived; roasted partridge, served with potatoes, peas and asparagus.

'Shot the birds myself, just this morning,' Lord Cawthorne said proudly, selecting several pink slices. Under the table, he fed scraps to his dogs, while gravy dripped from the curls of his moustache. Occasionally he would turn to Danny and shout slow questions in a booming voice.

'SO WHAT DO YOU MAKE OF THE ENGLISH WEATHER, PRINCE DANDIP?'

'I'm afraid he doesn't speak English, Your Lordship,' Mr Saddleworth said quietly. 'But he can hear. And his understanding is better than most.'

Lord Cawthorne frowned, swiping at his dripping moustache. 'How very peculiar. These foreigners must learn the language. Prove they're not barbarians. There'll be no educating them unless they speak English.'

'I couldn't agree more, Your Lordship. Well said.' Albright nodded vigorously. All evening, he'd been tripping over himself for Lord Cawthorne's attention, pouring out flattery as though it were cream.

Danny caught Hetty's glance and she rolled her eyes. It wasn't difficult to know what she was thinking. Her dislike of Albright was obvious. Looking down at his plate, he fought not to laugh. Instead, he concentrated on his food, scooping up mouthfuls with what he hoped was the right fork.

Ice cream and fruit sorbets followed the meat course. They'd been shaped to look like flower buds and Danny had to hold in a gasp when the crystal bowl was set in front of him. The crisp petals looked too beautiful to eat, but he managed it anyway, breaking off frozen pieces and letting them dissolve on his tongue.

Finally, the footmen brought in Stilton cheese, alongside apples and grapes. By the end, Danny's sides ached. Even he hadn't been able to finish every plate. He considered shovelling the leftovers into his napkin but he only had time to grab a couple of apples for Maharajah.

Lord Cawthorne rose from the table as the last dish was cleared. 'Perhaps now you'd like to see my menagerie.' It was nearer to an instruction than an invitation. 'I'm rather proud of it.'

'Is it not a little dark?' asked Mrs Applerow. She glanced outside nervously.

'Oh no, not at all, madam. My animals are all indoors. I'll show you.'

Stalking ahead, Lord Cawthorne led the way through a

large panelled hall before opening a door into a narrow corridor. Gas lamps, fixed at regular intervals, lit the way, and as they walked, shadows flickered on the wall. It seemed to Danny that they were moving further and further away from the main house.

At last, Lord Cawthorne pushed open a door. 'Here we are. I had this outbuilding connected up to the Hall, and then converted to house my collection. I'm sure you'll be impressed.'

Danny was the last to step out into the long, low room. And he wasn't prepared for what he found. Glass cases lined the walls, each filled with animals.

They were all dead.

Dead, stuffed and mounted. It was like being in a frozen zoo.

'Quite amazing, isn't it?' said Lord Cawthorne. 'My life's work.'

Stunned, Danny followed the others as they spread out into the room. His head swivelled, trying to take everything in.

The exhibits ranged from ordinary cats and dogs to creatures he recognized only because of the Wormwell auction. In one corner, a lion shared its space with a leaping tiger and a snarling hyena. In another, a crocodile, wolf and giant tortoise were circled around a small brown rabbit. Perhaps the most striking was a fully grown deer, complete with antlers that sat on its head like a crown.

In the centre of the room, the largest case held the most

bizarre exhibit – part zebra, part horse, as though leftover pieces of animals had been stitched together. Pushing his nose to the display window, Danny looked more closely. The creature stood proudly but its glass eyes were blank.

'A quagga,' said Lord Cawthorne, tapping his fingers on the glass. 'One of only twenty-three in the world on display. They're likely to be extinct soon, so it was a valuable find. It cost me a small fortune, I can tell you.'

Hetty began walking past the exhibits, reading aloud the labels as she went. 'Zebra, shot by Ambrose Cawthorne, eleventh of November 1870, Africa. Female baboon, shot by Ambrose Cawthorne, twenty-fourth of November 1868, Africa. Sea lion stranded and culled off the American coast, fifteenth of December 1871 . . .'

The more she read, the more dazed she sounded. And Danny knew why – because he felt exactly the same. Lord Cawthorne didn't love animals. He killed them. This was no menagerie. It was a graveyard.

'Why do you do this? Why ever would you want to?' Hetty's hands had risen to her hips.

'Henrietta! You're a guest here. Remember your manners.' Mr Saddleworth tried to pull her back, but she shrugged him off.

'That's quite all right, Saddleworth. Some people don't understand at first, but I'm happy to educate the girl.' Lord Cawthorne actually sounded glad of the opportunity. He cleared his throat.

'You see, my dear, there's nothing like the challenge of

hunting a wild animal. The most exciting moments of my life have been whilst big-game hunting in Africa. I remember once shooting a lioness. Even wounded, it still took days to finish her off.' He pointed. 'There she is, in that corner on the left. One of the most satisfying kills of my life.'

Mrs Applerow gave a soft murmur and held a handkerchief to her mouth. Her husband said nothing but he put an arm around her shoulders. Danny noticed they didn't get any closer to the exhibits.

'Of course these are not all hunting trophies,' Lord Cawthorne continued. 'I have to confess that some of the more exotic exhibits are from zoos and menageries, which is why I know Albright.'

He nodded to the other man. 'We have a business arrangement when his livestock is no longer of any use to him. Those too sick, too old or too expensive to keep. And, of course, those creatures which are no longer of any interest to the public.'

Lord Cawthorne was so matter-of-fact that at first Danny didn't understand what he meant. But then it became horribly clear.

'I have the animals brought here, shot, stuffed and mounted by a taxidermist. Walter Potter, one of the top men in the country. He's extremely skilled. Just look at the whiskers on the female ocelot and you'll appreciate his talent. He has a real gift for zoological creatures and I think they bring a touch of colour to my collection. It's quite remarkable, isn't it?'

No one responded. Perhaps Lord Cawthorne thought they were all speechless with wonder, but Albright was the only one who looked impressed. He was examining the ocelot closely, even though Danny knew he must have seen it many times before.

Then Hetty asked the question that Danny had been trying not to think about. 'What about Belle Vue? Do any of them come from Belle Vue?'

'No. I've none from there yet. But I hope to persuade Mr Jameson soon.' Lord Cawthorne smiled slyly. 'Of course, I'm not sure who I'll be doing business with in the future. We'll have to see who wins this bet.'

He glanced at his pocket watch. 'Speaking of which, I know you'll all be anxious to get some sleep. There are still seventy miles to go to reach Belle Vue, and I expect it'll be a dash to the finish. Isn't that right, Albright?'

'Possibly, Your Lordship. Although of course, I have no doubt about who'll end up the winner. No doubts at all.'

Everyone was quiet as they walked back along the corridor, or so it seemed to Danny. Mr Saddleworth put an arm around Hetty and whispered something into her ear. He didn't hear what was said but she tucked a hand into her father's arm. Their differences appeared forgotten. And despite a small spark of envy, Danny was glad.

An army of footmen guided the guests to their chambers. Danny's room was even grander than he could have imagined. Velvet curtains draped the windows, each wall was lined in patterned silk, and Persian rugs covered the floor. In the centre, the four-poster bed looked bigger than some rooms in Cowgate.

It was a poor boy's dream but Danny knew he couldn't relax and enjoy it. All he could think about was the Abbeystead menagerie – the dead eyes in dead faces. Restlessly, he prowled around the room, his fingers stroking across the finery. He picked up a silver picture frame then put it down again. He needed to do something. He couldn't stay here.

Easing open the door, Danny peered along the corridor then crept towards the stairs. Somewhere, a clock ticked loudly but there was no other noise. Lightly, he padded down the wide steps and almost bumped into a figure at the bottom. His heart jumped.

'Prince Dandip!' Arthur Albright leant casually against the balustrade. 'How fortunate! I'd hoped to have a private word.'

Danny didn't imagine there was anything Albright could say that he would want to hear, but curiosity stopped him from running. The menagerist stepped a little closer.

'We may have had our differences this past week but I've heard good things about you. You're a hard worker, I'm told. Clever, too. And I'm sure by now you've realized exactly what sort of a man Jameson is. A chancer with more dreams than business sense.'

Albright paused. Perhaps he was hoping for a reaction

but Danny kept his face blank. He didn't trust this man for a moment.

'So I'd like you to come and work at my menagerie in Leeds. I'll need good people once the Belle Vue collection arrives. And you're famous now. Forget Maharajah. Visitors will come just to see Prince Dandip. And I can make sure you reap the rewards.'

Stunned, Danny let the words sink in. The last thing he'd expected was a job offer. There must be some mistake. What was Albright up to? More publicity for his menagerie? Or was there another, more sinister reason?

'You don't have to answer now, but think about it. Here's something to help make up your mind.'

He pressed a coin into Danny's palm – a gold sovereign, just like the one Mr Jameson had given him at Waverley Station. Danny turned it over carefully, feeling the hard, round edges. It felt more like a burden than a comfort. But better to keep the money now and work out what Albright wanted later. He slipped the coin into his shirt cuff next to the first.

'Good. I hope that'll convince you. You can give me your answer tomorrow. And remember what I said: you've a richer future with me than at Belle Vue. And I've no intention of losing this bet.'

Albright's stare burnt into his back as Danny walked away; it wasn't pleasant. As soon as he could, he darted down another corridor, and then along a second hallway. It took several attempts, but eventually he found an unlocked door that opened on to the courtyard.

There was only one place he wanted to be.

Sidling around the outside of the main house, Danny passed the menagerie before reaching the adjoining stable block. Abbeystead's horses had already settled for the night, and apart from the occasional snuffle and snort, it was quiet.

In the far corner, a flickering lantern hung from a hook in the rafters. Below it, Sandev sat on a small wooden bench, a book in his hand and his legs stretched out. As Danny came closer, he shifted so there was enough room for them both to sit.

Nearby, Maharajah was just emerging from sleep. He only needed four hours a night, and often snored noisily much to Danny's amusement. The elephant climbed to his feet and trundled over, nudging Danny with his trunk.

Sandev watched. 'Mr Crimple is still in the kitchens looking for food but I suspect Maharajah would prefer whatever is in your pocket.'

Danny pulled out one of the apples that he'd taken from Lord Cawthorne's dinner table, and held it up. Whatever the outcome, the Elephant Race was nearly over. The notion was surprisingly sad. Just as Mr Jameson had promised, it had been more than a journey. It had been an adventure.

They sat in silence. Maharajah munched a second apple, Sandev occasionally turned another page of his book and Danny was happy just to sit. He had a lot to think about.

A few days ago, he'd had nothing. Now he had two job offers along with two gold sovereigns. He knew which one he wanted – and wanted more desperately than anything he could ever remember. But now, more than ever, his future hinged on the Elephant Race. The result would decide everything. For him and for Maharajah.

At least there was one certainty. In the morning, they would leave Abbeystead – and the strange, dead menagerie – far behind. It couldn't come soon enough.

If Danny had to guess, it must have been past midnight when he heard a noise outside. A metallic rattle and crash, as though someone had tripped over a badly placed bucket. Then silence. Beside him, Sandev put down his book. They both listened.

A horse snorted in one of the stalls. A door creaked on its hinge. And after that, there were footsteps. Danny was sure of it. They were the soft steps of someone who did not want to be found, and they were getting closer. He held his breath.

Once again it fell quiet.

Danny exchanged a glance with Sandev. The mahout didn't need to do anything except nod towards the door. Together, they rose to their feet and crept into the passageway that ran between the stalls. In the silence, it was possible to catch the rhythm of rapid breathing. Someone was still inside.

'Who is there?' Sandev's voice cracked the quiet.

Abruptly, a door banged, loud as a bullet. Now the footsteps weren't disguised. They were heavy and obvious. Danny didn't hesitate. He raced towards the noise. Sandev followed.

Side by side, they sprinted down the passageway. A little way ahead, a wall lantern picked out a slight outline but it was no more than a blurred silhouette. All Danny could be certain of was that the shadow belonged to a man and he was fast. He'd already reached the end of the stable block.

Then, just as he turned the corner, the figure stumbled and Danny saw something drop from his jacket. It clattered loudly on the wooden boards. Briefly, it looked as if the man would fall as well, but at the last moment, he regained his balance and ran into the yard. Danny followed. The gap was narrowing. They were going to catch him.

Suddenly, the man darted to the right, through a stone archway and into the Abbeystead gardens. It was a clever move. Paths criss-crossed the grounds and looped around trees and bushes. There were plenty of hiding places.

But this time Danny was not giving up. He was not going to let the stranger disappear until he found out what was going on.

Without stopping, he swung through the archway. Almost immediately, a cry ripped through the night. It was a raw sound, similar to the noise Danny had heard at Waverley Station when Maharajah had destroyed the carriage. Only this was a thousand times worse. Because this was the sound of an animal gone wild.

And it was coming from the stables.

Chapter Fifteen

ABBEYSTEAD HALL
16 April 1872

Danny knew he had no choice. He had to go back. They couldn't carry on the chase. He gave a final glance towards the gardens where the intruder had vanished, but the cries were getting worse.

Sandev had already turned around. Breathing hard, Danny followed, and something else became obvious. Clouds of smoke were billowing on the night breeze. The bitter taste filled his mouth. A steady plume rose from one of the hayloft windows.

The stables were on fire.

Sandev must have seen it too. He was racing ahead. 'Run to the house! I will go to Maharajah. You get help. Hurry!'

Danny ran. Whether you lived in a slum or a grand mansion, there was little more terrifying than fire. He'd seen it destroy whole streets in Edinburgh, blistering through tenements and gutting buildings until an entire neighbourhood had been reduced to ash.

But as he got closer, Danny saw the alarm had already been raised. Abbeystead's stablemaster was sprinting barefoot from one of the estate cottages. He stopped only to pull on his boots.

'I want those animals out of there now! I need everyone's help, I don't care who you are. We've got to be quick. Let's move!'

The yard buzzed with activity as quickly as the order was given. Grooms began dragging horses from the stable block. One stallion reared up, hooves clattering on the cobbles, his eyes wide and terrified.

Danny tried to slide past. All he wanted to do was get to Maharajah. He could still hear the elephant's cries, and Sandev had not come back. What was going on?

'Oi, you heard what Mr Barnabus said. Everyone has to help. Even if you're a prince. Here, take him.' Before Danny could refuse, a set of reins was thrust into his hands, and immediately, the stallion reared up again.

Wrapping the reins around his palms, Danny yanked down. Pain sliced through each shoulder and he had to use all his strength just to hold on. But to his relief, the horse obeyed, his hooves dancing skittishly on the cobbles. Danny tightened his grip and looked around. They stood in the centre of a storm.

Servants were spilling out of the main house, most still in bedclothes. Danny spotted Ogden dressed in a striped nightshirt, trying to organize the firefighting. It was hard to believe this man was the same dignified butler who'd calmly served up a seven-course dinner.

'Come on, you good-for-nothing idlers!' he yelled. 'I want a line of men over here, with buckets. Fill them from the kitchen pump. Get on with it!'

But Danny could tell that their efforts were already too little, too late. The fire had spread, licking across the stable roof to the neighbouring menagerie, and fanning smoke over Abbeystead. The heat was close to blistering. Sweat bathed Danny's top lip and trickled down his temples. And still there was no sign of Maharajah or Sandev. He had to find them.

Dragging on the reins, Danny pulled the frightened stallion away from the fire to the front formal gardens. Almost immediately, the horse broke free, galloping across the sweep of lawn that had looked so perfect when they'd first arrived. Danny watched, just long enough to make sure the animal was safe. Then he turned and ran.

The courtyard seemed even more crowded than before. On the far side, Lord Cawthorne and Arthur Albright had just emerged from the main house, both still dressed for dinner and looking as useful as toy soldiers at Waterloo. Danny made sure they didn't see him.

Pushing through the servants, he headed towards the

stables. The fire was burning fiercely at one end, but it hadn't yet spread to the stalls where Maharajah had been kept. A sudden, splintering crack split the air and sparks showered over the roof.

'I wouldn't go in there, Your Highness.' A groom shouted, raising his arms against the heat. 'It's not safe and the elephant's gone berserk. He's acting crazy. Someone's going to get hurt.'

But Danny ignored the warning. He didn't think even a royal command could have stopped him now. Shouldering open the door, he went inside.

The smoke was thick and black, much worse than in the courtyard. It was almost impossible to see more than a few yards. And it was even more difficult to breathe. Crouching low, Danny struggled out of his waistcoat and covered his mouth with the silk. Then he followed the noise. Maharajah's roars were still deafening and every so often they would be interrupted by a furious and repeated thumping. What was happening?

Blindly Danny scrambled on, scraping his hands and knees on the rough floorboards. At last, through the smoky haze, he spotted Sandev. The mahout stood among a group of Abbeystead's stable lads. And trapped in a corner, facing them, was Maharajah.

But Danny's relief lasted no longer than a heartbeat. Because this couldn't be Maharajah – the gentle animal who'd carried him from Edinburgh and rocked him with his trunk; who'd swung Hetty gently over the River Esk and let the village children tug his tail.

No. This creature was mad and savage and angry. His head rolled back, his ears flapped wildly, and the gold eyes seemed blind to everything. Against the wall, he was beating out a rhythm with his tusks. Pieces of brickwork crumbled to the floor.

'Danny!' Sandev had spotted him. His voice was little more than a whisper and coughs racked his body. Maharajah gave another bellow. 'He will not let me near him. He is terrified of the fire. We have to get him out.'

Danny inched closer. And he knew with bone-deep certainty that if ever there was a time for gentleness, this was it. Carefully, he drew the ankus from his belt and balanced it lightly between his fingers. He hesitated, trying to plan the best approach.

Sandev couldn't help. The mahout had collapsed into a corner after another violent coughing fit, his eyes now held only confusion. Then one of the grooms pushed forward. Danny recognized the stable lad who'd brought out the frightened stallion. He was stocky with wide shoulders and big hands.

'Let me at him. I'll sort it. What you need is a bit of muscle.'

No! Danny wanted to scream. No! He reached to pull the boy back but he wasn't quick enough. The groom was already marching straight at Maharajah with none of the patient care that Sandev had taught.

Maharajah brought down his head and lunged. His roar

was echoed by a scream as the lad was flung against the wall. He slumped to the floor, one arm twisted under his body at a peculiar angle. Danny wasn't sure if he was even alive.

'Good Lord, did you see that? The beast's a killer.'

The other men had begun backing away. One of them stopped to examine the fallen boy. 'Not yet, he isn't. He's still breathing. Come on, let's get him out!'

The injured groom regained consciousness long enough to scream in pain as he was lifted and carried outside. Danny watched them go but he didn't follow. He couldn't leave Maharajah or Sandev.

It was up to him to get them out.

Maharajah's cries were more subdued now that the stables were less crowded, although he was still thumping the wall furiously. It didn't seem to bring him any comfort.

Danny held the ankus low to the ground, and out of nowhere, a hum came from the back of his throat. If it had been some other time, he would have marvelled at the sound but now it didn't seem particularly important.

Moving slowly, he reached for the apple in his pocket. Above them, the building creaked.

It was strange; the noise should have frayed at his nerves but instead Danny felt calmer. The feeling seemed to spread out from his centre through to the tips of his fingers. He was careful not to charge directly at the elephant as the stable lad had done. Instead he approached from the side, edging closer, inch by inch.

He knew immediately when Maharajah realized who he

was. The dazed vision cleared and the gold eyes focused. Raising his trunk, the elephant explored Danny's face. And for the first time, the bellows stopped.

The relief was overwhelming but Danny stayed unhurried. He continued humming, unsure if it was helping but reluctant to stop. He almost shouted in triumph when the apple was swiped from his hand. Now he had Maharajah's full attention.

Briefly he glanced to where Sandev was slumped against the wall. He couldn't risk leaving him here until he came back later. The building was likely to collapse at any moment.

Stooping carefully, Danny wedged his body under Sandev's arm and pushed upwards. The mahout groaned but stood, leaning heavily against Danny's side. With luck, they could guide Maharajah through the debris together. It would be awkward but just possible.

Danny wrapped a hand around Sandev's waist and tightened his grip on the ankus with the other. He took a step, and felt Sandev move with him. The pace was slow but steady. *Come on*, Danny thought, *just a little further. Please.*

Suddenly, a blackened timber slipped from its fixture, and the roof groaned. Sandev didn't seem to notice but Maharajah's attention flickered then froze. He rocked his head again.

Forward and back. Forward and back.

Danny paused, trying not to panic, but inside he was praying like he'd never done before. Not knowing what else to do, he hummed a little louder. The sound seemed to float above the smoke. Maharajah stopped rocking. Slowly, he lumbered forward and together, they reached the door.

Almost immediately, a large wooden beam came crashing down behind them. It was where they had been standing only moments ago. Danny felt his knees buckle.

The smoke was still heavy when they burst out into the courtyard, but it was obvious that the fire was finally under control. The flames had been pushed back to a small area of the stables, and most of the servants were busy clearing the damage.

Danny was relieved to see Mr Saddleworth kneeling at the side of the injured groom. His medical bag was open. '. . . looks like he's suffered concussion and at least two broken bones but he should be fine. You need to take him to the main house. The village doctor will be there by now.'

He closed his bag and glanced up. 'Good Lord!'

Danny could only imagine what they must look like – Maharajah, emerging from the dark like a walking mountain, alongside a soot-scarred boy and a man who was very near to collapse.

'Let me.' Mr Saddleworth eased Sandev's weight away from Danny. 'It looks like he needs medical treatment.'

'No. No.' Sandev lifted his head weakly. His words were slurring. 'I cannot leave Maharajah.'

'You have to, Sandev. I'm not giving you a choice. The smoke's damaged your lungs.' Urgently, Mr Saddleworth signalled two nearby footmen. 'Take him to the main house. And make sure he sees the doctor. I reckon there'll be a few more patients by the time this night is over.'

The men left, propping up Sandev between them. Almost immediately a shout resounded around the courtyard.

'There he is!' The crowd parted, and Lord Cawthorne swept through. Albright followed, one step behind. 'This is all his fault.' Red-faced and spitting, Lord Cawthorne jabbed a finger at Maharajah. The elephant had begun an odd nervous sway. 'My life's work ruined, and that beast is to blame.'

'I'm sure you're right, Your Lordship.' Ogden lined up alongside his master and Danny's mouth loosened. 'No doubt the animal knocked over a lantern and caused the fire. My staff know better than to do such a thing.'

'And so do mine.' Now Barnabus had joined Lord Cawthorne and Albright. It was beginning to feel like a hanging jury. 'My grooms are more careful with the horses than they are with their own mothers. Besides, that animal needs punishing. He nearly killed one of my boys.'

Suddenly Danny realized what this was all about. The Abbeystead staff were looking for someone – or something – to blame. And it was better to point at Maharajah than towards one of their own. They were protecting themselves and their jobs. A small part of him understood, but mostly he was fiercely angry.

'If that's the case, then I suggest the solution is simple.' Albright stepped into the centre of the courtyard. He didn't need to shout. Abbeystead seemed to have fallen silent. 'The creature should be destroyed.'

A kick in the stomach would probably have hurt less, Danny imagined. Everything had fallen into Albright's hands; he had no reason to keep Maharajah alive. A dead animal couldn't win the Elephant Race.

'An excellent suggestion, and there's no need to wait. I'll do it myself. Get me a gun, Ogden. The largest one from my last hunting trip. It's in the cabinet.'

'Yes, Your Lordship.' The butler left at a run. Danny could actually feel the panic swelling inside. It seemed to rise up and block his throat. He looked around for help.

Mr Saddleworth was holding up his hands. 'Please, Lord Cawthorne, I ask you to reconsider. Maharajah has never harmed anyone before. I'm sure that whatever happened here was a dreadful accident. This is not the time to reach hasty decisions.'

'My decision is made, Saddleworth. And I'm not in the mood to argue. You know as well as I, that some animals need to be destroyed. Once they get a bloodlust, there's no stopping them.'

'But won't you—'

'No. I'm afraid, it's too late.'

The crowd parted as Ogden returned, the gun cradled in his palms. The barrel was longer than a man's arm, and the handle had been polished until it gleamed.

Settling the weapon on his shoulder, Lord Cawthorne took aim with the ease of someone who had done it many times before. He cocked the trigger.

And that was the moment Danny stepped in front of the gun.

This time, it wasn't an impulse – not like at Waverley Station when he'd grabbed the whip out of Albright's hands. No, this time Danny knew exactly what he was doing. Because he hadn't forgotten the Wormwell auction, or his first glimpse of Maharajah. He hadn't forgotten the curious sense of kinship, or the warmth of being held. And he hadn't forgotten being rescued from the River Esk. He owed Maharajah his life.

'Don't be a fool. Get out of my way!'

But Danny stayed exactly where he was. Because he knew that if he moved, Maharajah would die.

Chapter Sixteen

ABBEYSTEAD HALL

16 April 1872

'I said move,' Lord Cawthorne gestured with the gun. 'Or you'll get hurt.'

Danny stepped closer. He was within an arm's length of the barrel. From this position he not only blocked the weapon's line of sight but he could also push the muzzle off target.

'Obviously you don't understand, Your Highness.' Lord Cawthorne's face was so contorted with anger he was almost unrecognizable. 'MOVE!'

He pointed the gun at Danny's feet, and pulled the trigger. Dirt and stones sprayed up from the ground. The noise ricocheted around the courtyard, bouncing about in the silence.

Danny's confidence wavered. A damp trickle ran down his spine. He hadn't really believed Lord Cawthorne would shoot. How wrong he'd been. Then Maharajah let out a deafening roar. His ears fanned out, and he lifted his tusks so they stood up like spikes.

A shocked murmur rippled through the crowd. Abbeystead's servants had formed a half-circle around them but now they shuffled further away, some tripping in their haste. One of the housemaids began weeping.

And at that moment, Danny knew he was completely on his own. Even Mr Saddleworth was powerless. He'd already tried and failed. There was no one else to turn to for help. Fear fixed him like a nail.

Then the crowd parted for a thin man, wearing a flannel nightshirt and nightcap. Reverend Applerow must have come straight from his bed. Behind him was Mrs Applerow, similarly dressed. And at her side was Hetty, trembling in the cold. Danny had never been so glad to see anyone in his life.

'Good gracious, Your Lordship!' The vicar stared at the gun. 'What in heaven's name are you doing?'

'This beast started the fire.' Lord Cawthorne was reloading the weapon. He didn't even glance up. 'I'm simply making sure he never causes any more harm. Unfortunately, the Prince appears to be in the way.'

'My dear sir, this is not the way to settle an argument. Threatening a boy and an animal – it's madness. Have some Christian charity, please.'

'No. And I must ask you to stay out of this, Reverend. It's

none of your concern.' Lord Cawthrone raised the gun again and steadied the barrel.

At his shoulder, Albright nodded. 'His Lordship is quite correct. You know nothing about the situation, Applerow. This isn't the first time the animal has caused trouble. He has a history of destroying valuable property. Why I, myself, have seen him run mad in Edinburgh. On two separate occasions.'

Danny started to shake his head before Albright had even stopped speaking. That wasn't the whole story. He opened his mouth to shout out a denial but the only sound that emerged from his throat was an ugly grunt.

'Perhaps that's true, sir.' Reverend Applerow frowned. 'But I'm a man of God. And didn't God create all living creatures – animals as well as humans? No decision over life or death should be made in the heat of anger.'

'You may mean well, Reverend, but do go away.' Lord Cawthorne's finger tightened on the trigger, and Danny heard the gun lock. 'You're not needed here. This is my animal to kill.'

'No! NO!'

Across the courtyard, Hetty pulled free from Mrs Applerow. Weaving through the crowd, she ran towards Danny, and before anyone could stop her, she grabbed his hand. Warmth spiralled up into his chest. He wasn't alone. She'd said so; now he actually believed it. Behind them, Maharajah rocked and bellowed. But Danny felt strangely calm.

'Henrietta, come away. Now!' Mr Saddleworth didn't look calm. He looked terrified.

'I won't, Papa. Don't make me. I'm staying here.' Hetty twisted her fingers around Danny's until they were knotted so tightly together he thought it might be impossible to wrench them apart.

'Your Lordship. I'm begging you.' Mr Saddleworth had spun around, his eyes wide and frantic. 'Put down the gun so we can sort this out. My daughter ... she's all I have. And the boy ... they're just children. Please!'

'No. This animal needs to be dealt with. And you seem to have as much trouble controlling the elephant as you do your own daughter. I'll handle this.' Lord Cawthorne jerked his head at Danny and Hetty. 'Now move them out of my way, before I get my men to do it.'

Footsteps stomped across the flagstones and Danny was dimly aware of people pushing nearer. But they were only shadows at the edge of his vision, because every fragment of his focus was on the gun.

Reverend Applerow was speaking again. 'Your Lordship, you may be right. Perhaps the elephant has run mad. However, we need to address the question as gentlemen. I believe everyone deserves a fair hearing. And you have a reputation as a man of reason.'

Danny wondered if that was true. He half suspected the vicar was using flattery because logic had failed. If it worked, he didn't care. He kept his eyes on Lord Cawthorne's gun.

'So everyone is entitled to a hearing, are they? Well, in that case, let's hold a trial.'

'Put an elephant on trial?' The vicar sounded as astonished as Danny. Not since Mr Jameson had dreamt up the story of Prince Dandip had he heard anything more ridiculous. 'You mean in a court of law?'

'Why not? You're the local magistrate. You could arrange it.'

'But he's an animal!'

'You just said God made animals as well as humans. Then they should obey the same laws as the rest of us.' Lord Cawthorne made the idea sound almost reasonable. Moving his finger off the trigger, he lowered the gun slightly. Danny's breathing came a little easier. Beside him, Hetty squeezed his hand.

'Agree to put the animal on trial for starting the fire, and I'll put the gun away. Then when he's found guilty, I'll kill him myself. That should satisfy the courts. And the Church. In fact, I imagine the whole country will be grateful to me.'

Danny looked down. The gap between his chest and the gun was very narrow.

'Very well. If it's the only way that we can settle this as God-fearing Englishmen. I shall speak to the judge in Lancaster. The court of assize is currently sitting. We may be able to arrange it quickly.'

'The sooner the better. A message can go out tonight from Abbeystead. I want that animal dealt with.'

Abruptly Lord Cawthorne tossed the gun at Ogden, who staggered under its weight. Danny released a deep breath. The tight feeling around his chest loosened.

'Saddleworth, I'll have to withdraw my invitation for you to stay. I suggest you all find alternative rooms in Lancaster for the trial. And I must insist that the elephant is chained and guarded because it's obvious he can't be trusted. I'll have my men deal with it.'

Hetty only let go of Danny's hand when Lord Cawthorne had disappeared from sight. 'You did it!' she shouted. 'You saved Maharajah.'

'Don't you dare celebrate, Henrietta Saddleworth. That was the most stupid, foolish, reckless . . .' Mr Saddleworth was struggling for the right words. 'Don't you realize how dangerous it was? You could have been killed. Both of you.'

'But we weren't, were we? And if Danny hadn't stepped in, Maharajah would be dead by now. He's a hero . . .'

Danny didn't feel like a hero. Every nerve was stretched tight, his heart hammered and the backs of his knees felt soft. He wanted to sink into the ground. But Hetty wouldn't let him. She swung her arms around his chest and held on. And oddly, the prickling feeling that usually came whenever he was touched wasn't there.

But Mr Saddleworth was frowning. 'I'll have to send a telegram to Manchester at first light. Mr Jameson needs to get here as soon as possible.' He shook his head and took a deep breath. 'I'm sorry, Danny, you may have saved

Maharajah tonight but we'll still have to fight for him in court. And even if we win, he has to reach Belle Vue in little more than two days. I'm afraid everything's against us.'

Chapter Seventeen

LANCASTER CASTLE
17 April 1872

There was already a crowd outside Lancaster Castle when Danny arrived the next morning. He couldn't have dreamt of anywhere more intimidating to hold the trial.

The huge stone castle loomed high on top of a hill. Two towers sat on either side of the arched doorway and, tucked away at the back, was a small cobbled square where murderers and thieves were taken for hanging. It was grey and cold and frightening.

Outside, a small group of people were waving placards and shouting.

'Maharajah must die!'

'Kill the elephant before he kills us.'

One old man shook his fists at Danny and he had to jump back so as not to be hit. 'That beast is one of the devil's creatures. He be possessed by an evil spirit. I'm warning you. Death will follow you. Death and damnation.'

Danny wanted to scream at them to go away, and take their lies with them. The sick, anxious feeling had formed a hard ball in his stomach. He rubbed the spot where it hurt the most, but nothing he did seemed to make a difference.

'Come on, Danny. Don't let that nonsense bother you.' Mr Saddleworth pushed him past the protesters and through the castle gates. Crimple followed alongside Sandev who had recovered enough to walk – if not to talk.

Hetty scurried after them. 'Yes. There's no need to worry.' She touched his arm lightly. 'Everything will be fine.' But Danny could tell she didn't really believe it. Her face had lost its normal brightness, and her freckles stood out like warning signs.

Inside, the courtroom was even more impressive, with high walls of polished wood, and a judge's chair as big as a throne. It was already overflowing with people. Danny stopped and stared.

There were a few familiar faces – some friendly, some not. Alfred Kibble sat in the press box with the rest of the reporters. The Applerows had squeezed into the public gallery. And, of course, Arthur Albright had managed to grab a front row seat.

Right at the front was Mr Jameson who had just arrived from Manchester. He and Mr Saddleworth were talking in hushed tones.

'I don't like this, William. Maybe we could spare one day, if we pushed hard for the rest of the race. But the court clerk says the trial's more likely to roll into tomorrow. And that makes it near impossible.'

'Let's try and win the trial first, James. Then we can worry about the rest.'

Danny felt his knees weaken. He hadn't needed reminding of what was at stake. Pushing his way on to a bench, he sat down just as the courtroom doors swung open. Several men in white wigs and black gowns trooped inside: the lawyers had arrived. One led the way. He was tall and square-jawed, as handsome as an actor on the stage and almost as confident.

'That's Sir Harold Cooper-Temple,' whispered Hetty. She wedged herself next to Danny. Just behind them, Mr Saddleworth, Crimple and Sandev had crammed on to a bench. 'He's going to be arguing the case against Maharajah. Papa says he has a fearsome reputation. He was in Lancaster working on a murder trial, and Lord Cawthorne persuaded him to stay on.'

Trailing behind Sir Harold, a much younger man was blinking nervously. The sleeves of his gown were just short enough to reveal fraying cuffs and thin wrists. Halfway across the room, he wiped a hand across his forehead, and his wig slipped untidily over one ear.

'He's ours. His name's Leander Slank. Mr Jameson says

he was the only lawyer who was willing to take the case. And he's only costing a guinea a day.'

Danny winced. Already, he saw their chances of success sliding away.

'Please rise for His Honour Justice Cornelius Gulpidge.'

Everyone stood, so Danny did the same. He swallowed the lump in his throat. The man who held Maharajah's fate in his hands was finally here. Judge Gulpidge had a large nose, bushy eyebrows and looked like a man who enjoyed sending people to jail.

'Sit!' he barked, glaring down from his throne.

Everyone sat.

Sir Harold marched forward, brandishing a pile of newspapers. He bowed low. 'Your Honour, this is an unusual case. I suppose you could say it represents man versus animal. Or possibly "Our educated civilization against nature's savage barbarism".'

An excited murmur rippled around the public gallery. The words sounded grand and important; Danny didn't have a clue what they meant.

'However you wish to describe it, we should not underestimate the importance of this trial. The whole nation is watching us. Perhaps the entire empire. Britain's reputation as a civilized country is at stake.'

'Then perhaps you could get on with it, Sir Harold,' said the judge. He tapped his fingers on the arm of his chair. 'I do have other places to be. I'm needed in Blackpool on Friday.'

'Yes, of course, Your Honour.' The barrister cleared his throat, and produced a pair of metal-rimmed glasses. He perched them on the end of his nose. 'We are here to decide the fate of the defendant, Maharajah the Magnificent. A male elephant, approximately fifteen years of age, owned by the Belle Vue Zoological Gardens in Manchester. He is accused of attempted murder and deliberately setting fire to property.'

It was the first time Danny had heard the charges read out aloud. In the heavy silence of the court, they seemed even more frightening. There was no way of pretending this wasn't serious.

'For obvious reasons, the defendant cannot appear in court.' Sir Harold paused briefly for everyone to laugh. Danny clenched his teeth. 'So to begin, I'd like to show the court some newspaper reports. You will notice the similarity of the stories. If I can quote some of the headlines?'

The judge nodded, and Danny leant forward.

'The first is from *The Scotsman* – "Maharajah Runs Mad at Waverley". And another from *The Herald* – "Elephant Destroys Train Carriage". And again from *The Times* of London – "Street Boy Tames Wild Beast". In fact . . .' Grabbing a fistful of papers, Sir Harold waved them at the room. '. . . these are all first-hand accounts of the destruction which took place in Edinburgh, just six days ago. The elephant is repeatedly described as wild, savage and destructive.'

Gasps filled the room. Danny felt his heart stutter. A cold feeling seeped across his skin.

'I'm afraid it goes on, Your Honour. The following day there were yet more stories of the animal's violent behaviour. Once again *The Herald* describes how the elephant destroyed an entire street market. There are even claims that he attacked one of the market traders.'

For what seemed like hours, Sir Harold continued through the newspaper headlines one by one. The number was overwhelming. Mr Jameson's publicity campaign had been thorough – and every single story piled more evidence against Maharajah.

Danny was glad when the first witness was summoned. 'The court calls Mr Heywood Hardy.'

Anxiously, Danny watched. He wasn't certain how Mr Hardy could help but Mr Jameson had insisted that having a famous artist in court would impress the judge.

This time it was Mr Slank's turn to speak first. As he walked forward, some of his papers slipped to the floor, and he had to crawl under the table to pick them up. Danny willed him to hurry.

'Er . . . Mr Hardy, you met the Belle Vue party just outside Hawick and asked if you could paint Maharajah. Is that correct?' Mr Slank had regained most of his composure, but his chin was so low that he appeared to be talking to his chest.

'Yes, sir.'

'And how would you describe his behaviour?'

'I thought he was a very gentle animal. He appeared docile and well behaved. He stood quietly for about an hour while I did some sketches.'

'And you had no concerns about your own safety, or anyone else's?'

'No, sir. Not at all.'

Danny let himself relax back into his seat. This was better. Until then, he'd not been aware that he'd been leaning forward, balancing on the edge of the bench.

Then Sir Harold got to his feet. 'Mr Hardy, you are a painter of some fame, are you not? I believe the Queen is an admirer of your work? Many congratulations.'

'Thank you, sir. I try my best.' Mr Hardy was obviously flattered.

'And as an artist, you must be a keen observer of people – and of animals?'

'I like to think so.'

'So tell us, in your own words, what led to your decision to paint the elephant? Was there a particular event that triggered your interest?'

Now Mr Hardy looked uncomfortable. 'There had been a dispute, yes. It caught my attention.'

'Please don't be shy, Mr Hardy. This is a court of law. We must have every detail.'

Danny had edged forward again. He knew what was coming, and he couldn't do a thing to stop it.

'Very well.' The artist shuffled his feet. 'I was on a painting tour of Scotland, visiting some remote areas. Four days ago, I took a hired carriage from St Boswell, along with some other travellers. We stopped at a toll gate on the Hawick Road. There was some sort of delay. I couldn't believe my eyes when I saw an elephant. None of us could.'

Danny could see many in the courtroom were smiling with understanding. Encouraged, Mr Hardy continued. 'There was an argument underway, between the toll officer and the couple who were travelling with the animal. As I later discovered, they were Mr and Mrs Jameson. I believe there'd been a disagreement over the toll fee. I started to sketch the scene. It really was quite remarkable. I'm sure it will make an exceptional picture.'

'Get to the point please, Mr Hardy.'

Danny really wished he wouldn't. Beside him, Hetty tensed.

'Well, the argument continued until the elephant walked up to the toll gate and ripped it clean off its hinges. His strength was truly astounding. We were all amazed.'

'You describe the elephant's power very vividly. Would you say this was an animal capable of injuring or even killing a man?'

Danny was grateful that Mr Hardy looked horrified at the idea. 'I really couldn't say, sir.'

'I'm not asking you whether or not he killed someone, only whether you think he's capable of it. I'd like your opinion.'

Justice Gulpidge leant forward and glowered. 'This is a trial. You must answer Sir Harold's question.'

'Well, if I must.' Mr Hardy didn't look happy. 'From what I saw ... yes, I would say that he has the strength to kill a human being, but I just can't believe that he would.'

'Thank you, Mr Hardy. I've no more questions.'

The hum in the courtroom almost drowned out Sir Harold's words. The barrister sat down, looking smug. Danny could understand why. Everything had gone against Maharajah so far. He rubbed the side of his head where an ache was starting to spread.

Across the room, a clerk was delivering a message to Sir Harold. The lawyer's smile grew wider. He bounced up again.

'With your permission, Your Honour. I've just been informed that Mr Peppershank, the toll officer, is in court. I apologize for bringing him in at this point but he has only just arrived. And he can't stay for long.'

'Very well, Sir Harold. If this is your only opportunity.'

Despite his size, Samuel Peppershank seemed nervous as he was led to the witness box. His gaze shifted constantly around the room but he managed to avoid looking at Danny.

'The court can see that you're a big man,' Sir Harold began. 'A man able to fight his way out of most situations. But faced with this animal, Mr Peppershank, were you frightened for your own safety?'

'I was absolutely terrified. The beast was huge, with massive tusks. And his eyes were pure mean like he'd rip you apart. I feared for me very life.'

'And can you describe the damage he did to your toll?'

'Aye, sir. He tore up the gate. There was nothing left of it by the time he'd finished. And I was worried it would be me next. The state he was in, he could have ripped me to pieces.'

Ice coated Danny's insides. At the lawyers' table, Mr Jameson and Mr Slank had tilted their heads together in quiet discussion. He hoped they had a trick up their sleeves because this wasn't going well.

'Your Honour, I have a question for the witness. If I may?' Mr Slank got to his feet when the judge waved him on. 'Since you're under oath, Mr Peppershank, we must assume you're telling the truth.' Mr Slank's chin rose a little higher. 'But I am curious to know why, after this apparently terrifying incident, you asked Mr Hardy to paint your picture with Maharajah? It seems strange that you would want to be anywhere near an animal that you've just described as vicious and savage.'

Peppershank shifted uncomfortably. His gaze flickered around the room again. Briefly he caught the eye of someone sitting behind Danny. Danny turned but he couldn't work out who it could be.

'Well, er ... the beast had calmed down a wee bit by then. I thought I'd be safe. And the painting would be a canny wee souvenir for me house.'

Peppershank blushed as laughter rippled around the room. Danny's headache eased a fraction. At least they'd scored one hit.

But the worst was yet to come.

Lord Cawthorne was the next witness. There was a flutter of anticipation in the court while he was sworn in.

And as he described last night's events, Danny could see that everyone was caught up in the story.

'. . . and so, Your Lordship, how do you think the fire started?' asked Sir Harold.

'Well I know none of my staff were to blame. They'd lose their jobs if they were. And everyone saw the elephant turn wild. The only logical conclusion is that during his madness, the beast knocked over a lamp, and the flames spread.'

Lord Cawthorne's evidence had been clear, powerful and completely untrue – Danny was convinced of it. He'd thought about it until his head hurt, and he still didn't believe Maharajah could have caused the fire. The flames had started at the other side of the building, nowhere near where Maharajah had been sleeping. But the attack on the groom was less easy to explain. He'd seen it with his own eyes.

Danny's only hope was that Mr Slank could reduce the damage.

'I have to ask you why you wanted this trial, Your Lordship? Isn't it true that you were looking for someone to blame for the damage to your menagerie, and it suited you to point the finger at Maharajah.'

'I suggested this trial because I'm a fair man who believes in British justice.' Lord Cawthorne slammed his fist on the witness box. 'And I don't want the country fooled into thinking that animal is a national treasure. Maharajah is a menace. He almost killed my stable boy and started a fire that nearly destroyed an irreplaceable collection. If he was a man, he'd be hanged for what he did.'

When Lord Cawthorne stepped down, it was in complete silence. He'd told his story well. Danny couldn't pretend anything else. Gloom settled on his shoulders like a fog.

The stable lad was the last witness of the afternoon. Yesterday, he had looked strong and confident, but today he limped into court on crutches; his arm wrapped in a sling. No one could be in any doubt that he'd been seriously injured.

'I believe you are Master Tommy Sparrow, and that you've worked at the Abbeystead stables for the last two years.' Sir Harold looked up from his notes. 'Well, Master Sparrow, can you tell us what happened last night?'

'I was helpin' get the horses out, Your Royal Lordship, sir,' Tommy's voice was surprisingly soft and Danny had to strain to hear. 'The heat and the smoke were fair bad. But I've looked after those horses like they were babies, so I had to make sure they were all safe.'

'And what exactly did you do, Master Sparrow?'

'Well I'd gone back inside to make sure it was all clear. I saw the elephant – right at the far end. He looked like he'd gone wild. He was making an awful noise, like he was screamin'. He kept bangin' his tusks into the wall.'

He pointed at Danny. 'That boy there. Prince Dan Dip, I think his name is. He was in front of the elephant, with the other Indian bloke. They were waving a stick. But it didn't look to be doing much good. I tried to help, but the animal just tore into me. Knocked me right to the ground. I don't remember much after that. Only a lot of pain. The worst thing is I have to stay home for the next few weeks. And me mam's not happy.'

To Danny's disgust, everyone laughed. Tommy Sparrow had charmed the court. And just when it surely couldn't get any worse, Mr Slank asked his question.

'As someone who works with horses, Tommy, you'll know that animals hate fire. I suggest Maharajah didn't want to hurt you, but that he was simply frightened of the heat and the smoke. Wouldn't you agree?'

'Aye, I reckon he was scared. I know I was.' Tommy looked embarrassed. His eyes flickered down to the floor and back up again. 'But that animal, he frightened me more. He was just wild. I thought I was goin' to die. And I reckon I very nearly did.'

Chapter Eighteen

LANCASTER
17 April 1872

The trial had been as good as lost today. Danny didn't need the judge's verdict to know it. There was just no way of fighting the mountain of evidence that had built up against Maharajah, even with another day in court tomorrow.

Despair ate at his insides until Danny was sick with it. He rubbed the scars on his wrist. He didn't think he'd felt like this since the worst days in Cowgate.

He was sitting on the back step of the Castle Inn. It was a cheap, shabby hotel on the edge of Lancaster, but at least it was close to the warehouse where Maharajah had been locked up.

Not that Danny – or anyone else from Belle Vue – had been allowed near the elephant since they'd arrived in Lancaster. Two estate workers from Abbeystead had been told to guard Maharajah and they'd taken to the job with relish. Even Mr Saddleworth had not been let inside.

The lack of contact was surprisingly hard. For the last week, Danny had spent every waking hour with Maharajah. Now he felt lost, as though he no longer had any purpose. It was almost funny. For a common thief, he'd become surprisingly used to honest work. He picked up a stone and threw it as far as he could.

Behind him, a door opened and Mr Jameson came outside. He lit a cigar, blowing the cloud of smoke into the night sky. Together they sat and watched the fumes fade into the darkness. Finally, Mr Jameson broke the silence.

'At the start of all this, d'you remember what I said to you? That you had to treat Maharajah like he's the Crown Jewels?'

Danny nodded. It had only been a few days ago but so much had happened since then that it felt like years.

'Well, you've never let me down yet. I can see he's precious to you. More precious than any jewel. And I'm glad for that.'

The compliment should have filled Danny with pride but he knew Mr Jameson was leading up to something. He waited, fairly sure it was something he wouldn't want to hear.

'You're a bright lad, Danny. You must have guessed by

now that everythin's not been quite what it seemed. Even from the start, I had it planned – at Waverley Station and later when we set out from the pavilion in Edinburgh.' Mr Jameson chuckled, 'I've still never seen anythin' like Albright's face when Maharajah charged off. It was worth all that money I had to pay out.'

His grin faded and he gave another puff on his cigar. Danny tried hard to be patient. But it seemed a long time before the menagerist spoke again.

'The point is . . . I always said I wanted to make a splash. That I wanted to get Belle Vue in the papers. To make sure everyone was talkin' about us. Maharajah was just obeyin' orders. Creatin' drama. That animal hasn't got a mean bone in his body. It was my idea. I gave the orders and told Sandev what needed doin'. At the station. And then when we were starting off. The elephant just did as he was told.'

Mr Jameson shifted uncomfortably on the cold step. 'And I want to say I'm sorry. Sorry that it's come to this.'

It was confirmation of what Danny had already suspected but it didn't make it any easier to hear. Thanks to Mr Jameson's drive for publicity, Maharajah was trapped. The whole of the country believed he was wild and violent. When in reality, he'd simply been doing what he had been asked.

'It's difficult sometimes to admit when you're wrong. And I'll be honest with you, Danny, I'm no good at it.' Mr Jameson stubbed out his cigar on the step. 'But I'll put it right tomorrow in court. I'll tell the judge the truth. I've promised Ethel May. And I'll promise you. I will make it right.'

He got up and went inside. The door banged loudly behind him.

For several minutes, Danny sat alone in the darkness, trying to make sense of what he felt. Angry? Yes, he was definitely angry. But a part of him also felt betrayed – which was funny considering where he'd come from. He should be used to people lying and cheating. After all, he'd lived among thieves.

He wondered what to do. And in the end, there wasn't much of a choice. He couldn't watch Mr Jameson confess in court, and he wasn't going to risk Maharajah. The case against him was just too strong.

It was time to run.

Danny went straight to the room he was sharing with Sandev. Warily, he pushed open the door but it was empty. Rummaging under one of the beds, he pulled out the mahout's small suitcase and lifted the lid.

Like Danny, Sandev travelled light. There were a few changes of clothing, and a leather-bound book in a language which even he could tell was not English. He tipped everything out.

Quickly, he packed his own belongings into the case. In went the newspaper cartoon of Maharajah, the Wormwell publicity poster, one of the peacock feathers and a pair of silk and leather slippers. He added a couple of the apples that he now always carried for Maharajah.

The ankus wouldn't fit so Danny strapped it to one side with a leather belt. The two sovereigns were already safely tucked in his shirt cuff, along with the bundle of pennies. He shifted the case in his hands, testing the weight and then slipped out of the door. It was much more than he had arrived with.

At the warehouse, he was lucky. Only one guard was on patrol and it was easy to create a distraction with a stone through a window. Danny slipped into the building when the man went to investigate the noise.

Inside, the only light came from a single lantern. Lifting it from the hook, Danny crept to the far corner. Maharajah lay on his side, chains wrapped around each leg. The metal links sat just above the old scars. One must have rubbed through the skin because the surface looked shiny and sore.

Anger swept through Danny. His hands tightened into fists, the fingernails digging painfully into his palms. The powerful creature he'd first seen at the auction was gone. And in his place, was an animal who seemed almost frail, a shadow of what he had once been.

I will not let you die, he vowed. No one will harm you again.

At least Maharajah seemed to be resting. His eyes were closed, although occasionally the heavy lids fluttered as though he was being pulled out of sleep. Danny hated to disturb him but they needed to leave while it was still dark. He knelt and traced along the links of the first chain, searching for a lock.

'It is no good.'

The quiet words should have startled him but when Sandev walked out of the shadows, Danny wasn't really surprised. In his hurry, he'd left enough clues behind. Sandev must have followed him from the hotel.

'You know you cannot take him. He is not yours to take.' Sandev's voice was still hoarse from the smoke, and his chest rattled. 'And you will not even get past the guard.'

Deliberately, Danny turned his head away. He didn't want to listen. If he listened, he would have to give up, and he wasn't going to do that. He tugged on the chains again, stretching the links as far as they would go. They needed to get away, to run as far and as fast as possible.

'Listen to me.'

Danny could feel Sandev moving closer. With every step, escape grew more and more impossible. He wanted to stand up and push the mahout away.

'Where can you go? Where is there a place big enough to hide a thief and his elephant? You just have to trust that everything will come right. We all must. Even if the result is not everything that we might wish.'

To his embarrassment, Danny felt his shoulders judder. His breath was emerging in deep, dry sobs. For several moments, he couldn't make them stop. Every feeling that had been trapped inside wanted to explode out.

Sandev waited and said nothing. After a few moments, he reached for the suitcase. Slowly, Danny handed it over.

So this was the end of the adve[...] [...]
Maharajah would ever see Belle Vue. [...]
life had not just disappeared, it had sha[...]
The pain was unlike anything Danny had fe[...]
in some ways than being on the streets. That [...]
but this left a great, empty nothingness.

And now he had to say goodbye.

Danny trailed a hand over Maharajah's skin. It was warm in the cold night. He could see the rise and fall of the elephant's breathing, perhaps a little quicker than normal. Slipping an apple into his palm, he offered up the treat. But there was no reaction.

In the back of his mind, an alarm began to sound. Shrill and insistent. Something was wrong. Quickly, Danny moved to Maharajah's back leg. At first, it was hard to believe what he was seeing.

He brought the lantern closer, and touched the grey, wrinkled skin. It was sticky. He lifted his hand. Under the glare of the lamp, his fingertips were bright red. Blood. Leaking from a long, ugly gash that sliced across Maharajah's leg.

'What is it? What have you found?'

Wordlessly, Danny shuffled to one side, leaving Sandev enough room to sink to his knees. Just as Danny had, the mahout traced a palm along the bleeding wound – and something else became noticeable. The edges were straight and sharp. Maharajah's leg had not been rubbed open by one of the chains. He'd been cut with a knife.

heavens! No. No. This cannot be . . .' Sandev's
imal, serene expression had splintered. He seemed bewildered. Devastated. But behind all that, there was an
emotion that Danny couldn't quite decipher. He didn't
have time to work it out; Maharajah needed help.

Using a sleeve, Danny gently wiped the dirt from around
the wound. It was already partly closed and dried blood
had formed a crust over one side. And at that moment,
everything fell into place.

This injury had not just happened. It was at least a day
old. Maharajah must have been stabbed last night, at some
point during the fire. And if that was true, it explained his
temper. Pain, as well as fear, had driven him to lash out – to
knock Tommy Sparrow off his feet.

Danny turned over the suspicion in his mind, poking it
for holes, but he didn't need any more evidence to know
that it was true. The only question was: who had done it?

With a sudden jerk, Sandev pushed upright. His face
had tightened into angry lines.

'May God forgive the man who did this because I cannot. He deserves to know how pain feels.' He spat the words
like bullets. 'I will fetch Mr Saddleworth. You stay here.
And do not let anyone else near. No one.'

Danny didn't need the warning. He had no intention of
leaving, or of allowing anyone else within touching
distance. Lying on the floor, he stretched out along
Maharajah's side. He wasn't sure the elephant knew he was
there but it was reassuring to be close.

Occasionally Maharajah shuddered, causing ripples to run through his large body. But most of the time he was quiet, breathing in quick, shallow gasps. His energy seemed to be slowly seeping away. Curling closer, Danny hooked an arm across the tough skin, half afraid to let go in case Maharajah was lost for ever.

It was probably only a few minutes before Sandev returned, although it felt much longer. At his side were Mr Saddleworth and Hetty. The warehouse guard was trying to force them back outside. 'You can't come in here. I've me job to do . . .'

'I don't care what your job is,' Mr Saddleworth said. 'There's a sick animal in here who needs treatment. And I suspect I'm the only veterinary doctor within twenty miles. Besides, Judge Gulpidge wouldn't be pleased if he gave a court ruling on an animal who's already dead. And he will be, if I don't get to him soon.'

Sullenly, the guard let them through. Mr Saddleworth set his lantern near Maharajah and knelt to examine the cut.

'You're right, Sandev. This was done with a knife.' He peered closer. 'And I don't think it was an accident. It's too deliberate. The line follows the old injury almost exactly. I think whoever did it was trying to make it look like the scar had re-opened.'

Another powerful convulsion shook Maharajah. He lifted his head briefly but the effort seemed too much. He collapsed back down. The impact shook the floor, and Danny snapped his teeth against a cry.

Hetty gasped. 'Oh, Papa! Look at him. He's in such pain. Can't you help?'

Slowly, Mr Saddleworth stood and wrapped an arm around his daughter's shoulders. But when he answered, he was looking at Danny.

'I'll try my best although there may not be much I can do. It doesn't look good and you should prepare yourself. It's possible he might not survive.'

Chapter Nineteen

LANCASTER
17 April 1872

Danny watched as Mr Saddleworth unfastened his medical bag and took out an assortment of bottles and bandages. The glass vials clinked together importantly.

'I'm going to clean the wound and see how serious it is. But if there's infection, I'm afraid it may be too late.'

No one mentioned that even if Maharajah recovered, there was a good chance he wouldn't survive the court case. No one mentioned it, but Danny knew that all of them were thinking the same.

Mr Saddleworth washed his hands and started work. His movements were quick and efficient. Gently, he cleaned the remaining dirt around the cut using a damp cloth and tweezers. The scab rinsed away and fresh blood oozed. Maharajah's eyes flickered. He gave another cry, but Danny could tell there was no power in it.

'It's clear and there's no discharge so that's a good sign.' Mr Saddleworth dropped the tweezers into a bowl. 'I'm going to soak the area in chamomile water, then apply iodine. It needs to be done every day.'

There was something comforting about the way he worked, Danny thought. If anyone could save Maharajah, it was William Saddleworth. He was suddenly fiercely glad that he was here.

'I want to try to stitch the wound – to make sure the bleeding stops completely.' He glanced at Danny. 'Can you keep him calm? Like before, when we were at Abbeystead? I'm afraid it's going to hurt a great deal before it gets any better.'

Danny was already moving, glad of something to do. Kneeling by Maharajah's head, he looked into the gold eyes. They were half open and hazy with pain. He stroked the elephant's face and ears with long gentle movements, and hummed softly. Sandev sat near the back legs, holding them down while Mr Saddleworth worked. The mahout's normal, calm expression appeared to have settled back into place.

Maharajah shuddered as the needle pierced his skin, and Danny's anger bubbled.

Why had no one spotted the wound earlier? Yes, it had

been chaotic during the fire. The smoke had been blinding and no one from Belle Vue had been allowed near Maharajah since.

But surely Lord Cawthorne's men must have realized the elephant was injured when they brought him here? Perhaps they'd been paid not to care. Or more likely, they'd been too terrified of losing their jobs.

Mr Saddleworth continued sewing until a neat line of stitches was spaced along the cut.

'Just two more then I'm done.' Sweat had broken out across his brow. The needle was sharp, and the thread was more like wire than ordinary cotton. But the elephant's hide was tough. Danny could tell it wasn't easy work.

At last, Mr Saddleworth stood back and wiped his hands.

'That's it. I'll rub in a salve, and bandage it, but I can't do any more than that. It'll need cleaning daily. We have to prevent infection.' He looked at Danny. 'There's some swelling around the wound but if he's lucky it won't spread. If it does, there's not a lot I can do.'

'You were wonderful, Papa.' Hetty's pride was obvious. She wrapped an arm around her father's waist. Impulsively, Danny took a step towards them. The need to shake Mr Saddleworth's hand, to show his gratitude in some way, was overwhelming. Then as quickly as it had come, the moment was gone. It wasn't his place. He shuffled backwards.

'Thank you, Henrietta. But let's see if he makes it through the night, then I'll have a better idea of his chances.'

Mr Saddleworth rubbed his forehead. 'This was almost certainly deliberate. And it wouldn't surprise me if Arthur Albright was behind it. Perhaps we should speak to the police.'

Hetty nodded fiercely. 'Didn't I tell you, Papa? Albright's trying to sabotage the Elephant Race. I know it.'

'Miss Henrietta is right. That man is not to be trusted.' Sandev had risen from his position at Maharajah's side, and Danny realized he wasn't calm at all. He was coldly and furiously angry. 'And you must not forget about the intruder. The person we chased from the stables last night.'

Mr Saddleworth looked thoughtful. 'Yes, it's just a pity no one got a good look at him. If we knew who it was, we might be able to find out what's going on.'

Something stirred in Danny's consciousness. The fire and the stress of the court case had pushed it to the back of his mind. Now the memory returned. It might not be important – but there was a slim chance it could solve at least one puzzle. Anyway, he couldn't just sit here and wait for Maharajah to live. Or to die.

He had to do something to hold back the fear.

Danny picked up the ankus and tucked it into his belt. He edged towards the door, hoping no one was paying attention. A pull on his sleeve stopped him.

'Where are you going Danny?' Hetty's forehead was drawn into a frown. 'Didn't you hear what Papa said? Maharajah might not last through the night. You can't leave now. What if something happens?'

Danny unhooked her fingers from his arm. He knew how this must look – that he was running away just when he was needed most. But he couldn't explain. Besides, it might all come to nothing. He turned his back and ran out, into the night. And this time he prayed Hetty wouldn't follow.

Abbeystead lay three miles outside Lancaster, and Danny was close to collapse when he arrived in the courtyard. He'd strained every muscle to reach it.

Above him, the Hall was wrapped in darkness, except for a light that sparked on one of the outside terraces. Cautiously, Danny trailed along a garden wall and crouched behind a low hedge. He couldn't risk getting caught now. Not when he was so close.

'. . . so how do you think the trial's going?' It was Cawthorne's voice, which meant Albright probably wasn't far away. Danny waited patiently.

'Extremely well, Your Lordship. Sir Harold's a marvel. You needn't worry about the verdict.' Albright's reply held satisfaction. 'Of course, there was a time when I wanted Maharajah alive. He and the boy have become famous. They'd have been big attractions for my menagerie.'

'And now?'

'Now, I don't care whether the elephant lives or dies. All that matters to me is that he doesn't reach Belle Vue. This court case couldn't be more perfectly timed. And I have you to thank. I'm very grateful.'

'Grateful enough to grant me a favour? . . . After the

elephant is destroyed?'

'Yes, of course.' Albright chuckled, and it was as though a cold finger had traced a path down Danny's spine. 'I can guess what you want. After Maharajah is killed, his corpse is yours. You can do with him as you please. I'll have the rest of the Belle Vue menagerie. Although if the taxidermist does a good job, maybe Maharajah could make a guest appearance in Leeds.'

'Good fellow.' Danny didn't need to see Cawthorne to know he was smiling. 'That's just what I wanted to hear. The beast destroyed half my menagerie. It's only right he should be the star of my new collection. I'll order a new display case tomorrow.'

The men went inside but Danny didn't move. The sick despair that had been with him all day had spread into every part of his body. Somehow, he had to find a way to save Maharajah. And at the moment there was only the tiniest sliver of hope.

Danny had to pass the burnt menagerie to reach the stable block. Moonlight bounced off a broken window, and he could see the outlines of the dead animals frozen in their strange poses. Their glass eyes reflected what little light there was. He was glad he didn't have to go inside.

Instead, he crept towards what was left of the stables. Smoke was still rising from the ruins and the crumbling brickwork was warm to the touch. Last night he and Sandev had chased the intruder down the length of the building, past the horse stalls on either side.

Everything had been frantic and confused but one image stood out clearly: when the man had turned to escape, something had fallen from his jacket. This was what Danny had come back to find.

It was the only solid piece of evidence in this entire mess. And, if anything had survived, it had to be here, the furthest point from where the fire had started.

Kneeling, Danny searched blindly through the debris. He had no lantern so he was relying purely on touch and intuition. His hands brushed along the ground, and came away with nothing except rubble and ashes. This was useless. He wasn't even sure what he was looking for. But he wasn't going to give up yet.

Sweeping his arms wider, Danny pushed back the rubble and uncovered the wooden floor. There were cracks between the boards, just large enough for an object to slip through. Perhaps it had fallen underneath.

Danny lay face down and squeezed a hand through one of the gaps. He stretched as far as he could reach, before sweeping his fingers in a circle. Nothing but stones. He wriggled again, moving so he covered a slightly different area. This time, he brushed something much bigger than a pebble.

Slowly Danny pulled his hand back through the boards. In his palm was a fountain pen. Slim, elegant and ornately carved. He knew immediately who it belonged to because he had seen it once before. But now he was even more confused.

He'd wanted answers. Instead, he'd only found more questions.

Outside, a door slammed closed, and Danny nearly dropped the pen when rubble and glass crunched underfoot. He was not alone. Someone was searching through the ruins. And, whoever it was, Danny had no intention of being discovered. He had to disappear.

Returning the way that he'd come was no longer possible, and Danny didn't dare go back across the open courtyard where the moonlight would make him easy to spot. The best idea was to stay undercover, which left only Cawthorne's menagerie. Just the thought made his stomach clench.

The building had looked eerie enough from the outside, but inside, it felt even more sinister. The entire room was a tangle of shadows. And as Danny passed by, the dead animals stared at him from their smashed cases.

Several exhibits had fallen over, including the beautiful red deer, its antlers snapped and broken. Others, like the quagga, leaked damp stuffing across the floor. The smell of ashes and charred wool choked the air.

Suddenly, something flickered in the corner of his vision. Danny turned with a start then gulped a breath of relief. It was the lioness, lit up as the moon slid from behind a cloud. She looked ready to pounce but of course, it was only a trick of the shadows. Even so, he crept past carefully. Freedom wasn't far away. He just had to reach the door on the side wall.

And then, Danny realized he was being followed. It was difficult to explain why he was so certain. There were no warning sounds but the atmosphere felt different, like he was sharing the air with someone else.

He darted around a case of woodland animals, and waited. Seconds ticked away. Still nothing. He pressed himself more tightly against the cabinet, and felt a crack running from one corner of the glass to the other. It was barely an inch wide.

He pulled the fountain pen from his pocket and pushed it through the gap. It rolled behind a pine cone and stopped at the foot of a stuffed squirrel. Now he wondered at the impulse that made him do it.

The room stayed quiet. The only sound was his breathing. Perhaps whoever was following had given up. Should he risk it? He glanced at the door, knowing he was going to have to run. He took a step. And another.

A hand touched his shoulder. He tried to turn but the grip tightened and something large and heavy slammed down on the back of his neck. He fell forward. And then there was only darkness.

Chapter Twenty

ABBEYSTEAD
18 April 1872

Danny emerged into consciousness to find someone looking down at him. The face swam a little before coming into focus. Inspector Clarence Quick of the Edinburgh City Police. What was he doing here?

'Good morning, Your Highness.'

With a shock, Danny realized daylight was flooding into the room. He must have been out cold for hours. What had happened? The last thing he remembered was hiding in Cawthorne's menagerie. Stalling for time, he rubbed the back of his head and struggled to sit. The inspector allowed him some space – but not much.

'So you're Prince Dandip of Delhi? We've not been

officially introduced but I've heard a lot about you. I'm glad to meet you at last.'

Inspector Quick offered a handshake but Danny ignored it. He still wasn't sure what was going on. The inspector's eyebrows rose a fraction but he continued talking.

'I can't believe the number of miles I've clocked up on this case. First I arrive at Belle Vue, only to find Mr Jameson has already left for Lancaster. And when I get here, there's an elephant on trial for attempted murder.' He shook his head. 'I've been a policeman for twenty years and I thought I'd seen everything. But apparently not.'

Danny wondered if there was a point to this. More than anything he wanted to get back to Maharajah. He looked around for escape routes, trying to measure the distance to freedom. But even as he did, he knew it was useless. His head ached like an army was riding through his skull, and he was having trouble focusing.

'Anyway, you're a lucky young man. That's a nasty bump. And it was only by accident that we found you.'

Danny didn't feel lucky. Whoever had hit him had made a good job of it. He tried again to focus. This time with more success. A second face suddenly came into vision. Sandev was kneeling at his other side.

'It is true. When the inspector arrived last night, we told him about the intruder. And he was most keen to see Abbeystead for himself. He and I have been here since first light. Mr Saddleworth is looking after Maharajah.'

Danny's breath hiccupped at the mention of Maharajah. If the news was bad, he didn't think he wanted to know, but he forced himself to look at Sandev. To his relief, the mahout's mouth curved. It was as close to a smile as he was likely to make.

'All is well, Danny. Maharajah is alive. He survived the night. Mr Saddleworth says he should recover.'

It was as though someone had lifted a rock from his chest. Danny was surprised to feel his eyes prickle. He swiped a hand across his face and tried to concentrate on what the inspector was saying.

'. . . so as I understand it, Sandev says you and he chased an intruder on the night on the fire. And that during the pursuit, you both saw him drop something. He reckons you must have come back here to look for it.' Inspector Quick was watching Danny closely. 'Is he right?'

Warily, Danny nodded.

'And did you find it?'

Danny hesitated. He'd spent most of his life running away from the constables in Edinburgh. Sharing information with the police went against everything he'd ever known.

The inspector sighed. 'You're not making this easy for me, are you? Listen. I'm only interested in finding the man you were chasing. He's probably also responsible for that lump on the back of your head. Help me and I can help you.'

Danny caught Sandev's eye. The mahout nodded. 'I do not think we have a choice. We must trust Mr Quick.'

Unsteadily, Danny clambered to his feet. He drew the ankus from his belt and lifted it as high as he could. Inspector Quick jumped up but he was too late. Before the detective could wrench the ankus from his hand, Danny brought it crashing down.

Right on target.

The case of woodland animals shattered easily, showering broken glass across the floor. Carefully, Danny reached through the splinters and pulled the ink pen from its hiding place. He handed it to Inspector Quick who was looking slightly dazed.

'I won't ask you how it came to be there, but thank you.'

The detective held the pen up to the light. His examination seemed to take a long time. 'Do you know who this belongs to?' he asked at last.

Danny nodded, and a look of intense satisfaction flickered across the inspector's face. 'Then, Your Highness, you've just become my star witness.'

Chapter Twenty-one

'**T**he court calls Mr James Jameson to the stand.'

In the public gallery, Danny gripped the barrier as the menagerist made his way to the witness box. Regret tugged at his nerves. He should have fought harder for Maharajah. Whatever the cost. However difficult. Behind the scenes, events were unfolding that might change everything. But what if it all went wrong?

'You are Mr James Jameson of the Belle Vue Zoological Gardens in Manchester?' asked Sir Harold.

'That I am, sir.'

'And you are the owner of the elephant known as Maharajah the Magnificent.'

'I am, sir. I bought him at auction in Edinburgh just nine days ago.'

'So are you able to cast light on the beast's behaviour since then? I refer, of course, to what we have already heard in court – the events leading to the fire at Abbeystead Hall, and the serious injury to one of Lord Cawthorne's stable boys, a Master Tommy Sparrow.'

Sir Harold was obviously enjoying repeating the highlights of his case. He was striding back and forth across the courtroom floor as though he owned the entire castle. Danny hoped he choked on his grand speech.

'. . . And before then, let us not forget his repeated destruction of property and his terrifying temper. Perhaps you can enlighten us?'

'Sir, there are reasons for that. Very good reasons. And I want to explain,' Mr Jameson paused and looked straight at Danny. He pulled his shoulders back. 'It's not somethin' that I'm proud of, Your Honour. However, I have to own up because I can't—'

But he got no further. The door was thrown open. Inspector Quick marched in, trailed by an anxious-looking clerk. Danny's grip on the barrier tightened. His heart hammered in his chest. This was it.

The policeman went straight to the judge's bench and bowed.

'Please forgive the interruption, Your Honour. I'm Inspector Clarence Quick of the Edinburgh City Police. Some new evidence has come to light that's relevant to this case. Might I be allowed to explain?'

'This is most irregular. I'm really not at all certain . . .' Justice Gulpidge frowned. Danny held his breath. Everything relied on the inspector's story being made public here and now. If it wasn't, Maharajah was as good as dead.

The judge waved his hand. 'Oh, very well. Nothing about this case is normal. You may speak. But from the witness box. I'm sure I'll have some questions for you, and I want you under oath.'

'Thank you, sir. I'm grateful.'

Inspector Quick swapped places with Mr Jameson. Danny tried to read the policeman's expression but his face gave nothing away. It was impossible to tell if the news was good or bad.

'So what's this all about, Inspector?'

'I'm afraid it's rather a long story, but I believe it's connected to the events at Abbeystead Hall.'

'Well we appear to have the time now.' Justice Gulpidge leant back in his chair. 'I despair of ever making it to Blackpool. But you've intrigued me. Please continue.'

'Yes, sir. Let me start at the beginning . . .'

Inspector Quick scanned the room but he didn't nod at Danny. It was as though they'd never met, and just as quickly, his queasy feeling returned. This morning, the detective had promised nothing would go wrong if Danny cooperated. Had he been stupid to believe it?

'For the last two years, I've been on the trail of a criminal gang involved in everything from drug-running to child slavery. They're a vicious, unpleasant mob who call themselves...'

He paused and even though Danny knew what was coming he held his breath.

'... who call themselves the Leith Brotherhood. Their business is run from an illegal gambling den in Edinburgh. Security is tight and only members are allowed in and out. But, recently, I was told that one of the members – a man called Walter Wormwell – might be able to help us.'

The inspector turned to the judge. 'You may recognize the name, Your Honour. Mr Wormwell was the owner of a popular travelling menagerie. He was also a well-known gambler, although not a very successful one. He'd run up a great deal of debt.'

'Gambling's a fool's game,' said the judge. Danny couldn't disagree. The only reason they were in this court was because of a stupid bet.

'Yes, Your Honour. Well a few weeks ago, shortly before his death, Mr Wormwell struck lucky. He won a large sum of money at the club. My officers were tipped off. And we were confident we could persuade Mr Wormwell to identify the ringleader, and to give evidence against him.'

'Why on earth would he do that, Inspector?' It was a good question. Danny had wondered the same thing. On the face of it, there didn't seem much reason for Wormwell to help the police.

'The gambling is rigged, Your Honour. Fixed so no one

can win large sums. But something went wrong on this particular night and Mr Wormwell won a fortune. An entire year's profit from the whole of their operations. What's more, he walked out of the door with it. As you can imagine, the gangmaster wasn't pleased. In fact, the bodies of two of his henchmen were found floating in the Leith. I believed Mr Wormwell was also in danger. And I hoped he would help us, in return for police protection.'

He paused for a heartbeat.

'But we were too late. The Brotherhood got to him first.'

Danny watched the faces around the courtroom. The story was holding everyone spellbound, just as he and Sandev had been when Inspector Quick first explained the strange events that had brought him here.

Of course, Danny already knew part of it, thanks to Frank Scatcherd. But the King of Cowgate hadn't told the full truth. Wormwell had been a gambler, not a thief. And his death had not been an accident.

Justice Gulpidge leant closer. 'Go on, Inspector.'

'When we arrived at Mr Wormwell's home, we found him lying on his study floor, barely conscious. The room had been ransacked. Everything was torn apart. And the only word he seemed able to say was 'Maharajah'. Repeated over and over again. I'm afraid he died a short while later without saying anything more.'

A murmur swept through the public gallery. In the press seats, the reporters scribbled frantically.

'The doctors say Mr Wormwell almost certainly suffered

a heart seizure. Neighbours recall hearing raised voices a little earlier that night. Bangs, thuds and shouts. All the evidence suggests thugs had been sent to force Mr Wormwell to hand over his winnings. You might say he was terrified to death.'

'Good Lord! This is incredible.' The judge leant back in his chair. 'So I assume they found the money and ran?'

'No, Your Honour. They're still looking for it. Everyone is. The lawyers, his creditors, the Brotherhood. You see, we're talking about an extremely large amount of money. But my men have been through Wormwell's entire estate and there's no trace of where he hid it. No gold. No bank deposits. Nothing.'

'Good Lord!' said Justice Gulpidge again. Danny watched him rub the hook of his nose. 'This is all very fascinating but how does it link to this trial?'

'Your Honour, the only clue to the mystery is Maharajah. His name was all Mr Wormwell could say when he lay dying.' Inspector Quick paused again. Danny knew he was trying to make sure he chose the right words.

'I believe the gangmaster sent someone to follow Maharajah in the hope of discovering the money. And I'm convinced this person started the fire at Abbeystead as a distraction so he could get close.'

The inspector stepped to the front of the witness box and looked around the courtroom. 'If we uncover his identity, we'll solve not only this crime but break apart the entire gang – and get to the devil who's been pulling the strings.'

A shocked murmur rippled through the room. Danny could feel the mood change. Sir Harold was in excited discussion with Lord Cawthorne. Both men were gesturing furiously. Neither of them looked happy.

'Silence! I will have order in my court,' shouted the judge. 'Please continue, Inspector. I'm hoping there's been a development in this case since you've interrupted proceedings.'

'Indeed there has, Your Honour. An object was found in the remains of the Abbeystead stable block where the fire started.' Inspector Quick pulled the ink pen from his inside pocket. The clerk handed it to the judge. This was the moment Danny had been waiting for. He picked up the ankus from under his seat.

'I have two witnesses who say they saw this pen fall from the jacket of an intruder on the night of the fire. The man was prowling around the stables where Maharajah was being held. And thanks to one of those witnesses, I know who dropped it.'

Danny caught a flurry of movement on the far side of the room where the newspaper men sat. There were angry mutterings as people were shoved roughly aside. Someone was trying to push through the crush.

'Gentlemen of the press!' roared the judge. 'I understand these developments have caused a great deal of excitement but please will you stop disrupting my court.' He turned back to Inspector Quick. 'Is the witness reliable? Is he sure that he recognizes the pen? A great deal hangs on this evidence.'

'You may question the witness yourself, Your Honour. He's here.' The inspector pointed, and everyone swivelled round to stare at Danny. 'It was Prince Dandip of Delhi who chased the intruder.'

'His Highness? Good Lord! This case is really most unusual. Let him come forward.'

Danny scrambled up from his seat and approached the judge's bench. This was much harder than he'd imagined. Hundreds of eyes sharpened on his face. He lifted his chin, and tried to concentrate on breathing slowly.

'Well, Prince Dandip,' barked the judge. Up close, he was even fiercer. 'Are you certain you've seen this pen before?'

Danny nodded. He pointed to the carved markings that coiled from the pen nib to the end of the barrel. But the judge only looked confused. Frustrated, Danny glanced at Inspector Quick.

'Your Honour, he doesn't speak English, but I believe he's trying to draw your attention to the engravings. They're very distinctive. Quite memorable you might say.'

'And why's that, Inspector?'

'Because they're carved from ivory. Most significantly, ivory comes from the tusks of dead elephants. And as you know, the Prince has a particular interest in keeping elephants alive.'

Danny heard a ripple of laughter from the public gallery.

'I see.' The judge's mouth crinkled at the edges. He might even be smiling, but it was difficult to tell. 'So, Your Highness, are you able to tell us who this pen belongs to?'

Danny nodded again. He'd known immediately where he'd seen it before, although he still found it difficult to believe.

'Well . . .? Come along, I must have a name, Prince Dandip.'

Justice Gulpidge looked impatient. Perhaps, along with everyone else in the court, he knew they were on the brink of a revelation. Danny was pretty sure he was about to deliver one. Hooking one foot on to a nearby chair, he levered himself up on to the judge's bench. Papers slid beneath his silk slippers, and something ripped. He didn't look down.

'What on earth? This is not appropriate behaviour for a courtroom, Your Highness. You must get down immediately!'

But Danny ignored the command. At this height, he was able to see into the furthest corner of the room. He stretched out an arm. Then he pointed.

Straight at Alfred Kibble of the *Hawick Express*.

Chapter Twenty-two

LANCASTER CASTLE
18 April 1872

The court exploded into uproar. There was pushing and shoving and yelling. The noise was worse than a Friday night dog fight in Cowgate.

Through the chaos, Danny watched Kibble sprint to the edge of the balcony, leap over the press barrier and drop on to the prosecution bench. He ran along the top, dodging the arms reaching for him. By some miracle he was still on his feet when he reached the doorway.

Danny was surprised that Inspector Quick sat and did nothing. Then he realized why. Kibble flung open the doors. Two very large police constables stood on the other side. He wasn't going anywhere.

'Quiet, please. I must insist on quiet!'

Justice Gulpidge might as well have asked everyone to fly, Danny thought. Anyway, he doubted people could even hear him. Everyone in the public gallery had pushed forward for a better view, and most of them were shouting and pointing. Another fight had broken out in the press seats.

Between the two police officers, Alfred Kibble was struggling to break free. For a small man, he fought hard. But Danny could tell it was a losing battle, especially when one of the constables produced a set of handcuffs. His arms were pulled behind his back, and chained tightly. Danny almost felt sorry for him but then Kibble raised his head and stared. There was nothing friendly in his face this time. The wide, blue eyes were cold and hard.

A shiver rippled down Danny's back, and he was glad when the constables marched their prisoner out of the courtroom. Inspector Quick followed, smiling. 'Thank you,' he shouted.

It was the first time Danny had ever done anything to please the police. And he didn't regret it for a moment. Kibble deserved prison; Maharajah could have been killed in the fire. And if things had worked out differently, perhaps he and Sandev might have died too.

But best of all, he had set the police on the trail of Frank Scatcherd and the Leith Brotherhood. And that surely made up for all the wrongs he'd ever done.

*

It took a long time to restore order, and Danny had almost given up hope when the judge began issuing threats. 'May I remind you, this trial has not yet finished and I'm determined to reach a verdict. I shall evict anyone unable to stay quiet.'

The warning worked. There was complete silence when Mr Saddleworth entered the witness box. Danny slid into a seat next to Hetty and leant forward to listen.

'Please tell the court your qualifications, Mr Saddleworth,' said Mr Slank. His head was no longer buried in his papers much to Danny's relief.

'Certainly, sir. I am a member of the Royal College of Veterinary Surgeons. I have travelled throughout the world to treat animals and research treatments. Most recently I have been employed by Mr Jameson to work at the Belle Vue Zoological Gardens in Manchester. I shall be responsible for the health of the entire menagerie when we arrive.'

'And can you tell us what you found last evening?'

'I was called out to Maharajah by Sandev, one of his keepers. The animal was in considerable distress. On examination I found a deep cut on his left hind leg, approximately eight inches in length, almost certainly caused by a sharp blade.'

The hum from the public gallery forced Danny to crane forward. This was the first the court had heard about Maharajah's injury, and it seemed to be causing a stir.

'And do you believe this was an accident or that someone deliberately inflicted this injury?'

'It was definitely deliberate, sir, and I believe it's very likely that it happened on the night of the fire at Abbeystead. When the cut was discovered last night it was partly closed, indicating that it had happened approximately twenty-four hours earlier.'

'What would be the effects of that injury on the animal?'

'Normally, elephants are gentle creatures, but if hurt they can become aggressive. Maharajah would have been in pain, and likely to lash out at anyone in range. His fear of the fire would have made the situation much worse.'

This time the muttering around the room was louder. Danny wondered if people had begun to fit together the pieces of the puzzle. He hoped so.

Mr Saddleworth turned to the judge. 'I'm certain this led to what happened at Abbeystead. And as for Tommy Sparrow, he was simply in the wrong place at the wrong time. I believe—'

'If I could interrupt, Your Honour?' Sir Harold bounced up like an enthusiastic jack-in-the-box. Danny wished he could push the lid back down, and shut him away.

'Very well. Ask your question.'

'Thank you, Your Honour.'

Clutching the edges of his gown, the barrister rocked on his feet. Danny tensed. Sir Harold had the look of a man about to inflict a deadly blow.

'Mr Saddleworth, perhaps, on this one occasion, there was a medical reason for Maharajah's behaviour, but you must agree that he's still a danger to the public. In fact, the newspapers say he's been violent several times in the past week. The truth is simple – this elephant will attack again. Perhaps even kill someone. Isn't that correct?'

Almost without realizing it, Danny was on his feet. These were lies. Lies. Anyone who met Maharajah knew he was the kindest and gentlest of animals – bigger-hearted than most people he'd ever met. He wanted to shout it across the courtroom but, of course, he couldn't.

The judge glared at him. 'Will His Highness kindly sit down? This is a court of law, not a theatre.' Reluctantly, Danny sat. He put his hands beneath his knees so he wouldn't be tempted to leap up again. 'You may answer the question, Mr Saddleworth.'

'Your Honour, I disagree. Maharajah is not a killer. Before this, he had no history of hurting anyone. In fact, he's a very gentle animal. If you need proof, my daughter has a scrapbook of Maharajah's history with the Wormwell menagerie. It goes back several years, not just the last week. And there are many stories which show his docile nature, despite his great strength.'

Beside Danny, Hetty smiled triumphantly. And for the first time, he noticed that she held the book they'd found in the blacksmith's yard. She passed it to the judge's clerk.

Sir Harold scowled. He opened his mouth to speak but Justice Gulpidge interrupted. 'Thank you, Mr Saddleworth. Your evidence has been most useful.'

The judge peered down his nose. 'I believe we have now heard from all the witnesses in this case. I see no point in drawing this out any further. I shall retire to consider my verdict.' He motioned to his clerk. 'Mr Hepplebath, I'll take the newspapers with me. And the scrapbook.'

Along with the rest of the court, Danny stood as the judge left. The door had barely swung shut before speculation burst like a storm cloud. Mr Jameson shouted to Mr Slank above the noise. 'So what do you think? Have we done enough?'

Danny held his breath for the answer. His heart had swooped down to the bottom of his stomach.

'I'm not sure. Justice Gulpidge has a reputation as a tough judge, and he can be unpredictable. And Sir Harold . . . well, I'm afraid Sir Harold has never lost a case.'

The wait for the judge's decision was agonizing. For days, Danny had been wishing for time to slow down so they could reach Belle Vue, now he wanted it to speed up. But the clock wouldn't cooperate. The hands ticked round at the pace of a snail.

It was an hour before Justice Gulpidge returned. This time the judge didn't have to battle for silence.

'Ladies and gentlemen, this has been a quite exceptional case. In all my years in court, I can't remember anything similar.' He cleared his throat. 'There can be no doubt that on the night of the sixteenth of April, the elephant seriously injured Master Tommy Sparrow. Several people saw the incident and have described the animal's terrifying display of temper.'

Danny clenched his hands into fists until his knuckles turned white. This was not sounding good.

'Of course, there were other factors at work; factors which could reveal why the animal behaved in the way that he did. I refer to the Abbeystead fire, which the police believe was started deliberately by the person they now have in custody. And also to the presence of an unknown attacker who used a knife to injure the elephant.'

At least the judge had realized that there was more to this story than first appeared. Danny's night-time adventure had not been wasted. But would it be enough?

'Who would carry out such acts – and why – is not for this court to decide. However, there's no doubt they did happen. In coming to my decision I have had to weigh up both sides of this argument carefully, and I have to say, each made a strong case. Very strong indeed. But on balance . . .'

The faintest ripple had begun at the back of the court. Danny dug his fists into his thighs until it hurt. He wanted something else to concentrate on when the judge said Maharajah would have to die. He couldn't let himself hope for anything else.

'On balance . . .' Justice Gulpidge repeated. 'I find the elephant . . . not guilty! Maharajah is free to continue on to Belle Vue.'

Cheers rang from the public gallery. The press men raced for the doors to write their reports. Hetty's face was wet with tears; Mr Jameson clapped Mr Slank on the back and gave him a cigar, then handed another to Crimple.

Sandev and Mr Saddleworth shook hands, and then hugged one another.

But Danny sat in silence, his fists still tight against his sides. He'd never felt anything like this before. Nothing had ever meant so much. The relief made him dizzy, and he couldn't have stood even if he'd wanted to. Against all the odds, Maharajah was saved.

Angry voices cut through the bubble of happiness. Near the front bench, Lord Cawthorne was arguing with Sir Harold. His shouts echoed around the high castle walls.

'How could anyone lose this case? It was supposed to be impossible. I knew I should have killed that animal when I had the chance. To hell with being fair and humane.' He shoved Sir Harold's shoulder. 'And I hold you responsible. I was told you were the best. But you're nothing more than a puffed-up wig.'

As Danny watched, everything seemed to happen in slow motion. Lord Cawthorne swung a fist and hit Sir Harold on his square and perfect jaw. Shock flashed across the barrister's face then he sank to the floor like a flower in a gale.

Lord Cawthorne brought back his arm again, but this time one of the court clerks grabbed his wrist before he could throw another punch. He was led away, still shouting. Danny hoped he wouldn't be released for a very long time.

The courtroom cleared slowly. Danny was overwhelmed by the number of the people who wanted to shake his hand,

and he was slapped on the back too many times to count.

Finally, only the Belle Vue party remained. And one other, much less welcome, visitor. Arthur Albright. He was smiling. The same cold smile that Danny remembered from Abbeystead, and suddenly his happiness splintered into small worried pieces.

'Surely you must have realized the truth, Jameson? Or are you too much of a fool? This verdict makes no difference. You've still got over sixty miles to walk. With an elephant who's lame. You'll never get to Manchester by ten o'clock tomorrow. You've lost.'

The joy dropped from Mr Jameson's face. 'You can't still hold me to it? The trial's changed everythin'. No one can expect us to continue the Elephant Race after this. I thought we could cancel the bet. With no bad feelings . . .'

Danny didn't know whether Mr Jameson's shock was genuine or not. Perhaps he was clinging on to the last strands of hope.

'Whatever gave you that idea?' Albright slowed his words as though talking to a small child. 'That's not how it works. We agreed in front of witnesses. And you are honour-bound to pay up when you lose.'

'Won't you consider giving us a little more time, Arthur? Just a day? I ask you as a fellow businessman, as . . . as one colleague to another.' Danny could hear the desperation in Mr Jameson's voice. Inside, he felt the same. This couldn't be the end. They'd fought so hard to get this far.

'No. We're not colleagues. We're rivals. And soon we

won't even be that. You'd better get ready to pack up Maharajah and the rest of your animals. I'll be in Manchester to collect them by the end of the week. Belle Vue is finished. And so are you.'

Anger washed through Danny with the strength of a tidal wave. He was surprised by the power of it. Sliding a hand into his shirt cuff, he pulled out one of the gold sovereigns. Without a moment's hesitation, he threw the coin into the air. It bounced, rolled and settled at Albright's feet.

Albright bent to pick it up. The gold glinted briefly in his hand before disappearing into a pocket. 'So, you've chosen sides, Your Highness? I believe you'll come to regret picking Belle Vue. You can't win, you know. It's too late.'

The soles of his shiny leather boots squeaked as Albright stalked out, slamming the door behind him. In the court-room, everyone was quiet. Eventually, Mr Saddleworth walked across the room and lifted up the scrapbook from the judge's bench. He smoothed the wrinkled cover.

'I'm sorry, James, but Albright's right. The Elephant Race is over. It would take a miracle for us to get to Manchester on time now.'

If he lived to be a hundred, Danny knew he'd never forget the expression on Mr Jameson's face at that moment. Despair and guilt mixed with misery.

'I'm afraid I'm all out of miracles, William.' Mr Jameson sank his head into his hands. Hetty went to sit beside him and slipped an arm around his shoulders. 'I just don't know how I'm goin' to tell Ethel May. What am I goin' to say? I promised her Belle Vue would be safe. I said she shouldn't worry . . .'

Until then, Danny realized he'd only ever thought about his own future if they lost the bet. He hadn't considered what would happen to the others. Why would he? He hadn't cared about them. But at some point over the last few days that had changed.

These people were no longer strangers. Mr and Mrs Jameson stood to lose their business; Crimple and Mr Saddleworth would not have jobs, and Hetty was likely to be sent back to Edinburgh to live with her elderly aunt. Only Sandev's plans had not steered off course.

In the distance, footsteps tapped down the corridor – softly at first then louder as they came nearer. A boy appeared in the doorway, pushing back a cap from his flushed face. He was out of breath.

'Sir, are you Mr James Jameson? I've . . . I've a telegram for you. From Buckingham Palace.'

Danny knew he must have misheard, or perhaps it was someone's idea of a cruel joke. Mr Jameson barely even glanced up. 'For a moment there, I thought you said Buckingham Palace.'

'I did, sir.' The boy opened the bag strapped across one shoulder. 'Here it is.'

Mr Jameson hesitated then grabbed at the envelope, ripping open the seal with shaking hands. His eyes flicked across the telegram then returned to the top to start again.

'Good Lord!' The paper trembled slightly, but before it

could fall from his fingers, Hetty swooped.

'Henrietta!'

Danny was glad when Hetty ignored her father. At that moment, he would have handed over his last gold sovereign to find out what the message said.

She unfolded the paper and read the words aloud: "'From: Victoria, Queen of Great Britain and Ireland. To: Mr James Jameson, of the Belle Vue Zoological Gardens, Manchester, and His Highness Prince Dandip of Delhi,

"'We have followed the progress of Prince Dandip and Maharajah the Magnificent with much interest. Indeed, the Elephant Race appears to have captured the imagination of the whole country.

"'The accusations against Maharajah have been of great personal concern, and it was with deep relief that we heard of today's verdict. British justice has been served.

"'It has also come to our attention that there is a gentlemen's wager over the time taken for Maharajah to walk from Edinburgh to Manchester.

"'In the interests of fairness, and due to the delay caused by the trial, we suggest the new arrival date should be set at ten o'clock on the morning of the twenty-first of April. We will follow the race with continued interest. God speed."'

'And it's signed, "Victoria R.I."' Hetty looked up from the paper. A wide grin split her face. 'It looks like the Queen has given us another two days to get to Belle Vue.'

Chapter Twenty-three

LANCASTER CASTLE
18 April 1872

'God bless 'er Majesty!' Mr Jameson had come to life. He grabbed Hetty by the hands and swung her in circles. She giggled as her skirts flew out.

'We have a chance. I know we can do it. The newspapers are goin' to love this. The Queen has saved Belle Vue. We're still in the running.'

Danny watched them spin round and round. His smile stretched so wide that his jaw ached but he couldn't stop. Once again, the Elephant Race had been saved at the last minute. He remembered the first time he'd climbed on to Maharajah's back. The fear of falling, then the relief of rising back up, holding on and surviving. This didn't feel so very different.

Mr Jameson was flushed by the time he and Hetty came to a standstill. 'We'll set off this minute. We can get a few miles down the road before it gets dark.'

'No. I'm sorry. We can't.' Mr Saddleworth folded his arms across his chest. He sounded like a man who wasn't going to bend for anyone. Not even Mr Jameson.

'What d'you mean?'

'He means that Maharajah is still injured.' Sandev spoke quietly. 'Still in pain.'

Mr Saddleworth nodded. 'I've done as much as I can for him and he's improving. But healing is a delicate process. A few more hours of rest might make all the difference. I strongly advise we don't move him tonight.'

The suggestion made sense but Danny itched to get going. He had a sudden, urgent feeling that every second was going to count. It pricked as sharply as needles.

'Oh, very well, I suppose a few hours won't set us back that much. But we'll start early tomorrow,' Mr Jameson grinned and rubbed his hands. 'Now I've got to speak to Albright and give him the good news.'

Once again, Danny and the Belle Vue party got ready to set off at dawn. Mr Jameson was in high spirits. He'd been to tell Albright about the Queen's telegram.

'He threw his pocket watch across the room, he did. It's a good job I took Justice Gulpidge with me, or I reckon he'd have thrown me too. But of course, he had to agree. Who could possibly say no to Her Majesty? The Elephant Race is back on.'

Mr Jameson's enthusiasm was almost enough to ease Danny's doubts. Thank goodness the menagerist had decided not to head back to Belle Vue by train. At the moment, he seemed to be the only one totally certain of success.

They were in the warehouse loading the wagon when Inspector Quick appeared in the doorway. Danny had not seen him since Kibble's arrest in court, and he'd been burning to know what had happened since.

'Congratulations. I hear you've been given more time to get to Manchester.'

The inspector had to step through piles of crates and boxes to reach them. After the trial, Maharajah had been swamped with food parcels from well-wishers. Even now, gifts were still arriving, tied up in fancy ribbons and coloured bows. Danny imagined this must be what Christmas felt like – presents stacked up to his knees. He and Hetty had already munched through a basket of currant cakes.

'Thank you, Inspector. I'm confident we'll get there on time. You can put a few pence on it if you'd like.'

The detective laughed. 'Perhaps not. I have it on good authority that gambling's a fool's game.'

'And as I keep saying,' said Mr Saddleworth. 'We're going to struggle to reach Belle Vue by Sunday morning. Maharajah's not back to full strength yet. It'll be tough going.'

As much as Danny would have liked to deny it, Hetty's father was right. No one really knew how Maharajah would cope. He didn't seem to be in any pain. The cries had stopped, and after several hours of sleep he'd recovered enough to walk. But his long, loping steps were awkward, and his back leg dragged. On top of that, there were still more than sixty miles to go.

'Well, I wish you luck.' Inspector Quick took a seat on one of the crates. 'I'm here because I wanted to tell you this in person. Kibble's been talking.'

Danny had been trying not to look as though he was eavesdropping. Now he gave up pretending, and gathered with the others to listen. Even Crimple drifted closer.

'As we suspected, Kibble's part of the Leith Brotherhood, the gang we've been after. Best of all, he knows all their names and all their secrets.'

The inspector stretched out his legs and let a smile crease his face. 'We've a good chance of catching them – of breaking the whole ring apart. And I have to thank you all. Particularly you, Your Highness. Without you this wouldn't have happened.'

Danny wasn't sure how to take the compliment, so he shrugged and tried to look as though pride wasn't swelling his chest. Hetty smirked at him, and rolled her eyes.

'Kibble admits to almost everything.' Inspector Quick ticked off the list on his fingers. 'Following you, searching your rooms at the inn in Stow, ransacking the wagon, starting the fire at Abbeystead. He was looking for Wormwell's money.'

He glanced again at Danny. 'Kibble was also the man who knocked you out. He realized he'd dropped something that could identify him, and he wanted it back. I imagine he searched you while you were unconscious.'

Automatically, Danny reached around to touch the back of his head. The bruise was still tender. He was doubly glad that Kibble hadn't found anything. He thanked whatever impulse had made him hide the ivory pen.

'But why pretend to be a newspaper man?' asked Mr Jameson. 'I practically told him me life story when we got stuck at that toll near Hawick. He wouldn't stop asking questions.'

'Yes, and he did the same to Danny and me.' Hetty said indignantly. 'He asked all sorts of things, about Mr Wormwell and Maharajah. He said he was writing a story for *The Times* of London!'

The inspector laughed. 'Posing as a reporter was a good way of asking questions and following you without attracting suspicion. He wanted to find out what you knew about the missing fortune, and whether you had anything else belonging to Maharajah. Equipment, costumes, papers and such like. Anything at all that might have led him to the money.'

Hetty leant forward. 'What about the fire? Why do that?'

'As I suspected, it was supposed to be a distraction. He

hadn't been able to get close to Maharajah. One of you was always with him, even at night, and he was getting impatient. So he started the fire to lure away Sandev and Prince Dandip but it went wrong. They spotted him and gave chase. In the meantime, the fire spread.'

Looking back, Danny couldn't believe he'd fallen for Kibble's innocent act. Every word had been false. He'd been stupid not to realize it earlier.

'The big mystery is the whereabouts of the money. Kibble didn't find it, not even when he searched the wagon. Or so he says. At the moment he's in no position to lie. He wants to save himself from the hangman's noose. Information is just pouring out of him. It's making my job very easy.'

'But why hurt Maharajah?' asked Mr Saddleworth.

Danny held his breath. This was the answer he most wanted to hear. Injuring Maharajah didn't make any sense, and it was difficult to imagine when Kibble would have had the opportunity.

'Well that's the odd thing.' Inspector Quick frowned. 'He swears he had nothing to do with it. He says his mother loves the menageries and would skin him alive if he harmed any of the animals. In fact, Mother Kibble is a big admirer of the elephant. Apparently she's seen Maharajah in Liverpool. Twice.'

Mr Jameson snorted. 'Well if he didn't do it, who did?'

The same question was already worrying Danny. Arthur Albright had the most obvious motive, but he couldn't get rid of the idea that Scatcherd and the Leith Brotherhood might also be involved.

'I'm afraid I don't know. Kibble could easily be lying. He may have had an accomplice. But we're working on him. The truth will come out. And if you can think of anything that might help us find Wormwell's money, let me know. It's always good to finish a case with everything solved.'

'Knowing Walter Wormwell, my guess is he spent it as quickly as he won it. I doubt you'll ever find it.'

'You may be right, Mr Jameson.' Inspector Quick stood up. 'Once again, thank you. And good luck for the rest of the journey. Perhaps I'll make a trip to Belle Vue when this is all over. Mrs Quick is very fond of the menageries.'

He shook Mr Jameson's hand, and said goodbye to the others. But when he came to Danny, he paused. 'Prince Dandip, might I have a word? In private.'

Danny swallowed but nothing could dislodge the knot in his throat. It felt like a fist. He nodded.

'Whoever you are I'm certain you're no prince.'

It was the first thing Inspector Quick said when they were alone. Danny's pulse pounded. He flicked a glance around. The policeman had managed to trap him in a small corner of the warehouse. He had nowhere to run.

'Don't worry, lad. I've told you before I don't care who you are. And I meant it.' There was a pause. 'But I am interested in what else you might know. Am I right in thinking that you're from Edinburgh?'

Slowly Danny nodded.

'I thought so.' The inspector smiled. 'I've been racking my brains to think why you look so familiar. Then last night I remembered. Take away that peculiar hat of yours, and rub a bit of dirt into your face, and you'd be that boy at the Wormwell auction.'

It wasn't a question so Danny didn't feel the need to respond. He watched the inspector carefully, wondering what was coming next.

'Are you familiar with an area in Edinburgh called Cowgate?'

Suspicion flared, hot and strong, but Danny tried to damp it down. So far the inspector had done all that he'd promised. Maharajah was free because of what had been revealed in court. There was no need to worry. He tilted his head in acknowledgement.

'Then it's occurred to me you might know the leader of the Brotherhood. Kibble claims he's called Frank Scatcherd, also known as the King of Cowgate. A vicious piece of work, from what I hear. Ever come across him?'

Danny felt a tremor; it was so strong that he wondered why his whole body wasn't shaking. He had hoped Kibble's confession would be enough to put the King behind bars, because any other possibility filled him with horror.

He rubbed his wrist – perhaps it was time to take a risk. Because, for the first time in his life, he was in the presence of someone who had the power to do something.

Before he could change his mind, Danny pushed up his

sleeve. Carved into his skin were two letters. Even after several months, the marks were still red and ugly. And, although he couldn't read, he knew what they stood for.

'FS'. Frank Scatcherd.

The inspector didn't hide his shock. Reaching out, he pulled Danny's wrist into the light and turned it so he could see the scars from every angle.

'He did this to you?' he asked at last.

Danny nodded. He would have liked to tug his arm free but he didn't; it seemed more important to make sure Inspector Quick understood.

'Good grief, lad. This must have hurt like blazes. It looks as though he dug out the letters with a knife. Like a brand.'

Danny nodded again. He'd tried to block out the memory so many times – to pretend that it had happened to someone else, and not to him. But at inconvenient moments, his mind would flash back.

Last year, Scatcherd had sent for him. He'd wanted an errand done, and for a single, stupid moment Danny had been flattered to be chosen. It meant he was the best; so good that even the King of Cowgate needed him.

The job should have been easy. He'd been smuggled into a grand house by a Brotherhood henchman. It had been past midnight, and the owner and his wife were away from home. All he'd had to do was sneak into the bedchamber and grab the woman's jewels. Simple for anyone so quick and light-fingered. But then the little girl had sat up in bed.

Danny hadn't noticed her before. She'd been lying, half

hidden under the sheets. Her mouth had dropped open. And she'd screamed. And screamed. And screamed.

So he'd run. Empty-handed.

He'd known there would be trouble. But Scatcherd's rage had been icy. He'd pulled out a knife and sunk it into Danny's wrist. The pain had been beyond anything Danny had ever felt before, and he must have passed out because he couldn't remember much after that.

When he was able to focus again, his shirt had been red with blood and Scatcherd was grinning. 'That's so you won't forget that you're mine, Boy. You belong to me, just like the rest of Cowgate. And I don't like it when my people fail.'

Hastily, Danny shoved down his sleeve. He didn't want to think about it any more. Inspector Quick was still watching, but now the lines of his crumpled face had softened.

'It looks like you've more reason to want Scatcherd behind bars than me. Do you know where I could find him?'

Danny shook his head. Scatcherd had always been careful. No one but his closest associates knew where he lived, and usually he'd appear when people least expected – it was all part of keeping his victims terrified and off-balance.

'Well, you've no need to worry, lad. I've got men searching the whole of Edinburgh. And now I've a witness who's willing to testify against him. He won't be able to harm you again. I give you my word.'

When they finally left Lancaster, Danny was on foot. Maharajah couldn't carry any extra load because of his injury. Only his show harness stayed in place, but the glass jewels were tarnished, and several beads had cracked and fallen, leaving gaps in the collar. It looked as tired and worn as they all felt.

The first few miles were tense. Danny watched anxiously for any sign that the cut had reopened. But Maharajah seemed unconcerned, marching along with only a slight drag of his back leg. As time passed with no problems, Danny felt a little happier, and he let himself think about Inspector Quick's promise. He was only just beginning to realize what it meant.

The inspector knew – or, at least, suspected – who he was and what he had done to make a living. But apparently the Edinburgh City Police weren't interested in a small-time pickpocket. They were too busy chasing bigger prey. Frank Scatcherd and the Leith Brotherhood.

Which meant for the first time in a long while, Danny might not have to look over his shoulder to check who was there. He was free. Free from the constant fear of being caught. It was like standing on top of a high mountain looking down on nothing but space – wonderful and just a little breathtaking.

'So I was wrong. It wasn't Crimple. Or Albright.' Danny jerked, startled out of his thoughts. Hetty had been so quiet he had almost forgotten she was there. 'It was Kibble who caused all those problems for us. And Papa is convinced he stabbed Maharajah too. He and Mr Jameson say, that now Kibble's in prison, we won't have any more trouble.'

Hetty frowned. She looked like someone trying to unravel a particularly complicated tangle of knots. Danny understood how she felt. Together they walked a little further down the road. Then she stopped, as abruptly as if she'd hit a brick wall.

'But it doesn't make sense, does it? Not all of it anyway. Why would Kibble hurt Maharajah? There wouldn't be any point. He'd be likely to attract more attention, not less. Exactly what he didn't want. And I still don't trust Crimple. There's something shifty about him. Do we even know where he was when the fire started?'

Danny tried to think back. When he'd arrived at the stables Crimple hadn't been there, but Sandev had said he'd gone to look for food in the kitchens. Could he have had time to double back and stab Maharajah? He supposed it was just possible.

'Then there's Wormwell's missing money. Where is it? Why has nobody found it?' Hetty had started walking again. Suddenly she spun round so that she stared him full in the face. Her eyes flared. 'Because if it is with Maharajah, it must be right under our noses. Don't you think?'

Chapter Twenty-four

ON THE ROAD TO BOLTON
19 April 1872

Trouble came again in a way Danny would never have predicted. They'd stopped at a farm for food and rest. The yard was already small, but now it was crowded by a wagon, one large elephant and six tired people.

'Get out of me way, boy,' Crimple said as they both reached for the handle on the water pump. His rough shove sent Danny skimming along the ground like a kicked stone.

Almost immediately, a bellow erupted, and Danny's stomach dipped. He knew that cry, but there was no time to react. Maharajah moved so quickly that his victim was taken by surprise.

One moment Crimple was standing, and the next, he lay sprawled across the floor. The elephant stood over him, tusks raised. In the yard, everyone froze, like carved pieces on a chessboard. No one seemed quite certain of their next move.

'What's he doin'?' Crimple was wide-eyed and panicked. 'Get him away from me.'

It was Sandev who moved first. Raising his ankus, he whistled sharply. But to Danny's shock, Maharajah stayed exactly where he was.

'Why isn't he shiftin'? Do somethin' quick!' Crimple tried to scramble backwards. He didn't get far before a deafening blast rumbled across the yard. And Danny knew that if anyone had forgotten Maharajah was a wild animal, this was meant to be a reminder.

Sandev tried again, blowing a piercing signal that seemed to split the air in half. But still Maharajah didn't step back. Instead, he shook his head, snapping both large ears against his body. Slowly, Sandev lowered his ankus.

'This is ridiculous. We haven't come this far to let a temper tantrum stop us now.' Mr Jameson stabbed a finger in Danny's direction. 'You have a go, Danny. Maybe he'll listen.'

Danny swallowed. If Sandev hadn't been able to persuade Maharajah, he doubted he could. Reluctantly, he stepped forward and drew the ankus from his belt. But when he met Sandev's gaze, he paused. Awkward and uncertain. It was as though, quite by accident, he'd slipped into someone else's shoes, and the fit wasn't entirely comfortable

To his surprise, Sandev gave a quick, decisive nod, and stepped back. 'Yes. You try, Danny.'

Carefully, Danny lifted the ankus and immediately, Maharajah raised his head. The clever, gold eyes inspected him; Danny knew to hold his ground. He whistled. Not a shrill blast like Sandev's, but a soft gentle signal. Maharajah seemed to listen. And, for a moment, it was just the two of them.

Then Maharajah stepped back and away from Crimple.

The keeper staggered to his feet. 'What were that all about? I didn't do anythin'.'

'Of course you did.' Hetty's hands were braced on her hips again. 'You knocked Danny clean over. I saw you, even if no one else did. Maharajah was just protecting him. It's your own fault. You should stay away from them. From both of them.'

'Henrietta! Keep out of this.'

'But, Papa!'

'I warned you – no more of this. It's finished. Come on, help me feed the horses.'

Mr Saddleworth grabbed Hetty's elbow and steered her away, while Crimple limped off to the wagon with Mr Jameson. It left Danny alone with Sandev. He stood there, suddenly not quite certain what to do with himself. He wondered if he should apologize in some way, although he wasn't sure exactly why. Or for what.

Sandev took the decision out of his hands.

'You care about him.'

Danny nodded, although it hadn't been a question.

'Thank you.' Bringing his palms together, Sandev bowed very low, just as he had at the Wormwell auction. 'I thank you for all that you have done for him. For discovering that he was hurt at Abbeystead. For helping me on the night of the fire. For stepping in front of Lord Cawthorne's gun. For all of it. Thank you. I will not forget.'

The warmth left by Sandev's words lasted for several miles. Danny still wasn't sure what had happened in the farmyard, but he did know that finally he had proved himself to the one person who cared about Maharajah as much as he did. It was a good feeling. But it didn't last.

Maharajah was slowing down. As night fell, his brisk pace dropped to a trundle. Every step was slow and sluggish as though he was wading through thick layers of pain. And suddenly, Danny couldn't bear to watch. He whistled. Maharajah stopped and behind them, the wagon came to a standstill.

'What's the matter?' Mr Jameson shouted.

Danny lifted a lantern and pointed to the dressing on Maharajah's leg. Spots of blood were expanding into large red circles. Most likely the cut had been pulled apart in the farmyard. In his head, he chalked up another black mark against Crimple.

Mr Saddleworth knelt to examine the wound. 'Some of

the stitches have torn,' he said. 'I'll re-sew them but I can't keep doing it. He needs proper rest to allow the cut to heal.'

'No, there's no time for that. We have to get to Bolton. He can have a break then.'

To Danny's surprise, Mr Jameson was already hurrying back to the wagon. Perhaps, he hadn't realized Maharajah couldn't go on like this. Danny had to make him understand. He grabbed Mr Jameson's arm before he could settle into his seat.

Pointing at Maharajah, Danny shook his head. Then he did it again, criss-crossing his hands across his chest to make sure the message was clear. 'No.' he wanted to shout. 'No. NO!'

'I'm sorry, Danny.' Sighing, Mr Jameson curved an arm around one shoulder. Danny supposed it was meant to be comforting.

'I don't like this any more than you do. But if Albright wins the bet, Belle Vue belongs to him, and you know about his deal with Cawthorne. There'll be a glass case waitin' at Abbeystead, and Maharajah won't be goin' into it alive. We have to carry on. At least this way he has a fightin' chance. Don't you see?'

Danny could still feel the tremors vibrating through his body. He looked around at the others – Hetty and her father, Crimple and Sandev – but every face showed shades of the same resignation. And Danny realized that, almost without him noticing, a huge chasm had opened up at their feet.

They couldn't go forward; and they couldn't go back either. They were caught between two impossible choices without a map to guide them. So when Mr Jameson made the signal to continue, he didn't object again. What would be the point? There was danger in every direction.

They arrived in Bolton just before eleven o'clock on Saturday morning. The town was already busy and everyone stared. This time Maharajah and Prince Dandip weren't the only ones attracting attention. After a night on the road, they were all rumpled and grubby. More like tramps than travelling royalty.

Taking turns with the others, Danny had tried to snatch sleep in the back of the wagon. But the jolt of the road kept him awake for most of the night; and worry ruined any chance of sleep for the rest.

Leading Maharajah away from the crowds, Danny followed the wagon into the shelter of an empty churchyard. The elephant pulled down a branch and began eating the leaves. His limp was more obvious but there was no sign of fresh bleeding.

'We'll stop here,' declared Mr Jameson. 'Only for an hour, enough time to get somethin' to eat. Meet back here at noon. Not a minute later.'

The last order held a snap of impatience. Everyone's tempers were threadbare, and tiredness had teased away at the edges. There were less than twenty-four hours to go.

Mr Saddleworth began filling a bucket from the church

pump. 'Henrietta! Come here. I need your help.'

But Danny could see Hetty's attention was firmly fixed elsewhere. Crimple was slinking across the yard and everything about him looked slippery, from the quick movement of his eyes to the tense set of his shoulders.

'I'm sure he's up to something.' Hetty lowered her voice to a whisper. 'Where do you think he's going?'

Danny didn't have any idea. The keeper had been unsettled since yesterday, and he kept shooting wary glances at Maharajah as though expecting another attack.

Hetty sighed. 'I wish we could follow him, but Papa won't let me out of his sight.'

Danny hesitated. His first instinct was to stay with Maharajah but this might be the last chance to find out what was going on. He pointed to his chest, and then gestured towards Crimple.

Frowning, Hetty bit her lip. 'Are you sure?'

He nodded.

'Then you'd better be quick, or you'll lose him.' She stood on tiptoe and kissed his cheek. 'Good luck!'

During his years on the streets, Danny had had plenty of practice at being stealthy. One of the most important lessons for a pickpocket was to blend in; to move without being noticed.

So he wriggled out of his brightly-coloured waistcoat, removed the turban and toed off his slippers. Grabbing a basket from the wagon, he stuffed his clothes inside so they looked like laundry. Then he hunched his shoulders and lost an inch in height.

Now he was able to slip through the crowds quite easily. No one stared at him like they stared at Prince Dandip. He was just a boy on his way to the washerwoman.

Walking quickly, he followed Crimple. Occasionally the keeper glanced back but Danny was prepared. He hid behind people, knelt to examine something on the floor, or lifted the basket to cover his face. It worked. The further Crimple went, the more he relaxed.

They passed a line of shops. Then a pub. A picture of a white horse swung above the door. Crimple ducked inside. Danny crouched in the shadows and waited. Ten minutes later he was still waiting.

Fidgeting, he scanned the busy street. On the opposite corner, a hansom cab had stopped outside a grand hotel. A passenger climbed out, and the hotel doorman nodded a greeting. The man turned to reply, and Danny's eyes widened. It was Arthur Albright.

Quickly, he worked through the possibilities. Was Albright here to meet Crimple? Were they planning another delay to the Elephant Race? Or were they already celebrating their success? The only way to get answers was to find a way inside. And he was going to have to bluff.

Using a shop window as a mirror, Danny tugged on his royal costume and brushed down the silk. The turban was the trickiest to get right but he managed it on the second attempt. He stuck two peacock feathers in the top, and they fell limply across his forehead. He only hoped he'd still be recognized as Prince Dandip.

Pretending a confidence he didn't quite feel, Danny strode up the hotel steps. For one moment, the doorman frowned but then his face cleared.

'I'm sorry, Your Highness. We'd heard you were passing through town but we weren't expecting you here. Welcome to the Adelphi.'

Dipping his head politely, Danny strode through the open door. His pulse slammed against his skin. But the reception desk was empty and, although the hall was lined with doors, only one was ajar. Danny peered through the gap into a large sitting room. A fire smouldered in the grate and sofas faced towards the heat. He slid inside, as quiet as smoke.

Albright stood at the opposite end of the room, leaning against the fireplace. He was looking down at someone sitting in a high-backed, leather chair.

'. . . finally the plan appears to be working. No thanks to you. Failing to inform Jameson about the damaged bridge hardly caused any delays, and the boy stopped you from being stranded in the river for too long. It's just a pity he was rescued from the water so quickly.'

Danny's hands curled into fists. Just as Hetty had suspected, Albright had been paying someone to stop the Elephant Race. Not every mishap and catastrophe had been Alfred Kibble's fault. The delays had been part of Albright's plan – even his fall into the river.

'As for your friend, Peppershank – he's a fool. He barely stopped you for five minutes at the toll gate. And stealing Saddleworth's map was pointless. I'm not sure why you even bothered.'

Albright paused but whoever sat in the chair said nothing. Danny leant out a little further from the alcove where he was hiding. It made no difference. He still couldn't see who it was. Crimple? Could he have sneaked out of the pub without Danny knowing?

'Anyway, here's what we agreed.' Albright drew a cloth pouch from his jacket. 'It's all there. Count it if you like.'

'Do you think I would take your money now? After what you did?'

Danny jerked, only just stopping the cry that welled in his throat. The voice was hoarse from breathing in smoke but it was still utterly unmistakable.

Albright snorted. 'Don't be so sentimental – he's just an elephant. And thanks to your incompetence, I had to make the most of every opportunity. By taking off on that wild goose chase with the boy, you made it easy. Even the fire helped. The beast was surprisingly trusting, right up until the moment I stuck the blade in. You've trained him well.'

Danny pressed his fingers against his lips to hold in a cry.

'You promised you would not hurt him.' The voice had grown rougher.

'Then I lied.'

'You asked only for delays to the journey. If I had known what you would do, I would not have agreed to this.'

'That's your problem not mine.'

'Yes. To my great sorrow it is.'

Abruptly, the man in the chair stood, his reflection clearly visible in the mirror hanging over the fireplace.

Sandev.

Betrayal, cold as frost, numbed Danny's insides. He still didn't want to believe it. Even with the evidence of his own eyes and ears, it seemed preposterous. As if someone had suddenly announced the sky had turned green.

It was a split-second before Danny realized his mistake. He was able to see Sandev, but Sandev could also see him. Their eyes caught in the glass, frozen in reflected shock, and then Danny scrambled upright.

Albright turned. 'Stop!' he shouted. For a large man, he was surprisingly quick. In a few steps, he'd reached the door and slammed it shut. Danny grabbed for the handle but there was no contest as to who was stronger. However hard Danny tugged, the door refused to open.

Sinking to his knees, he struggled for breath, drawing out the moment until he felt Albright ease back. Immediately, Danny dived to the side. He'd almost wriggled free when a hand clipped his cheek, splitting the skin.

Desperately, Danny kicked out. It didn't work. His arms were pinned behind his back and a fist gripped his neck. It brought back memories of the Wormwell auction. He was trapped again.

Taking a gulp of air, he lifted his chin. Above him, Albright was smiling, but Sandev stood to one side, silent and solemn-faced. It was impossible to know what he was thinking.

'How wonderful to see you again, Your Highness.' Albright was mocking. 'So now you know all our secrets. Sandev and I have enjoyed an interesting partnership over the last week. It wasn't difficult to persuade him.'

Sandev's dark eyes blinked but he said nothing. Danny was glad. His treachery was far worse than anything that Alfred Kibble had done. Kibble had been a stranger, but Sandev was someone he'd grown to trust.

'Everything is coming together perfectly. The Elephant Race is collapsing. In fact, I'm told it's barely even a walk, more of a stumble. They won't get much further. And by this time tomorrow, I'll be in Belle Vue to claim my winnings.' Albright smiled. 'And to reveal the real truth about Prince Dandip of Delhi.'

Danny started in surprise.

'Oh yes, I've known about you for some time. I kept your secret when I stood to benefit. My zoological gardens would have been happy to welcome Prince Dandip and Maharajah as our new star acts. But since you've proved so loyal to Jameson and his tinpot menagerie, I think it's time to reveal the real story. I expect Jameson's reputation will be ruined, right along with Belle Vue.'

Instinctively, Danny tried kicking backwards with his heels. But the grip around his neck only tightened. Albright seemed to find his struggles amusing.

'Perhaps you can do one last favour for me, Sandev. I'll

give you another fifty guineas if you take the boy.' Albright narrowed his eyes. 'And as soon as the Belle Vue menagerie is signed over to me, you can have Maharajah as well. The job's yours. Chief elephant keeper at the Yorkshire Zoological Gardens. It's exactly what you wanted.'

Sandev's gaze held Danny's. Danny willed him to say no. 'Very well.'

'Good! I don't care what you do with the boy, as long as I don't see him again. And just to make sure no one follows, perhaps I'll spread a little rumour.'

Albright turned back to Danny. 'I don't expect it will take much to convince Jameson that you've run back to Edinburgh. And I can't imagine anyone will look for you. A dumb mute can't possibly inspire much affection.'

Danny fought hard to escape, lashing out with his legs and scratching at anything he could reach. But against two grown men, it was impossible.

Half an hour later, he was lying in the back of a cart, his hands and feet bound tightly. Then the world went dark as a tarpaulin was thrown across his body. The cart began to move.

And any chance of escape disappeared.

Chapter Twenty-five

SOMEWHERE IN LANCASHIRE
20 April 1872

The cart stopped much sooner than Danny expected. The heavy canvas was wrenched back and he blinked against the brightness. The sun had cast Sandev into shadow – and the shadow held a small, curved dagger.

Suddenly, Sandev raised his arm. Panicked, Danny tried to roll away but the ropes made movement impossible. The blade sliced down, and he felt the ties around his wrists loosen then fall. A few seconds later, the same happened at his feet.

Sandev put a hand under each of Danny's shoulders and dragged him from the cart. He slid awkwardly to the ground. The sudden freedom sent a burning sensation through his trembling limbs.

'Do not worry. You are safe here.'

Danny didn't feel safe. He felt as though his world had been tipped upside down and shaken hard. Keeping his head down, he stared at the swollen skin around his ankles – and waited. The silence seemed oddly fragile.

'I imagine you want to know why.'

Danny looked up. Sandev stood over him, his face filled with all the emotion that had been missing in the last few days. An uncomfortable mix of guilt, anger and regret.

'When Mr Wormwell died, I had no work. No home. I hoped to find a job at Belle Vue, caring for Maharajah. It is what I have always done. And what I have always wanted to do. Then you appeared at the train station. A street boy. And everything changed.'

The cracks in Sandev's damaged voice had deepened. 'Mr Jameson wanted you. And the publicity that you would bring. He did not need me – except to teach you how to do my job. All those years I cared for Maharajah. All the time I spent training him. And it was worth nothing.'

Danny flinched. He was not going to feel guilty. This was not his fault. He thought about the times he'd been desperate for food. A little warmth. He'd stolen and he'd lied. He'd done things that now filled him with shame. But he'd never knowingly hurt anyone.

'Then Mr Albright made an offer. He wanted me to delay the Elephant Race. In return, he would give me back Maharajah, to care for at his menagerie. It was all I ever wanted.'

Sandev shifted a little. Now the passion had disappeared, instead his face looked tired. 'But I will tell you this... I would not hurt Maharajah. And I will never forgive the man who did. Never.'

Abruptly, Sandev pivoted on his heel and pulled himself back up on to the cart. 'Follow the road to the north, and go back to where you belong. I have not forgotten what I owe you. But let me deal with Arthur Albright.'

It was a moment before Danny realized what was happening. Standing shakily, he reached for the side of the wagon, but it was too late. The horses were already moving. The cart rattled down the road and Danny stood, watching while it disappeared into the distance. He felt bruised, battered and betrayed. And that was when he was sick.

Judging by the position of the sun, it was probably mid-afternoon, and Danny was still no nearer to civilization. An hour or so had passed since Sandev had let him go, but Danny wasn't heading north.

He was going south. Towards Manchester and Belle Vue. The shock of Sandev's betrayal still burnt, but he was not giving up yet.

Behind him, Danny heard the first sign of life. A large carriage, which had definitely seen better days, bumped along the rough ground. Danny crouched down, shielded by hedgerows. He was fairly sure that neither Sandev nor Albright could be on board but he needed to be certain.

The carriage rumbled closer. Nothing about the driver

looked familiar, so he stepped directly into its path. The driver yanked at the reins but the carriage didn't stop. It kept rolling forwards. On and on and on.

Now it was so close Danny was sure he could feel the brush of the horses' whiskers against his skin. He closed his eyes and thought of Maharajah. The coach groaned then stopped.

'What're you doing, lad? I almost killed you.'

The driver scrambled down from his seat, sounding more upset than angry. And suddenly, Danny was hit by cold reality. What on earth had he been thinking? He was a mute. A useless mute. How was he going to explain that he needed help?

Danny edged back a little but he needn't have worried. The man was staring at him as awestruck as a religious convert.

'Oh, my dear Lord. I don't believe my eyes.' He pushed his hat back from his forehead and rapped loudly on the side of the carriage. 'Oi, Mary. You'll never believe this. That prince who we saw in Lancaster? The one with the elephant? Well he's right here. Come and see.'

The door swung open and a chain of small children toppled out. A woman emerged last – creased, rumpled and clutching a baby. She gazed at Danny, with the same wonder as her husband.

'Oh my word, Jeremiah. You're right. It's Prince Dandip. I'd recognize him anywhere.' She fell into a curtsy then almost immediately bobbed up and swirled around. Danny felt dizzy just watching. 'Where's the elephant?'

'It looks like he's all by himself. No sign of anyone else. He just appeared out of nowhere. Stepped right in front of me. I very nearly ran him over.'

'Good heavens. You mean we almost killed a prince!' Wide-eyed, the woman fanned herself then sank into another curtsy. This time, she didn't get up. Giggling, the children stared at Danny. One of the boys started sucking a finger. No one spoke. Everyone seemed to be waiting for him to make the first move.

Hastily, Danny smoothed his face into the aloof royal expression that he had perfected on the road from Edinburgh. He had no idea what he looked like. The cut on his cheek throbbed, and his wrists were red and sore. But dirty and dishevelled as he was, he was still dressed as an Indian prince. He gestured for the woman to rise. She bounced up immediately.

'Oh, I've gone all of a dither. You must forgive my manners, Your Honoured Majesty. I'm Mary Hamp, this is Mr Hamp and these are our children.' She elbowed her husband in the ribs. 'Jeremiah, come on! Introduce everybody to His Royal Excellency.'

'Yes, dear.'

Mr Hamp lined up the children in front of Danny, in order of size. They shuffled into position as if they had done this many times before.

'This is our oldest, Joshua, then there's the twins, James and Jacob, and the girls, Jessica, and little Jemima. And the baby's John.'

The Hamps obviously expected some sort of response so Danny went down the line, nodding solemnly as every child bobbed up and down. Thank goodness, it seemed to satisfy their parents. They looked on proudly.

'I'm not sure if you'll be understanding me,' said Mr Hamp after Danny had finally wrestled his fingers from the baby's fist. He'd obviously decided he needed to speak slowly because it took him a long time to reach the end of each sentence.

'But since you haven't got your elephant, you're welcome to travel on with us until the nearest town. We're headed to Manchester to visit my wife's mother, but we're stopping at Bolton on the way. Does that suit you, Your Royal 'Ness?'

For a brief moment, Danny was almost overwhelmed by doubt. Impatiently, he shook it off. He had to get back to Maharajah, Hetty and the others. The urgency of it snapped at his heels. He managed to nod his head graciously.

A few minutes later, he was sitting in the midst of the Hamp family as the carriage trundled on. The baby bounced happily on his lap.

'Oh, I can't tell you what an honour it is for us to have you here. Isn't it, children? No one at home will believe it when I tell them. I can hardly believe it myself.'

Danny kept nodding and smiling. His face was beginning to ache but he was overwhelmed with gratitude. As travelling companions, the Hamps were all that he could have wished for – open, accepting and trusting. They didn't seem at all surprised to find an Indian prince wandering alone in the English countryside.

The coach was not such a blessing. There was little padding and it rattled along as though a wheel might roll loose at any moment. Danny felt every dip and rut through his bones. Around three hours probably passed before they arrived in Bolton. Parts of him felt like it had been three days.

Through a mixture of gestures and nods, Danny guided them to the outskirts of the town. He was fairly sure this was where the Belle Vue party had stopped. The church certainly looked familiar. He clambered down and looked around.

Yes, the churchyard was the same. Those were the trees that Maharajah had chewed, and the water pump where Mr Saddleworth had filled the bucket. But the yard was completely empty. The wagon was gone, and only wheel tracks showed it had ever been there at all.

Still, even if no one had stayed behind for him, perhaps they'd left a marker. A sign. Anything to show they'd been thinking of him. Danny searched, trying to pretend he wasn't desperate. Nothing. And then, even knowing it was useless, he searched again.

Abruptly, he was aware how very foolish he must look.

'I'm sorry, Your Highness.' Mrs Hamp's face was soft with sympathy. 'I think they've gone.'

Danny wanted to deny it but he couldn't. They hadn't waited. How stupid to have imagined that anyone would. Whatever story Albright had spread, they'd believed it.

Even Hetty. He was on his own again. He slumped beside the Hamps' wagon, and ground the heels of his hands into his eyes until sparks appeared behind the lids.

Once long ago, there had been a cake in the baker's window on Princes Street. It was covered in thick sugar and topped with a glistening cherry. Every day, for more than a week, he'd walked past to have a look, imaging the sweet, rich taste. Then, one day, the baker had been distracted so he'd grabbed his chance.

Later, when he'd run far enough to feel safe, he'd taken a bite, only to spit it out immediately. The sugar was a layer of salt, the cherry was a red bead, and the sponge was so old it had hardened into brick. The treat that he had craved so much was nothing but a fantasy and a disappointment. If this was any different, Danny couldn't see how.

An arm edged around his shoulders.

'Never mind, Your Highness. We can take you to Manchester with us. Can't we Jeremiah?'

'Of course, my dear. No question about it.'

Danny wasn't sure he wanted to go, but there was no reason to stay here. He let the family haul him back into the wagon. As they rattled through the streets, he gazed out of the window but he could have been anywhere because he saw nothing.

Danny never found out whether the Hamps had planned to travel through the night to reach Manchester. Or whether they helped him out of sheer kindness.

They were a rowdy family and once the children forgot to be shy, they climbed all over him, pulling at his turban and examining the peacock feather curiously. He wasn't allowed time to brood – or to wonder what might happen when he got to Belle Vue.

So he played peek-a-boo with the baby, and listened to the girls singing rhymes, while the boys rolled clay marbles on the wagon floor. It was cramped and noisy but eventually one by one the children dropped off to sleep, their bodies curled around one another. Even Mrs Hamp snored gently for a few hours. Danny envied them.

He didn't know what it was like to be part of a family, but sometimes, he dreamt about it. The woman always had the same face – young, pretty with warm dark eyes, and skin the same colour as his own. And she sang to him.

'. . . *the lilies so pale, and the roses so fair . . .*'

Or something similar. It occurred to Danny now, that it was the same tune he'd hummed to calm Maharajah. And the same song Mrs Jameson had sung that first night in Edinburgh when he'd been too nervous to trust her.

'. . . *and the myrtle so bright with its emerald dew . . .*'

At other times, the dream woman would cough into a handkerchief and leave it blood-red. He remembered her with confusion more than sadness. To be truthful, he wasn't entirely sure who she was. Although, occasionally, he wondered if she might have been his mother.

His earliest memory was definitely not a dream. He'd been small, perhaps no older than five or six. Mr and Mrs

Dilworth had looked after him then. Although he didn't know why, or how he'd come to live with them, only that the dream woman wasn't there any more.

One night, they'd taken him to a building with lots of windows. He was told to wriggle down a coal chute because he was the smallest, and then to sneak through the cellar to prise open the back door.

He remembered dropping down into the tight, narrow hole. His hands had been black with soot and he'd been terrified of getting stuck. Then, of course, he had. He'd banged and kicked but no one had come so he'd had to wriggle free by himself. When he did manage to open the door, it had been an effort not to cry.

But later, when they got back to the Dilworths' room in Cowgate, he'd been given a peppermint for being a good boy. And for weeks afterwards, there'd been plenty of money for food.

Then he'd grown bigger and he wasn't so useful. Another, smaller boy had come along to replace him, and the Dilworths didn't have room for him any more. So he'd learnt to make his own way, stealing from pockets and purses because there was nothing else he was good at.

At dawn, Danny climbed out of the wagon and took a turn sitting next to Mr Hamp at the reins. From here, he got his first view of Manchester.

Even on a Sunday, tall chimneys belched out smoke from the factories. There were rows of shops and the occasional green splash of a public square. Building seemed to be underway in every corner. Mr Hamp pointed out the new town hall rising up from the ground and Danny marvelled at its sheer size. Eventually, the road turned east towards Belle Vue.

'I'll take you as near as I can.' Mr Hamp had to shout over the peal of bells ringing for the start of morning service. It was a day off for most families, which usually meant a visit to the church or to the pub. But even to Danny, this didn't feel like a normal Sunday.

Excitement quickened the air, and the nearer they got to Belle Vue, the busier the roads became. Eventually, Mr Hamp pulled on the reins and stopped the carriage.

'I think you'd better travel on foot from here, Your Majesty. I can't get any closer. The crowds are just too tight. Hyde Road goes right to the zoological gardens, and it looks like everyone's heading to Belle Vue.' He flashed a grin. 'They've come to see you. You'd better get going.'

Danny didn't move. He couldn't. That yawning chasm was at his feet again. It was time to make a decision. Just one short week ago, he'd vowed not to depend on others; to think only of himself and to run at the first sign of trouble. But everything was different now. Less straightforward. More confusing. Other things had begun to matter. Other people. And then, of course, there was Maharajah. He couldn't walk away now.

The entire Hamp family scrambled out to say goodbye. Danny wished he could thank them properly. Reaching up, he tugged the last feather from his turban and handed it to Mr Hamp. It had been bent in the fight with Albright but he didn't have anything else.

Then he remembered Mr Jameson's sovereign. Slipping the coin from his shirt cuff, he pushed it into Mrs Hamp's palm before he could think better of it.

'Oh, Your Highness. There's really no need. We wanted to help. But thank you. Thank you!'

She bobbed another curtsy then abandoned politeness and pulled Danny into her arms. He made himself relax into the hug. Sometimes it was easier to let himself be touched, and he was getting better at it. Finally, she let him go but the warmth lingered like heat on a summer evening.

'God speed, Prince Dandip. I promise we'll come and see you at Belle Vue one day soon.'

They were still watching and waving as Danny melted into the crowd. Eventually, when he turned to look, even the top of Mr Hamp's head wasn't visible any more.

He was on his own again.

Quickly, Danny snaked through the press of bodies. This was as familiar to him as breathing. He was back to being Boy, owning only what he stood up in and eaves-dropping for gossip.

'Did you get a good look at him?'

'Couldn't see nowt in this crowd. I'm goin' to try to get inside Belle Vue. They're chargin' a shilling entrance fee but I reckon it'll be worth it.'

'Not sure I'd bother. Rumour is he's not goin' to make it.

They had a mile to go when they passed by here and he didn't look good.'

'Well I hope he gets there on time. The missus won't be too happy if we have to go to Leeds for the menagerie. It'll cost a bleedin' fortune!'

Danny moved faster but it was becoming more difficult. The crowd was packed so tightly there was barely any wriggle room and further on, people had stopped altogether. But he wasn't turning back now. Crouching low, he dived into the crush. Then, with elbows spread, he slithered between legs and knees, earning several kicks for his trouble. Finally, he emerged at the front.

The road ahead had been cleared, and rows of police officers were stopping spectators from pressing forward. But Danny didn't spare them much more than a glance because in the middle of the clearing, lying on his side, was Maharajah.

He wasn't moving.

Instinctively, Danny started running, heart pounding in his chest. But a strong hand grabbed his arm.

'Where d'you think you're going, lad? It's not a place for you. The animal's dying. He'll have to be put out of his misery.'

The words didn't make sense. The constable must be confused. Maharajah couldn't die. He'd been slowing down but he wasn't sick. Or not so sick that he wouldn't recover. Danny was certain of it. Besides, they were too close to Belle Vue to fail. It must be a mistake. It must be.

Danny pulled back from the iron grip. Perhaps panic made him stronger because suddenly he was free. He slipped under the policeman's arm. 'Oi, what're you doing? Get back here. Stop that boy! Stop him!'

A hand reached to catch him, and then another. But Danny dodged them, easily. He had to get to Maharajah. He didn't care about anything else. He ran quicker. There was nobody between them now. He was moving so fast that he practically slid the last few yards. And then he was on his knees next to Maharajah.

Trembling, Danny reached to stroke the wrinkled skin. Maharajah was barely breathing. His chest moved up and down, in fluttering, shallow gasps – and there was no sign that he knew Danny was there at all.

Danny blinked against the prick of tears. A rough, choking sound came from the back of his throat. No. No, this was not the end. They were not giving up. They were not.

'Danny. Danny!'

He'd been so focused on Maharajah that he hadn't even seen Hetty. In a blur of movement she knelt, threw her arms around his neck, and clung tight. He was nearly bowled over.

'Where were you? We looked everywhere. And we waited for as long as we could. And a bit longer after that.' The relief in her voice made Danny wonder why he had ever doubted he'd be missed. He buried his face in her hair, and was sure he felt a sob.

'They said you'd been seen getting on a train to Edinburgh. But I didn't believe it. Not for a single moment. I knew you wouldn't run away. But everything's been going wrong since you left. Crimple came back, then Sandev disappeared, and we couldn't find you. But now you're here. You're here!'

Abruptly she scrambled upright, tugging Danny along with her. He allowed it because it felt good. 'Look, Papa, look. Didn't I tell you Danny would be back? I told you he wouldn't leave us. I said so.'

'You did, Hetty.' It was the first time Danny had ever heard Mr Saddleworth use his daughter's nickname; the name she liked best. 'It's good to see you, lad. I'm glad you're here. Maharajah missed you. We all missed you.'

Slowly, Hetty relaxed her grip and tipped her head to look at him properly. Danny watched her expression change. 'Oh my good Lord!' She touched his cheek. The cut still hurt, and Danny suspected bruising was starting to show. 'What happened? Did Crimple do this? This is my fault, isn't it? I shouldn't have let you go. I should have . . .'

But Danny stopped listening. A familiar face was staring out from the crowd. Then people surged forward again, and he disappeared. It was only the briefest glimpse, but the solemn face had been unmistakable. Sandev was here.

Chapter Twenty-six

HYDE ROAD, MANCHESTER
21 April 1872

Roughly, Danny pushed away from Hetty. She staggered back, looking confused and hurt. But he didn't have time to stop and put it right. He had to make Maharajah move.

Because whatever had brought Sandev here, Danny was going to make certain the Elephant Race wouldn't finish without a fight.

He sank to his knees, but Maharajah didn't stir. His breathing was no more than a tired whisper. Burying his face under the elephant's trunk, Danny butted his forehead gently against the rough skin. There was no reaction but he didn't stop. He pushed again, desperate for some sign.

'I'm sorry, Danny. We've tried everything.' Hetty's voice was sticky with tears. 'But he's given up.'

Beside him, Mr Saddleworth knelt in the mud. 'You've saved him once. Maybe now's the time to let go. Sometimes it's kinder.'

No. Danny wasn't going to let Maharajah surrender. There was too much at stake for both of them, and this time they would fight together. They were big enough and strong enough and clever enough to do it. He wasn't going to quietly accept what someone else had decided was going to happen.

Danny wriggled so that his entire body lay against Maharajah's head and trunk. His pulse raced, and the sound of his heartbeat thumped loudly in his ears. He had to force himself to be calm. To think.

What could he do?

He tried what had always worked before – humming, turning the sound into a soft whistle that blew on to the elephant's long lashes. Maharajah's eyes fluttered open. Danny was so close he could see the circle of gold expand and contract.

'Keep going, Danny!' Hetty shouted. 'He's moving!'

But Maharajah's lids had already closed.

'Have another try,' Mr Saddleworth squeezed his shoulder. 'I don't pretend to know why, but you got a reaction. Do it again. We still have ten minutes before ten o'clock.'

Danny repeated the sound. Nothing. He tried again. No

movement. He wondered if he was fooling himself. Was he just dragging out the pain and making everything worse?

Then without warning, Maharajah's eyes blinked open, and this time, they stayed fixed on Danny. He released the breath he'd been holding.

Shifting slightly, the elephant raised his trunk and wrapped it around Danny's neck. They stayed like that for what felt hours but was probably only seconds. Hetty gave a half-sob. Mr Saddleworth put an arm around her shoulders and she turned into his chest.

'Well done, Danny. Keep going. You can do it.'

Around them, the crowd had fallen silent. Everyone was watching, perhaps they were expecting a miracle. Danny was going to try his best to make sure one happened.

Without taking his eyes from the elephant's face, Danny wriggled out of the embrace and stood. He waited, willing all his strength into Maharajah. A full minute passed. People grew restless, feet began to shuffle. Danny held up the ankus – not at the elephant but at the crowd. He needed quiet.

Then Maharajah began to move. His front feet battled to get a hold on the ground. Danny's hands gripped the cane so hard he worried it might snap. This was taking too long.

And then just when defeat looked certain, the elephant's legs straightened. With obvious effort Maharajah pulled the rest of his body upright. He was unsteady but standing. Danny's fists relaxed. He lowered the ankus.

'Move those people,' Mr Saddleworth shouted to the

constables. 'Get them out of the way. At once!'

The police began to clear the road and suddenly, there it was – a stage, decorated with bunting and banners, and swarming with guests. Belle Vue. The end of the Elephant Race. After all these miles, it was just a few steps away.

Mr Jameson and Albright stood on the platform. They hadn't noticed Maharajah was on his feet. But Danny knew the moment they realized. Mr Jameson smiled a smile so wide that it seemed to spread from ear to ear.

'I knew you wouldn't let me down, lad, I knew it,' he shouted, climbing down the steps of the stage. Behind him, Albright seemed to have frozen, his face filled with shocked disbelief. Then the spell broke, and he clambered after Mr Jameson.

'Stop! You're too late. It's already ten o'clock. It's over. You've lost.'

But it wasn't true. The Belle Vue clock hadn't struck the hour. There was still time. If Maharajah could reach the gates before the last chime rang they could still win.

Then Danny heard the first clang.

ONE.

Frantically, he pointed his ankus and whistled. Maharajah stumbled slightly, still unsure of his balance.

TWO.

Unsteadily, Maharajah weaved forward a few steps.

THREE.

They were definitely making progress. But as the road continued to clear, Danny saw Sandev darting through the crowd. What was he doing?

FOUR.

Danny's throat dried to dust.

FIVE.

Maharajah was still trying but his steps were getting more erratic. Danny's hands were slippery with sweat.

SIX.

More progress. But just to their left, Sandev was pushing forward, ignoring police orders for people to move back.

SEVEN.

Maharajah staggered on. The Belle Vue gates were less than ten yards away.

'Yes. You can do it. Come on!' yelled Mr Jameson. He and Albright stood on either side of Maharajah, like an angel and a devil on each shoulder.

EIGHT.

They were so close to the finish. Danny felt a new rush of hope.

NINE.

Several steps forward this time. Almost there.

TEN!

The clock chimed for the last time. But Maharajah was already over the line. Wasn't he?

'NO!' Sandev broke past the last of the spectators. Unsure what to expect, Danny turned – and all he could see was the small, curved dagger clutched in Sandev's hand.

Danny flung himself against Maharajah's side and shut his eyes. He waited but nothing happened. Cautiously, he raised his eyelids, and this time he saw what he hadn't noticed before. Sandev wasn't heading for Maharajah. Or for Danny.

Only luck, and a last-minute stagger, saved Arthur Albright. The dagger sliced harmlessly through the air, passing a bare inch from his chest. Sandev lifted his arm again, but it was too late. A constable was already wrestling the knife from his hand.

'What in heaven's name?' One of the guests had stalked from the stage, Danny knew he must be someone important. Rows of medals decorated his red military jacket, and a white sash ran from one shoulder to the opposite hip.

Arms outstretched, Mr Jameson scurried forwards. 'I do apologize, Lord Sefton. I have no idea what's happenin'.'

'Then I demand you find out, sir. When I was invited here as Her Majesty's representative, I certainly didn't expect this!'

Now another policeman had joined the first. Together they wrenched Sandev's arms behind his back, and forced him to his knees. It wasn't much of a fight. The mahout wasn't struggling. Everything about him had turned blank and remote.

Albright was red with rage. 'What's the meaning of this, Jameson? This is one of your keepers. He tried to attack me. I could have been killed.'

'I had nothin' to do with it. I don't know why he tried to hurt you, but it was not at my askin'. He's been missin' since yesterday.'

'Don't deny it. I've witnesses. Everyone knows he's been working for you. I'll have him charged with attempted murder. And you along with him. I'll chase it through the courts. This is one crime you won't wriggle out of.'

'How dare you accuse me—'

'Gentlemen, please,' Lord Sefton interrupted. The medals glinted on his chest. 'These are serious allegations. Have you any evidence, Mr Albright?'

'What do you mean? It's obvious. Jameson realized he was about to lose the bet so he ordered his keeper to attack me.' Danny's mouth dropped open at the lie. Vigorously, he shook his head but no one was watching.

'No!' The damaged voice was soft, but everyone heard it just the same. 'That is not true.'

'What do you mean, Sandev?' Something about Mr Jameson's bewilderment made Danny move closer to his side.

'I did come here to hurt Mr Albright. But not because I was told to. I came here because he was the one who stabbed Maharajah. And he needed to know how the pain felt.'

'What? This is nonsense!'

But Sandev ignored the protest. 'Mr Albright offered me money and a job at his menagerie. In return, he wanted me to make sure the Elephant Race failed.' Sandev's eyes flicked down for a moment before moving back to Mr Jameson. 'To my shame, I agreed.'

'Lies. All lies.' Albright spluttered. 'You can't believe him.'

'But nothing I did satisfied him so he did it himself.' Sandev's voice was getting stronger. Louder. 'He stabbed Maharajah on the night of the fire. And yesterday, he paid me to make sure the boy disappeared. I took Danny away to keep him safe.'

'Danny? Is this true?'

Carefully, Danny nodded. The cut on his cheek throbbed, but it didn't matter now. All that mattered was making sure everyone knew the truth.

'This is absurd. I'm sorry I just can't let this fantasy continue. The man needs to be put behind bars.' Albright sounded panicked. The jaws of the trap were closing in on him.

'It is true. And I wish on all that I hold dear, that it wasn't.'

Mr Jameson looked devastated. 'I don't understand, Sandev. I'd have given you a job if you'd asked. I thought–I thought you had other plans. If I'd known . . . we could have sorted this out between us. I could have—'

'No. I heard you at the station in Edinburgh. You said you did not need me. You said you had the boy.' For a brief moment Sandev's eyes caught Danny's. They were filled with a sad acceptance. 'But it makes no difference now. Maharajah is no longer mine. He belongs to Danny. The elephant thief.' Slumping, Sandev's face turned blank again. He didn't react, even when the officers cuffed his wrists behind his back.

'Why are we listening to this fantastical story? The

man's a liar.' Albright had regained a little of his confidence. 'And the boy's a fraud. Just look at him. He's not a prince. He's a dirty thief, an orphan picked off the streets. He's got no more royal blood than I have. It's all been a lie. One of Jameson's tricks . . .'

Lord Sefton drew himself up to full height and gripped the handle of his sword. It wasn't difficult for Danny to imagine the blade against his neck. His heart banged inside his ribs. Was this the end of Prince Dandip?

'Preposterous!' Amazed, Danny stared at Lord Sefton. He was practically bellowing. 'The Queen herself sent a telegram praising His Highness and Maharajah, and congratulating them on their court victory. Are you saying she is part of a conspiracy? Part of a confidence trick? Good grief, sir. Have you no respect?'

'You can't really believe . . .?'

'I can and I do. One only has to look beyond his pitiful clothes to see that the boy is high-born. Merely by his gallant actions, the Queen was able to recognize a fellow royal. A person of noble blood. And let me tell you this – Her Majesty cannot be fooled.'

Danny might have laughed if his entire world had not been hanging by a thread.

'You little beggar! This is all your fault.' Albright lunged. Danny didn't manage to dodge in time. Fists grabbed at his shirt and shook hard. His head bounced painfully on his neck.

'Let go of His Highness immediately, sir!' With one

firm, gloved hand, Lord Sefton pushed Albright away. 'I believe you have questions to answer. Officers, please make sure Mr Albright isn't tempted to wander off. I'll be extremely unhappy if he disappears without giving me a full explanation. He can wait in the cells.'

Danny would have liked to watch Albright being led away just to make sure he was really gone, but Lord Sefton was gesturing towards the stage.

'Please, gentlemen. There's an audience waiting. I suggest we get on with making the announcement official. Congratulations, Your Highness. Mr Jameson. You've won.'

Chapter Twenty-seven

BELLE VUE ZOOLOGICAL GARDENS, MANCHESTER
21 April 1872

The list of Danny's adventures over the last ten days sounded too incredible to be true. He'd survived a stampede, near drowning, fire, assault and kidnapping. He'd sat through a court trial, posed for a painting and received a telegram from the Queen. It had been the most extraordinary week of his life.

But if there was ever a chance to repeat a single moment, Danny would pick this one. Nothing could ever be as exciting again.

Crowds lined every corner of Belle Vue. Wherever he looked there were people – on top of the gates, along the avenue of trees, past the deer park, the maze and the monkey house, all the way to the boating lake. In some places spectators were packed six deep.

And every one of them wanted to see him. Him and Maharajah. Because they had won. Together they had finished the Elephant Race and saved Belle Vue. It felt . . . well, Danny didn't even have the words for how it felt.

'Three cheers for Prince Dandip,' someone in the crowd yelled. 'Hip. Hip . . .'

'Hurrah! HURRAH!'

Danny held up his ankus like the leader of a marching band, and waved. He was walking just ahead of the wagon, along one of the paths that criss-crossed the park. Mrs Jameson had unearthed his last surviving costume, and three new peacock feathers bobbed from his turban. It could only have been more perfect if Maharajah had been at his side, but he was recovering in Belle Vue's new elephant house. Mr Saddleworth had said he would be fine, with enough rest and care.

The victory parade made slow progress through the park. It didn't matter. Danny was cheered and clapped, until his head reeled. Eventually the wagon stopped, and they were surrounded by people and goodwill. And Danny couldn't help thinking of Sandev.

The mahout would have enjoyed hearing the crowd shouting Maharajah's name; and he'd have been pleased to see how much the elephant was loved. But pride and fool- ishness had cost him all that he most wanted. And in that moment, Danny could only feel pity.

'Hurrah for Prince Dandip. For he's a jolly, good fellow ... For he's a jolly, good fellow ...'

The song rang in his ears until he couldn't hear anything else.

It was late evening by the time the celebrations ended. The last revellers were practically pushed outside by the ground keepers – or so it seemed to Danny. Mr Jameson had invited all the staff to a celebration in the main show hall, and no one wanted to be late.

Even Crimple hurried off looking less sour than usual – but that may have been because of Hetty. She'd apologized. 'My Aunt Augusta always says I'm too impulsive. I'm sorry I ever doubted you, Mr Crimple. I was wrong.'

The park felt bigger after the crowds had gone. Danny watched an empty bottle roll and clink into the gutter. Bunting fluttered from the trees and a single toy balloon drifted down the avenue. One by one, the gas lamps were snuffed out until Belle Vue stood in twilight.

Then only Danny, Mr and Mrs Jameson, Hetty and her father remained. Together, they strolled past the bandstand towards the lake, where the Wormwell wagon now stood, battered and grubby.

'What a day. It doesn't get much better than that.' Mr Jameson released a puff of cigar smoke.

His wife tucked her hand into his. 'You did well, Jamie. You've made Belle Vue the most famous menagerie in the entire empire. I'm proud of you.'

To Danny's surprise, Mr Jameson scowled and his shoulders dropped. He gazed across the lake as though he could see beyond the horizon.

'No, me darlin', I was a lucky fool. And I know it. If I'd thought a bit more, maybe Sandev would never have got caught up in this. But I let the whole idea run away with me. The trouble is I can't promise not to do it again. You know me, Ethel May.'

'I do. And I married you anyway. But no more fantastical tales, Jamie. No risking Belle Vue. Just good, honest, hard work. Please.'

'I'll try, me pet. I'll try.'

Mrs Jameson looked as though she might say more but thought better of it. She smiled instead, and Mr Jameson smiled back. Watching them, Danny felt like he'd intruded on a private moment – one he wished he could be part of.

'Come here, Danny. Help me up.' Mr Jameson grabbed Danny's shoulder and boosted himself on to the edge of the wagon.

'I want to say somethin' to you all.' He opened his arms wide. 'Whatever else happened, the Elephant Race brought together the very finest of people. I couldn't have selected better for Belle Vue than you folk right here. The best and the most loyal.'

He pointed at each of them. 'William, the greatest medical man in the whole country. Miss Henrietta, blessed with a clever brain and the gift of puttin' up with more than one old fool.'

Mr Jameson paused and a smile took over his face, deepening the fan of wrinkles around his eyes. 'And Danny, a prince among thieves. Let me tell you, lad, the day I caught you stealin' at the auction, was the luckiest day of me life.'

Danny wished with every part of himself that he could say something with as much meaning as Mr Jameson had to him. But the words still wouldn't come. Perhaps they never would.

'The truth is, I need all of you. It's not just about right this minute. It's about the future. I want Belle Vue to be here for another hundred years or more. There's never goin' to be another place like it, let me tell you. I've got plans. Big plans.'

Mrs Jameson threw up her hands and settled them on her hips. 'Oh, Jamie! You promised me . . .'

'Don't you worry, me dove. Just trust me. Now that Albright's busy with the police, nothin' can stop us. I've a feeling we're on the up. And I'm hardly ever wrong. Am I, Danny?'

Danny didn't think he needed to nod but he did anyway.

'Come on, it's time to introduce you to the rest of Belle Vue. Let's go and join the party.'

As they walked back through the zoological gardens, Danny listened to the night sounds. A growl from one of the tigers, chattering from the monkeys, and squawks from the cage of exotic birds. It was magical, as though he'd been washed up on the shores of a strange, enchanted land. He wondered if he'd ever get used to it.

'Look, Danny.' Hetty pointed to a poster, pasted on to the side of one of the zoo enclosures. 'It's Maharajah!'

There had not been enough time to get new publicity material so Mr Jameson had ordered that the old Royal Number One Menagerie advertising should be dotted around the park. Wormwell's name had been crossed out but other than that, this poster looked the same as the one Danny had folded away to keep as a souvenir.

'It's strange.' Hetty stood at his side. 'Wormwell's money still hasn't turned up. I looked for it when you didn't come back. Poked around in that box of papers. But there was nothing. Perhaps Maharajah didn't have anything to do with it after all.'

Tilting his head, Danny looked at the picture again and all of a sudden he knew. He knew exactly where Wormwell had hidden his winnings. The answer had been in plain sight all the time. It was so obvious, why hadn't he realized before?

He tugged Hetty's arm, pulling her back as the others walked on.

'What is it? What's the matter?'

Danny jabbed at the outline of Maharajah with his finger.

'Yes, I'm looking but I don't understand.'

Frustrated, Danny traced the picture again. Why couldn't she see? He gave up trying. They were going to have to find it for themselves. He grabbed Hetty again, half dragging her towards the elephant house.

'What are you doing?' She was giggling, still giddy from the celebrations. 'Where are you taking me?'

Danny didn't stop. He pulled her through the park, their hands tangled together like tree roots. Faster and faster. By the time they reached the enclosure, they were going so quickly he had to catch the gate to stop them from tipping over.

They were both laughing when they found Maharajah, lying alone in one of the corner pens. It was quiet. The keepers must have already headed off to join the celebrations. Maharajah didn't seem to mind. He was too busy munching on sugar cane. Kneeling in the straw, Danny stroked his face. The gold eyes blinked sleepily, then he coiled his trunk around Danny's neck and pulled him close. As always, it felt warm and safe and comfortable.

At last Danny drew back. It was time to find out if he was right.

Maharajah's circus harness hung from a hook at one side of the pen. Carefully, Danny lifted it down and slid his fingers under the large, red bead that hung from the centre. The jewel was difficult to unfasten but he managed it eventually. He smoothed his thumb over the surface to clear the dirt that had built up from the journey.

This close, it looked very different from the rest of the paste and glass harness. It wasn't gaudy like the costume jewellery he used to steal from the music hall girls in Edinburgh. Despite the cheap setting, this stone had a rich, elegant beauty. It had been cut into a pear shape, with triangular edges that turned the light into a deep and luminous red. Danny didn't have to be an expert to know it was worth a fortune.

This was Walter Wormwell's legacy.

Hetty leant over. 'Oh, my goodness. Is that a real ruby?'

Danny was almost certain it was. He nodded. Cautiously, she touched the stone. 'I can't believe it. You found it! Right under our noses all this time.'

Danny smiled. It really had been that close. On the old poster, Maharajah had been wearing the jewelled circus collar but there had been no red bead dangling from the centre.

Wormwell must have used his winnings to buy the ruby – maybe from one of the merchant sailors down by the Leith docks; or perhaps he'd met someone who needed cash more desperately than he had. But then most cleverly of all, Wormwell had hidden it in plain sight. Hanging from the harness.

Danny supposed it must have seemed like a good plan. The Royal Number One Menagerie travelled all over the country. Wormwell could have sold the ruby whenever enough time and distance had passed. There'd be no paper trails left in bank accounts and lawyers' offices. Nothing for anyone to find.

Hetty bounced impatiently. Excitement made it impossible for her to stand still. 'Come on! We have to tell everybody. Show them what you've found.'

She raced out of the stall. Danny followed more slowly,

the toes of his slippers scuffed on the ground. He looked at the ruby again. Perhaps Hetty didn't realize there were other choices.

In his hands, Danny held a fortune that didn't belong to anyone – not the Leith Brotherhood who'd originally let it slip from their fingers; not the gambler who had won it; and not the police inspector who thought it lost for good.

Danny could leave now, walk away with the ruby and never come back. This discovery would change his life. He'd be rich. Stinkingly, disgustingly, incredibly rich. Or he could stay here in Belle Vue with these people who had become friends. He had nothing in common with them, except for a great adventure and an elephant.

He lifted the jewel a little higher so the lantern light shot red sparks across his palm. Then a whimper drifted through the enclosure.

Hetty was silhouetted in the open doorway, her eyes wide and frightened. A man stood behind her, so close that she seemed to be wearing him as a cloak. One large hand was wrapped around her throat, and fingermarks already stained her skin.

It was the one person Danny hoped never to see again. Frank Scatcherd.

Danny stopped. He couldn't move. Fear pierced his chest like a hook. His palms were damp. How could this have happened? Scatcherd was supposed to be in Edinburgh. Even now, an army of police officers were combing through the city looking for him.

Yet here he was. An unwanted guest on what had been the best day of Danny's life.

Roughly, Scatcherd pushed Hetty back inside the elephant house. She stumbled but the headlock kept her upright. Only just. Danny could tell she was trying hard to be brave. Her face was pale and she was biting her lip as though to hold in a scream.

'Did you think I'd trust Alfred Kibble to do this on his own? Not a chance, Boy. If you need something done right, you have to do it yourself.'

For a moment, Scatcherd relaxed his grip on Hetty's jaw. She tried to pull away, but he only laughed and squeezed even harder. Danny knew the signs. Scatcherd was playing, like a cat teasing a butterfly. Danny tried not to let his fear show. He willed Hetty to do the same.

'I've been following you for a while now, Boy. Or should I say, "Your Royal Highness"?' Scatcherd snorted. 'A prince! I've never laughed so much. You've managed to fool a lot of people. But I know who you are. Don't I, Boy? You're nothing.'

No, Danny wanted to shout. He'd lived for so long without a name, a home or a family, that he might have believed it once. But not any more. In the last few days, he had started to dream of something better.

'But I'm not here to talk about old times. It sounds to me like you've found what I've been looking for. You'd better hand it over.'

Abruptly, Scatcherd wrenched his fist higher so Hetty

had to stand on tiptoes to ease the pressure on her neck. This time she couldn't stop the sob from escaping. 'You see, one twist is all it would take to break your lady friend's throat. And she's a pretty wee thing. I'd hate to do it.'

And suddenly, Danny's panic and fear disappeared.

And whatever had been broken inside began working again as if all it had needed was one brutal kick at the right time and in the right spot.

'No!' he shouted. The word was raw and rusty because it had been dragged from a pit somewhere deep inside. And the difference from all those other times was that he didn't have to think about it. Or work at it. It just happened. 'NO!'

Head down, Danny ran. Even if he'd wanted to, he couldn't have stopped. Anger drove him, steaming through his muscles to work his arms and legs like pistons. A roar rumbled through the elephant house, and Danny knew it must have come from him because he could feel the vibrations in his chest. And then his forehead smacked hard into Scatcherd's ribs.

It was difficult to tell who was the most startled. The impact jolted through Danny, and Scatcherd yelled in pain. They both crashed to the ground, bringing Hetty down with them.

The three of them tangled across the stone floor in a mess of arms and legs. When they stopped rolling, Danny was lying on his stomach, his chin pressed into one shoulder. But Scatcherd must have relaxed his hold on

Hetty because she was scrambling up.

Danny felt a rush of relief.

'Run!' he yelled. His voice sounded strange, as though he'd borrowed it from someone else and it wasn't quite the right fit. But now he'd started talking he wasn't going to stop. 'RUN!'

A fist to his temple prevented Danny from saying any more. The pain was blinding but he was aware enough to know that Hetty was sprinting out of the enclosure. Then his mouth and cheek were pressed into the dirt, and he couldn't move. Scatcherd sat on his spine. And this time, he held a knife.

'Where is it, Boy? I know you've got it.'

Breathing hard, Danny let his muscles relax. His best weapon was the knowledge that Scatcherd didn't expect him to fight back. He raised a hand to show surrender and the King eased off a fraction. There was only a second to act.

Gathering every ounce of strength, Danny launched himself on to his elbows and flipped over. Sharp and quick. The move knocked Scatcherd off balance. He fell heavily across the stone floor, and sprawled there, winded. Danny wasn't going to wait for the next punch. He scrambled to his feet but before he could take a step, a hand shot out and grabbed his ankle. Only luck stopped him from falling straight back down again.

Desperately, he yanked loose but Scatcherd was already lashing out with the knife. Twisting round, Danny brought his foot down hard and the blade fell from Scatcherd's fist.

He kicked again and the knife spun away, out of reach.

'You'll regret that.'

Clutching his injured hand, Scatcherd struggled upright. He aimed a boot at Danny's knees. Danny managed to avoid the worst of it by dodging to one side. But the blow was enough to send a judder through every bone. He groaned. And as if in answer, a trumpeting noise blasted through the enclosure.

Danny listened, amazed. It was Maharajah, sounding out a warning. In Cowgate, he'd never had anyone to watch his back. Nobody had ever cared enough before – and now he had an elephant!

But Maharajah was weak and injured. Danny wasn't going to drag him into this fight. 'Stay,' he whistled. 'Stay.'

He only hoped Maharajah would obey because it was time to show Scatcherd that everything had changed. *That he had changed.*

Chapter Twenty-eight

BELLE VUE ZOOLOGICAL GARDENS, MANCHESTER
21 April 1872

The fight was going to be ugly. Scatcherd might be large and heavy but Danny was quick and crafty. And the one thing he wasn't any more, was frightened. Hetty was safe and, at the moment, so was Maharajah. That was all that mattered. He had to make sure it stayed that way.

Danny raised his fists, and bent into a crouch like he'd seen the bare-knuckle boxers do on fight nights in Cowgate. Scatcherd did the same. For several minutes, they shuffled around the enclosure like clumsy dancers. A few steps forward, a few steps back. Dust kicked up from the floor, and only their heavy breathing punctured the silence.

Then Danny swung a punch, it missed and Scatcherd laughed. He wasn't laughing when Danny swung a second blow and raised his knee at the same time. Bent double, Scatcherd hissed, 'I'll make you sorry for that.'

Danny didn't reply. He was saving his energy. Using his arms and legs and feet, he made contact wherever he could. A clip to the chest. A strike to the hip. But it didn't take long for Scatcherd to recover and, when he did, his punches were strong and accurate. Of course, he'd had more practice.

After one sharp jab, Danny's left eye began to swell shut. Another cut joined the bruise on his cheek, and his ribs ached from a blow to the chest. Judging by the pain, he thought he'd probably broken at least one bone. But the last punch was the worst.

It hit the side of his skull, just above his ear, and stabbed through his head. He crumpled to the floor. Everything hurt. He wanted to close his eyes but Scatcherd loomed over him.

'You've surprised me, Boy.' He pressed a knee into Danny's ribs and pushed down. The pain was almost unbearable. 'You don't normally put up much of a fight. It looks as though you've discovered your guts as well as your voice. Now for the last time – give me the jewel.'

Disorientated, Danny didn't understand at first and then he realized the ruby was still clutched in his fist. Throughout the fight, he hadn't let go. It was the only advantage he had left.

He lifted his hand just a fraction and stared into Scatcherd's face.

'No,' he said and flicked his fingers. The ruby skidded across the enclosure floor. In the darkness, it was impossible to see exactly where it had landed. Danny only hoped the search would keep Scatcherd busy for a while.

'That was a mistake, Boy. Now I'll have to go and look for it.' Scatcherd got up and grabbed a lantern. The burning pressure on Danny's chest eased a fraction. 'But don't think this is over yet. You know I don't like it when people disobey me.'

The last words were accompanied by a kick to the ribs and a new burst of pain. Danny's throat tightened against a scream. But the fact that he didn't cry out was surely a victory. Wasn't it?

He waited a heartbeat then, clenching his teeth, rolled on to his stomach, and slowly lifted to his knees. It felt like a blacksmith was hammering away in his head, while another poked hot irons into his chest. He could barely see through his swollen eye. In this condition, he'd never be able to make it out of the elephant house. He couldn't even stand. And there was probably not much time before Scatcherd returned to finish what he'd started. Panic surged, hot and urgent.

How could he escape?

Pivoting, Danny tried to see through the blur. In the corner, Scatcherd was still scrabbling about in the dirt. But a few feet away, to his left, something metallic glinted on the stone floor. The knife. It was close, but not close enough. Could he reach it?

He had to try.

Danny dragged himself along the floor. The effort was almost too much but he wasn't giving up now. He stretched out a hand, feeling the strain through every muscle. Just a little further. His fingertips brushed the knife then hooked around it. Gradually, he eased the blade into his palm, and tucked it behind his back, out of sight. He sat, panting as though he'd run a race.

Just in time.

With a shout, Scatcherd grabbed at something in the shadows and lifted it up into the lamp light. There was a flicker of luminous red.

'Looks as if you were right, Boy.' Scatcherd hadn't moved his eyes from the ruby. 'Wormwell was cleverer than I thought. This must be worth a fortune. I'll get my money back and more.'

He slipped the jewel into his jacket, and climbed to his feet. Then all Danny could hear was the tap-tap of boots walking towards him. A tight band of panic squeezed his chest. But behind his back, he held the knife. He tightened his grip on the handle. It slid a little in his damp palm.

'Now I warned you, didn't I? I said we weren't finished yet. And you know me, I always like to leave you with something. A little souvenir to make sure you don't forget who owns you.'

Scatcherd reached out and wrenched Danny upright by

the shoulders. Pain burnt down his side, and the hammering in his head grew louder. But he stayed upright. He knew what he had to do and he only had one chance.

'Scared, Boy?' Almost gently, Scatcherd slid his knuckles along the line of Danny's jaw, and into the soft skin. He pressed hard until it seemed to Danny that bone pushed directly into bone. With a little more pressure, they might even fuse together.

'NO!' Before he could change his mind, Danny pulled the knife from its hiding place. Against Scatcherd's throat, it looked jagged and cruel. Surely, the King would turn and run? Isn't that what bullies did when people fought back?

But of course, Scatcherd didn't do what was expected. A smile spread across his face as though he'd just been told a joke. His fist dropped loosely to his side.

'Go on, Boy. Do it. If you dare.'

'Not . . . Boy.' Danny wanted to be strong and confident but the words sounded weak and feeble. To his horror, the knife trembled in his hand. Scatcherd's smile widened.

'I can call you whatever I want. You belong to me. Remember? Those letters on your wrist prove it. And what is mine, stays mine.'

Danny shook his head. 'No.' This time, his voice was stronger. 'NO.'

'Then convince me.' To Danny's surprise, Scatcherd spread his arms wide. Now his body was an open target. 'Have a go. Prove that you're as good as me. That Prince

Dandip can beat the King of Cowgate.' He lifted his lip in a sneer. 'Take a stab. I dare you.'

For a moment, Danny was tempted. He was just so tired. Blood and sweat ran down his forehead, into his eyes. Every part of his body ached. More than anything, he wanted all this to be over. Then he could sleep until the pain went away.

He turned the knife in his palm, testing its weight as if the only decision left to be made was where it would hurt the most. And then through his blurred vision he saw the marks on his wrist, and he realized something.

He didn't have to prove anything. To anyone. Because he was entirely happy with the person he'd become. And if he let himself be dragged back into Scatcherd's world, he would lose all that he had found.

Killing Scatcherd would mean a lifetime behind bars. It would mean leaving Maharajah and Belle Vue. Hetty and the Jamesons. Everything and everyone he had come to care about.

'No. NO!' Danny dropped his arm, and spat the words like bullets. 'You are not . . . not worth it.'

This time, there was no doubting that Scatcherd was angry. With a roar, he lurched forward. Perhaps that was why he didn't hear the footsteps.

But Danny did.

Or were they only in his imagination? For a moment he wasn't completely sure. And then Scatcherd's fist closed around his throat, and he couldn't get his next breath. The knife dropped from his fingers, and blood filled his eyes.

'Stop! Get off him!'

Danny heard Hetty but he couldn't see her and, for some reason, that bothered him more than anything else. Suddenly, the pressure around his neck eased. And he fell to the ground, gasping.

When his vision cleared again, everyone was there. Hetty and Mr Saddleworth, Mr and Mrs Jameson, even Nelson Crimple. And at the door of his pen, Maharajah was on his feet. Caught in the middle was Scatcherd. The King of Cowgate was cornered. He couldn't run anywhere. There were too many people between him and escape.

Danny watched the realization sink in, quickly followed by disbelief. It was very possibly the first time Scatcherd had ever been trapped. He spun round to where Danny sprawled on the floor.

'You think you belong here? Don't be stupid, Boy. These people will throw you away like yesterday's fish bones. They don't want you. You're nothing to them. Noth—'

With a quick, precise movement, Mr Saddleworth swung the ankus and caught Scatcherd neatly on the back of the neck. Face forward, he fell unconscious into the dirt. For a heartbeat they all stared at his body. He didn't stir. Then Hetty bent and yanked his head by the hair.

'Henrietta!'

Obediently, she let go and Scatcherd's forehead bounced on the stone. 'That's for hurting Danny,' she said. Then did it again. 'And that's for hurting me.'

Danny wanted to laugh but his bottom lip was split so the chuckle emerged as a moan. Picking up her skirts, Mrs Jameson ran to his side.

'Oh, my dear Lord, Danny. Just look at you!'

She knelt in a puff of petticoats and lifted his head on to her lap, not seeming to care that he was bloody and dirty. Danny sank into the softness. He never wanted to move again. And when Mrs Jameson stroked a hand across his brow, he lay there. And enjoyed it.

'What in heaven's name is this all about, Danny?' Mr Jameson crouched beside them. 'You look as if you've gone twenty rounds with Bare Knuckles Broughton. And who's that bloke?'

'No one.' Danny spoke slowly. He was still getting used to the peculiar creak of his voice. 'No one important.'

Mrs Jameson was staring at him as if he'd worked miracles. A wide smile spread across her face. 'Danny! You're talking!'

'Of course, he is, Ethel May. Haven't I always told you he's not dumb?' Mr Jameson was indignant. 'And what's all this nonsense about where you belong? I can tell you exactly where you belong. Right here.' He looked at his wife. 'Shall we tell him, me dove?'

'Yes, Jamie. I think now would be the perfect time.'

Mr Jameson cleared his throat, opened his mouth and closed it again. Danny was surprised; he wasn't normally lost for words. His wife gave him a nudge with her elbow. She looked a little nervous. 'Go on, Jamie. Say it.'

'Well it's like this, Danny. Me and Mrs Jameson haven't been blessed with children. We were never that lucky. But we've been thinking about all you've done for us. And for Maharajah and Belle Vue. And so we'd like you to come to live with us. In our house. And for you not just to be called Danny. But to be called Danny Jameson.' He paused. 'That is, if you want to?'

This time, Danny thought he actually heard the herald of angels. The angels he hadn't really believed in two weeks ago at Waverley Station. Now they were singing. There wasn't a chance he was going to miss this opportunity. His heart rose in his chest.

'Yes,' he said. And then louder, so no one could be in any doubt. 'YES!'

Thanks to Maharajah, he had everything he'd ever wanted. Friends, a family. Even his voice. Briefly, Danny relaxed the fingers of his left fist, revealing a flash of luminous red. It was still there. He smiled with the side of his mouth that didn't hurt.

In the end, it had been easy to steal back the ruby from Scatcherd's jacket during that last tussle. After all, hadn't Mr Jameson said he was a prince among thieves?

And tomorrow, when he felt better, Danny would tell the Jamesons about Wormwell's legacy. And what it would mean for Belle Vue. And for their plans for the future. He closed his eyes, letting his mind dream of all the possibilities.

ABOUT THE BOOK

I first saw Maharajah in the Manchester Museum ten years ago. His skeleton was on display alongside a brief history. I never forgot the story – or him.

Maharajah had been part of a travelling circus, Wombwell's Royal Number One Menagerie, until April 1872, when he was sold at auction in Edinburgh. He was bought for £680 (about £30,000 today) by James Jennison, owner of the Belle Vue Zoological Gardens in Manchester.

But moments after boarding the train to his new home, Maharajah destroyed his railway carriage. Instead, his keeper, Lorenzo Lawrence, decided they would walk from Edinburgh to Manchester. It took them ten days.

In reality, the walk was fairly uneventful. In my book, it isn't. But the common theme is the affection that Maharajah inspired during the journey – and for a long time afterwards. In fact, such was his popularity that the Victorian artist Heywood Hardy is thought to have used him as inspiration for his painting, *The Disputed Toll*.

I borrowed many of these true events and real people to help create *The Elephant Thief*, but one confession: the real Maharajah was an Asian elephant, not African. He died in 1882 from pneumonia after ten years at Belle Vue. His skeleton was put on display, and when Belle Vue eventually closed, he moved to the Manchester Museum where visitors can still marvel at him today.

ACKNOWLEDGEMENTS

As I have realized, writing a book takes more than just one person and I want to thank all those who helped me. To my mum – the first person to read the story, and the first person to believe it was any good. To Dad, Brenda and Mark, whose enthusiasm and interest drove me on.

Thanks also to the author, Brian Keaney, whose guidance steered me off the wrong path on to the right one. And to my agent, David Smith, who understood the story straight away. To family, friends and all at BBC Radio Manchester for their support.

My gratitude to David Barnaby, author of *The Elephant Who Walked to Manchester*. His account was invaluable. And also to the Manchester Museum, where I first learnt about Maharajah. As well as to Philip Kerr, and Amanda and Cecilia Taylor for their knowledge of Edinburgh – any mistakes are my own, or creative liberties.

A special thank you to all those at Chicken House – Barry Cunningham, Rachel Leyshon, Rachel Hickman, Jazz Bartlett, Laura Myers, Kesia Lupo, Esther Waller, Elinor Bagenal and Sarah Wilson – for their patience and encouragement, and to Claire McKenna.

And most of all, thank you to my husband, AJ, and children, Alexandra and Ben, who have put up with my constant disappearances (both physical and mental) over the last few years – and have supported me anyway. Now you can finally read it. It's for you.

doodle
dog